T0243211

PRE-APPROVED FOR HAUNTING

AND OTHER STORIES

ALSO BY PATRICK BARB

Gargantuana's Ghost

Turn

Helicopter Parenting in the Age of Drone Warfare

PRE-APPROVED FOR HAUNTING

AND OTHER STORIES

PATRICK BARB

FOREWORD BY RICHARD THOMAS

+ KEYLIGHT
BOOKS
AN IMPRINT
OF TURNER
PUBLISHING

KEYLIGHT BOOKS
AN IMPRINT OF TURNER PUBLISHING COMPANY
Nashville, Tennessee
www.turnerpublishing.com

Pre-Approved for Haunting: And Other Stories

Copyright © 2023 by Patrick Barb. All rights reserved.

This book or any part thereof may not be reproduced or transmitted in any form or by any means, electronic or mechanical, including photocopying, recording, or by any information storage and retrieval system, without permission in writing from the publisher. This is a work of fiction. All the characters and events portrayed in this book are either products of the author's imagination or are used fictitiously.

Cover and Book Design by William Ruoto

Library of Congress Cataloging-in-Publication Data
Names: Barb, Patrick, author.
Title: Pre-approved for haunting / Patrick Barb.
Description: First Edition. | Nashville, Tennessee : Keylight Books, [2023]
Identifiers: LCCN 2022032723 (print) | LCCN 2022032724 (ebook) | ISBN
  9781684429486 (hardcover) | ISBN 9781684429479 (paperback) | ISBN
  9781684429493 (epub)
Subjects: LCSH: Anxiety. | Nostalgia. | Violence.
Classification: LCC BF575.A6 B29 2023 (print) | LCC BF575.A6 (ebook) |
  DDC 152.4/6—dc23/eng/20230322
LC record available at https://lccn.loc.gov/2022032723
LC ebook record available at https://lccn.loc.gov/2022032724

Printed in the United States of America

FOR MOM AND DAD:
I'VE COME A LONG WAY FROM STICK FIGURE
DRAWINGS AND DICTATED STORIES WRITTEN
DOWN ON A YELLOW LEGAL PAD, HUH?

CONTENTS

FOREWORD

I first met Patrick when he signed up for my Short Story Mechanics class. I've been an author for fourteen years now but have only been teaching for about ten. Quite often when I teach this class I see a range of talent and effort—some come into it, see the assignment, get the feedback, and disappear. These students form about 25 percent of the class. Others complete the individual lessons, but never turn in the final story—another 25 percent. And then the rest (50 percent) turn in the final story. It's these students I keep an eye on, to see if they might have what it takes. I contemplate their voice, their choices, the depth of story, and whether or not they applied what was taught and improved over the class. I'm looking to see if they have any talent, any vision, any originality. Patrick was one of those authors. Not only did he turn in his story, and do well, but he went on to take my other classes—Contemporary Dark Fiction and my Advanced Creative Writing Workshop. (And he's signed up for my novel-in-a-year class as well, for 2023). What does this all tell me about Patrick? Quite a few things. Let me elaborate, and maybe it'll help to see why he may be an author you want to keep an eye on as well, an emerging voice, a talent.

One of the things I've always admired about Patrick, going back some four years now, is his work ethic. He put his butt in the chair, did the heavy lifting, and didn't complain. Those are the best students, and, I've found, usually the best authors—because they understand it's not easy to write short stories. Patrick turned his work in on time, embraced each assignment, and really worked hard to make the most of every opportunity. He did the extra work, perused the secondary articles and stories, and bought books by those voices that inspired him. It's that energy and discipline that often leads to success.

Another aspect of Patrick's study has been his openness to criticism, lessons, and suggestions. Over the years, as Patrick has grown and improved as an author, I've seen him apply what's been offered. I teach Freytag's Triangle (or Pyramid) as the structure for fiction, and it's been exciting watching Patrick put it all together—the title, narrative hook, inciting incident, internal and external conflicts, rising tension, climax, resolution, change, and denouement. Along the way I've seen the lightbulb moments, the aha revelations as he figured out how to complete a story with all of the essential elements. I've seen him hone his craft, putting in his 10,000 hours in order to improve and evolve. I've spoken with Stephen Graham Jones about this in the past, and we both had that moment somewhere around the fiftieth story we wrote, where we said to ourselves "Oh, now I think I know how to write a short story." It takes practice, it takes imagination, and it takes vision. Not only have I seen Patrick put it all together over my classes, but I've seen him continue to grow and evolve on his own as well. This collection is a perfect example of that hard work.

I think the third part of Patrick's study and craft that I really admire is his imagination and willingness to take chances on the page. I'll get into more specifics in a minute when I discuss the collection, but I've always admired the way Patrick has tapped into the expectation and requirements of various genres while still pushing to be original and unique. It's not easy to find that intersection between classic and innovative, between accessible and surprising. Over the years, I've edited a magazine (*Gamut*) and a small press (Dark House Press), and one thing I see all the time is fiction that is cliché, expected, and unoriginal. New authors, or writers who aren't quite as talented, start out writing (in my experience) by imitating others, by tapping into classic myths, monsters, and plots. And there is nothing wrong with that. I mean, we all have to start somewhere. But if you want to break into a top market like *Nightmare* or *The Dark* or *Cemetery Dance* or *Clarkesworld*, you have to build from that original inspiration and then do something original with it—you have to do *more*, you have to go *farther*. And that's something I've always enjoyed in Patrick's work—he pulls me into his stories with character, tension, setting, and conflict, but then surprises me with his unique visions, his variations on themes, his originality and depth. That's not an easy thing to do.

As I continue to read Patrick's work, I'm excited for the future. I know that he's just getting started, which is already very impressive. I know that I became a different author before and after watching *Black Mirror* and various A24 films, such as *Hereditary*, *The Witch*, *Enemy*, and *Under the Skin*. I know I changed as a writer after reading China Miéville, Haruki Murakami, Cormac McCarthy, Jeff VanderMeer, Jack Ketchum, Chuck Palahniuk, Priya Sharma, Usman Malik, Brian Hodge, Alyssa Wong, Benjamin Percy, Kelly Robson, A. C. Wise, Brian Evenson, Craig Clevenger, and the aforementioned Stephen Graham Jones—just to name a few. So as far as Patrick's work and voice? He's just getting started.

Let's talk about this collection, shall we?

The first part of this collection I'd like to talk about is what I call the "classic" horror stories. These are tales that lean in and nod toward the past, tapping into elements of the genre that are to be expected—the places and monsters that we've come to associate with horror. What I like about these stories is that they are familiar, and by "familiar" I mean accessible. They pull you in with a comforting presence, tapping into aspects of slashers and old school horror stories, this embrace you recognize from past encounters. Now, that doesn't mean they stop there, only that these are the access points, right? When I talk to my students about genres—whether it's horror, fantasy, science fiction, thrillers, magical realism, transgressive fiction, neo-noir, new-weird, or literary stories—I ask them to make sure they are fulfilling the expectation of the genre. What does horror ask of us? What does it promise to deliver? What do I mean by that? If you went to McDonald's and ordered a Big Mac, you'd expect to get a Big Mac whether you were in Chicago, New York, or Paris, correct? Now, if you ordered that Big Mac and got a venison burger with brie on top, you might not be very happy. But at least it's a cheeseburger, right? It's a variation on a theme. And it might be good. Now, if you ordered that burger and got *sushi*, I expect you would be upset, even if the sushi was good. But what if you ordered that cheeseburger and got a screwdriver? Now that would be disappointing. Frustrating. Infuriating. That's what I'm talking about here. Its's easy to see the classic horror that inspired stories like "There Is No Bunk #7"—I mean, summer camp, yeah? That's *Friday the 13th* territory, and so many other books and films. But as this story leans more into *The Cabin in the Woods* and otherworldly possibilities, we go beyond the usual slasher fare and into uncharted territory. Set in a similar world, we have "The Giallo Kid in the Cataclysm's Campgrounds." Without spoiling much here, as it's in the opening lines, I like the update of the Homer Simpson mask, which immediately puts us in an uncomfortable place, between classic animation and the masked horrors of films like *The Strangers*, *The Purge*, and *Texas Chainsaw Massacre*. Who doesn't want to root for the last final girl, and other classic elements of horror? Twists and turns keep us on our toes. When it comes to zombies and the undead, as well as ghosts, I love the originality in what could have been a derivative tale in "Rose from the Ashes," where the visual of snorting the dead's ashes leads to some surprising encounters. The bargaining, the danger, the unexpected—a fun ride for sure. We tap into another ghost story in the title tale from this collection "Pre-Approved for Haunting." So much has been done with ghost stories, but the idea that the haunting hasn't been cemented yet, that the horror is still coming, that the main characters can *see* the future, but may be unable to stop it? I hate it when that happens. That's classic horror, and it gets under my skin every time. The mariachi band, the recurring presence and themes, the way it rolls forward, the desire to avoid it—such a compelling story. One of my favorites in the collection. And I'd be remiss if I didn't talk about the variation on a theme that is "Iggy Crane and the Headless Horse Girl." The setting here is a nice twist on a standard summer camp—the riding lessons, the four girls that partner together as one, Iggy being pulled into the story, her lust and desire for the headmistress, and the inevitable truth behind the video the kids have shared with her. Another story that really stayed with me, starting with the classic imagery of *The Legend of Sleepy Hollow*, and then taking it in an updated, contemporary direction. These are all stories that begin someplace we recognize, but then do something fresh and different, luring us in with promises of familiar horrors, before pushing us into the shadows where something else entirely lurks, waiting to surprise and unsettle us.

Another group of stories that really appealed to me were tales that start out someplace grounded in realism, but end up somewhere supernatural.

When I think of the films and books and stories that have really stayed with me over the years, especially in horror, I think of those that set up the narrative in a realistic way, overflowing with authority and authenticity, building a world defined by science, society, rules, and laws. It could be the opening scenes of *The Shining*, where we see the car driving up the mountain, the family dynamic unfurling, a history of abuse, the father going to a job interview, all of it feeling grounded in the normal—a man and his wife struggling to get by, a kid who has suffered at his father's quick tongue and uncorked violence. But there is so much coming, way beyond the solitude and isolation of a snowed-in hotel in the off-season. I think of the opening to *The Exorcist*—not Regan peeing on the floor in the middle of the dinner party. No, go back farther in your memory. I'm talking about the archaeological dig in Iraq, the calls to worship at the end of the day, dogs fighting in a feral frenzy as a statue of the demon Pazuzu is unearthed. We see the struggle, the violence, the heat, and it resonates, it *ripples* with a pulsing horror that fades as we transition to a house in Georgetown. But it is not forgotten. I'm thinking about the opening to Stephen King's *The Stand*, as a family flees a lab experiment gone wrong, crashing into a gas station, the virus spreading outward. When we start with something as simple as the story "Lost Boy Found in His Bear Suit," we laugh at the kid, who is unwilling to take off the costume, just glad he is alive. But as we look at the details—the child sticky with honey and salmon smeared on his lips—we start to wonder what exactly they are bringing home, and if it's still a boy. And while we might think of *The Picture of Dorian Gray* when reading "A Portrait of the Artist as an Angry God (in Landscape)," this story is something else entirely. Quite possibly my favorite story in the collection, the bloodline from father to son, the paintings and all they have to offer, the slow descent into madness and uncertainty—it all pulses and ripples outward in a gradually building, slowly unraveling, eventually disturbing story that pulls no punches. It reminds me of the art by Simon Stålenhag that went on to inspire the television show *Tales from the Loop*. The depth and layers in "The Crack in the Ceiling" start out with the unsettling opening line of, "At the end of every week, our town hangs burning bodies from the Ceiling so we'll remember what stars looked like." You're already grounded in one reality rife with tension and horror, but it's not until we get to the final words of the last line that the truth is revealed with a disturbing note reminiscent of the end of *The Mist* or *The Village*—so disturbing, expanding outward in a growing horror. There is a similar vibe in the story "Putting Down Roots," which gives Arbor Day a whole new meaning. It's always interesting to revisit our roots in fiction, to have the horror story go home, for a reunion, or gathering, or special event. But if we look at tales like *Midsommar* or *Get Out*, we can see how these quite often go horribly wrong.

The final set of stories I wanted to talk about have to do with cosmic horror and the new-weird. In the last couple of years, I've written quite a few stories that fit into this category, tapping into the uncanny, the unsettling, the weird, and Lovecraftian. Everything from old gods to expanding chaos to doppelgangers and the unknowable. It's one of my greatest fears, when it comes to horror—insanity, things on the periphery of my vision, the idea that this is all an illusion, the visions and creatures and people that aren't quite right, as I stop to wonder if there might be something else entirely going on here. "Have You Seen My Missing Pet?" is a good example of how the weird gets rolling, starting with a rainy night, an old man, and a missing pet. We of course keep thinking *dog*, but he continues to correct us: "I never said he was a dog." We go from leash to dog to something more, and then when it appears, when the baby is in danger, when it all goes to hell, then what? It's like a nursery rhyme in a class horror movie—it takes on a whole new life, these lyrics and melodies, or when you utter a phrase like ". . . the makings of a very good boy." Truly unsettling, as it telescopes out into the future, the horror continuing. There is the metafictional story, "I Will Not Read Your Haunted Script," which invites us in with the humor and intimacy I mentioned before, joking about this history of repeated events as it starts to go south, escalating into something much more. I always think of sly, grinning, intimate horror (such as the work of Stephen Graham Jones) as pulling us in closely so that, instead of the monster stabbing us in the back or some killer shooting us from a great distance, the darkness leans in close as it slides the blade between our ribs, up close and personal, laughing the whole time. It's coming from within the house! Soylent Green is people! Turns out it was the father, the neighbor, the coach all along. Done right (and I think Patrick has achieved that here), the inclusion of the script in the story, the formatting looking great, the haunted words on the page pulling us in closer, then out of the script, then back into it again, until we are trapped, too close, under its spell? Brilliant. I tried to do a similar thing in my story, "In His House," getting you to recite a phrase three times (like saying Beetlejuice, Beetlejuice, Beetlejuice!) so that the spell was invoked, the promises made, the deal signed and closed, forever. This has that feel, that constriction, that claustrophobia. Another favorite in this collection, for sure. The only thing worse than paranoia is when the fears come true, right? In "The Other Half of the Battle," we aren't sure which side are the "good guys," as we go back and forth between bullies and soldiers, to heroes and allies, balancing the realism of kids playing by a freezer with the war unfurling just out of sight finally come home to roost. It's easy to make fun of conspiracy theories in the dark, deep corners of the woods, until the tank comes rolling over the hill, pushing down trees, the reality emerging from the mist in all its horror and glory. Then what? You pick a side? One of the visuals I hate the most in horror is cutting, punctures, and self-abuse of any kind—everything from the carrot scene in *Color Out of Space* to the nail on the steps in *A Quiet Place* to the pica in *Swallow*. So, of course, "Shattered" is a story that really pushed my buttons. What starts as mere body horror with the broken glass in the opening scene, turns into something much more—an uprising that comes out of breaking a glass ceiling, using the shards to transform, reminiscent of the film *Men*. It doesn't matter if Norman says no. He does as he is told. A lesser author would have stopped with the visceral, unsettling imagery. But as I've said before, one of Patrick's strengths is pushing beyond that, into new territory, the initial unsettling feeling not nearly enough, wanting more for his readers—a chill, a haunting, a memory that causes the skin to flush, an image that can't be shaken, as we keep one eye on the shadows forming in the upper corner of our bedroom, the other on the closed door, with the knob that just started to move.

I hope my comments here have given you some indication of the breadth, depth, originality, and emotion that goes into Patrick Barb's work. Think of this like reading an early copy of *Carrie*, the one Stephen King's wife pulled out of the trash. She smoothed out the wrinkled pages, dusted it off, and sat down to read it. Turns out it was pretty good. There are stories in here that will stay with me for a long time. And yet . . . I feel like Patrick's best work may still be ahead of him. So sign up, get on board, strap in, and buckle up. There are horrors in these pages that pay homage to past classics, while pushing into new space. There are uncanny tales that keep shifting and morphing the longer you look at them, refusing to sit still. There are moments that feel like they could be happening to you, today, or next door, or just down the road—nothing special—as the darkness slowly expands into something quite unknowable. Hold on to that early Picasso sketch, that debut album from the Quarrymen, that black and white experimental film from Christopher Nolan. We have our inciting incident now, the moment after which things will never be the same. As you sit at the mouth of madness, know that you've been warned. What has been seen can't be unseen. This is only the beginning.

—Richard Thomas
Chicago, IL
June 16, 2022

PRE-APPROVED FOR HAUNTING

AND OTHER STORIES

LOST BOY FOUND IN HIS BEAR SUIT

Three days after he went missing in the woods, they found the boy alive. He was sticky with wild honey, and chunks of salmon were smeared around his lips. The fuzzy collar of his teddy bear jumpsuit, the only outfit he'd wear to bed, was worn and matted.

But he was alive and that's what mattered.

His parents were supposed to wait back at the makeshift command center the authorities established at the 4-H Center. But after a restless night spent holding hands across the gap between two cots made up with Army surplus sheets, they weren't going to wait behind.

"Don't be surprised if he looks different. Being out in these woods for that long, at his age," Park Ranger Steve told them.

The boy played with leaves on the forest floor as his parents approached with the park ranger. One of the EMTs had pushed the jumpsuit's hood, with its teddy-bear ears, off his head. The boy turned at the sound of shoes crunching through the underbrush. He smiled. His mouth opened wide with the effortless enthusiasm only small children can achieve.

Reheated coffee stung his mother's esophagus before passing through her pale, chapped lips. Pain inside her mouth and horror inside her head drove the woman to her knees. Unsure of whose comfort to prioritize, the father rubbed her shoulders but kept staring over at his boy.

The now crying child looked more like an abandoned plaything than the dimpled sprite who'd kissed his stubbly cheeks and called him "Dad-doo." The boy pulled the hood back up. The fabric cast a shadow over his face, coating his eyes in a bottomless black.

After the EMTs and Park Ranger Steve got everyone calmed, they explained to the boy's parents that the wriggling white "worms" falling from his smiling mouth weren't maggots. They were grubs. Larva. "Hell if we know how he got to 'em."

Somewhat reassured, the boy's parents walked over and scooped him up in their arms. He was theirs once again. Their little lost boy found in his bear suit. Each tried to find a tiny hand inside the stitched-on paw coverings at the ends of his sleeves. But he growled, teeth snapping, and pulled his hands back further into his mud-caked fuzzy outfit.

He wriggled and squirmed in their arms. He seemed stronger than they'd been told to expect. The boy broke free and fell the short distance from their grasp to the ground. He landed on padded feet and ran.

Everyone sprinted to catch up with him. His parents ran that much harder than the others, perhaps fearing they wouldn't find him again if they let him run too far. But he eventually stopped. After pushing aside some broken branches, they found him standing by a dark cave entrance. A slight breeze pushed the bear ears down against the top of the hood.

"She's sleeping now."

Flashlight at the ready, Park Ranger Steve nodded toward the cave entrance. He'd already seen the scat, with the bones and bits of hair, as they'd made their approach. He'd heard the stories from older rangers, the ones about an old bear sow whose cubs were killed out of season by some hunters. Campfire tales said she'd take human children to even the score.

But that story had been around for ages, details changing with every retelling. The old mama bear, if she'd ever lived at all, would be long dead.

Then again, the cave was right there.

The boy's parents shook their heads. It was their call, and they didn't want to know what was inside. They only wanted their boy back home. Away from the cave. Away from the woods.

They returned to the Jeep. The boy passed out almost immediately and slept between his parents in the back seat. They wrapped him in a foil rescue blanket, ignoring the tightness of his stretched-thin skin and the stiff black and brown hairs growing out from under the scrapes and scratches on his tiny body.

The Jeep's engine growled, then roared. Its tires threw dirt and rocks back behind them. Its tracks, like claw marks, were left to show that they'd been there.

A PORTRAIT OF THE ARTIST AS AN ANGRY GOD
(IN LANDSCAPE)

Jake needed to destroy the oil painting hanging above the bed in his room at the Sand Dollar Inn. *Or, at least, corrupt it.* The unframed canvas jutted from a wall doubly-stained by salty sea air and the lingering curls of cigarette smoke.

As a working artist and veteran horror comic book creator, Jake always traveled with his supplies. For this year's trip to the Sand Dollar, he'd brought paint brushes (animal hair to synthetic, fat to skinny, coarse to smooth), gloss, paint thinner, and crusted-over squeezable tubes of acrylic paint left wrinkled from overuse. And, of course, he'd brought his sketchbook.

He approached with the book open in hand and stood close enough that he could reach out and touch the canvas.

Why shouldn't I? It's got my name on it, after all.

His surname "Varmette" appeared in cursive in the canvas's lower right-hand corner. But it wasn't his work. Both painting and signature belonged to his late father.

Jacob Varmette *Senior*. To Jake, he was "Senior" or "The Old Man." To the countless fans who swore by his paintings and came to his annual art workshop at the beach, he was "Jacob." He'd never received critical notice, his paintings were never displayed in the galleries of New York, Tokyo, Miami, or Paris, and no celebrities filled their overpriced homes with his works, but the absence of those signifiers of fame didn't prevent the elder Varmette from amassing renown in less highbrow corners of the world.

To wit, Jacob Sr.'s paintings were all over the Sand Dollar. Every morning, during his tenure running the workshop, Senior took his students to paint the dunes and coastline behind the hotel. After each lesson, he'd spin his easel around to let his students "ooh" and "ahh" at firsthand exposure to a Jacob Varmette original. Then, he'd give the painting to the front desk staff. Soon enough, another "Original Varmette" would hang inside the hotel.

The paintings' omnipresence made Jake's own creative "project" that much more ambitious. He intended to add one of his "monsters" to every single Jacob Varmette painting at the Sand Dollar. Jake had started the "work" before his father passed, a minor act of rebellion after Senior rolled his eyes at the news he'd be taking over as artist on the relaunch of the cult-favorite "Bog Monster" comic. "Oh good," he'd said. "Just make sure it doesn't interfere with your participation in our workshop classes."

That was the way it'd always gone for Jake. His art, his accomplishments, they remained in the shadow of his father's mass market appeal. Injecting a little of his rougher-edged style into the old man's work seemed like a reasonable trade-off for that sort of dismissal. Of course, then he'd liked his renegade art project so much that every year following, the tradition continued. Now, with his old man gone for over a year, Jake figured that changing the paintings was the real reason he'd decided to keep the "Jacob Varmette Painting Workshop Weekend" going.

That and the money.

"Let's see what you left me this time, Senior."

While his father's signature sat in the corner of the canvas as usual, the rest of the painting diverged from his typical output. Like it came from a storybook's pages, this piece depicted a rustic village in the shadow of a snow-capped mountain range. Senior used sweeping brushstrokes for the snow. In the village, he mixed alizarin crimson with yellow ochre for thatched roofs of peasant hovels otherwise rendered in muddy browns and grays.

The villagers were impressionistic, half-realized faceless beings. Jake hated them.

"Good old dad, never aspiring to anything above lowest common denominator, even outside his comfort zone."

Jake opened his sketchbook. On page after page, foreboding shadow-draped monstrosities sketched in his signature horror artist style awaited consideration. He ran his fingertips along his cheeks and down to his chin, smoothing the wiry brown and gray hairs of the beard he'd grown to distance himself from immediate comments about his resemblance to Jacob Senior.

Altering one of Senior's paintings was simple—Jake picked a monster and painted it into the landscape. He delighted in blending lines, shadows, and colors so his beasts fit into Senior's canvases seamlessly. He could mimic his father's style so well that no one—particularly not the housekeeping staff of the Sand Dollar—noticed.

And even if they did, what were *they* gonna do to the dead artist's son?

He pulled out paint tubes by their rolled-up ends and released his selections onto the bedspread. Shaking from a sudden chill that certainly came from the room's air conditioning, Jake started his addition.

Moments later, the inaugural paint selection dribbled from the tip of Jake's brush. He glanced at the alarm clock. With plenty of time before the Welcome Banquet, Jake licked his lips.

He went about his task like a mad Doctor Frankenstein grafting a malignant tumor onto an unwilling but paralyzed patient. Sometimes his brush touched the canvas so hard paint splattered down onto the headboard and sprinkled the sheets. Finishing with one color, Jake went over to the bathroom, where he filled the complementary drinking glass with clear cold water from the tap and washed out the brush.

Clink-clink-clink.

The brush's dented metal ferrule struck the rim of the glass, playing a soothing, hypnotic lullaby.

Jake came down from a creation fever dream, finding his face and chest sticky with perspiration. Paint droplets freckled his knuckles and palms.

On the bedside table, the room phone rattled in its cradle. Jake let it ring while admiring his handiwork. His new addition rose above Senior's quaint, homely village.

Brrrring. Brring.

Jake finally grabbed the phone before the sustained ringing could shake the handset loose from the dock.

"Hello?"

"Mr. Varmette . . ."

The voice of the nervous-sounding kid who'd checked him in down-stairs was easy to recognize. It was the second year he'd worked at the Sand Dollar. The previous summer, the kid had been the picture-perfect portrait of middle-American unexceptionalism—blonde hair, pastel Polo shirts with a sand dollar embroidered on the pocket in silver and white thread, and a look in his eyes that screamed, *Is this enough?!* That look alone was all Jake needed to take a shine to the kid.

When he'd checked in for the current workshop, Jake had gotten quite a surprise. The kid had swapped his Polos and Sunday School Hitler Youth haircut for a black t-shirt emblazoned with the incomprehensible logo of some Swedish death metal band and a royal-blue mohawk towering above a face pierced and threaded with metal that sparkled wherever sunlight touched it.

"Yes?"

"Mr. Varmette, your workshop attendees are waiting in our dining area. They're asking if you'll be join—"

Jake checked the blank face of his alarm clock. He followed the cord from the back of the machine, down to the floor. The plug had come out and hung just short of the socket. "Shit."

"Should I tell them you'll be a few minutes?"

"I'll be right there."

Jake hung up. He went to the bathroom to splash cold water on his face and scrub his beard with a hand towel. Still feeling cold, he went over to check the A/C.

But it was already off. Jake slapped the side of the plastic and metal box that contained the air controls. The clang of thumb and forefinger against the encasement reminded him of tribal drums in an old black-and-white jungle adventure film, something with a giant monster waiting behind some ominous barrier.

With no answers regarding the room's temperature coming, Jake left the room. He turned back at the door to tip an imaginary hat to the pitiful painted villagers, leaving them at the mercy of his towering beast. Out in the hallway, he stood holding the door handle for a moment longer than he'd intended. He could see over to the bed where the painting hung. He was sure he'd positioned the monster's head facing to the right, looking down at the village.

But now the creature appeared to look to the left. *Strange.* Jake shrugged and let the door swing closed in front of his face.

Jake swam against the current, heading for the front desk instead of the dining area. A smile broke out under the metal covering the blue-haired kid's face.

"Mister Varmette, your party's waiting for you over in the—"

Jake interrupted. "Please, call me Jake."

The kid repeated the name like he wasn't quite sure what to do with it. "Jake . . ."

"Listen, could I get someone from housekeeping to change the sheets on my bed?"

"Sure thing, Mister Varmette I mean, Jake. I'll call now."

"No rush."

"Y-y-yes s-s-sir."

Jake took a deep breath, prepared for an onslaught of awkwardness at the Welcome Dinner.

Jake woke up shivering. Eyes crusty with sleep, he slapped blindly for sheets flattened under his form. Housekeeping had, indeed, come in and tucked a fresh set of linens onto the bed. Jake had passed out right on top of them. Hands shaking, teeth chattering, he wondered if housekeeping had turned on the A/C whenever they'd changed the sheets.

Once the comforter was loose, Jake flung it from the bed and let the momentum carry his body out as well before heading for the bathroom. The previous night's bad decisions came back with a vengeance. Soon enough, Jake felt like he'd turned himself inside out.

Releasing the toilet from his sloppy, desperate embrace, Jake stood on uncertain feet and spread his hands flat on the counter. Through narrowed eyelids, he studied his reflection. His bushy, unkempt madman's beard, bloodshot eyes, and sunken cheeks were a far cry from the neat and clean look he'd sported when Senior first brought him in to help with the workshop.

Back then, there was no Jake, at least not as far as Senior's adoring fans were concerned. There was Jacob Jr., a role Jake played as well as he could for as long as he had to. He'd thought he needed the old man's blessing for making his art. But even when he tried for it, Jake never felt that approval. With that realization, he'd thrown Jacob Jr. away, a derivative creation he wanted no part of.

A half-hazy memory came to Jake, dredged up from the moments before his head had hit the pillows. Adrenaline and fear propelled him out of the bathroom. The painting waited for him.

There were the trees, the mountains, the fairy-tale village populated by anonymous faceless blobs. *But his monster!* It no longer towered above the trees as it headed down from the mountains, lumbering toward the village.

Something looking like Jake's monster remained on the canvas, but it was now tied down with thick ropes and heavy, rusted chains, which were attached to stakes driven into the ice. Blood spilled from the creature's open mouth, a thick and syrupy reddish-green painted on with the consistency of spilled cough medicine.

Jake hoped touching the canvas would provide answers where sight failed. But he didn't feel fresh paint under his fingers as he ran his hand over the snow-white fields, brown and green trees, gray and silver mountains.

When he tried pulling his hand back, something tugged at his skin like a prickly briar. He pulled again—harder—and his hand came free. Twisted, rope burn patterns appeared on Jake's pale, puckered palm.

"Son of a bitch."

Jake squinted at what looked like tiny fibers embedded in his skin. He bit down on a piece lodged under his thumbnail and tugged until it came out between his teeth. He spat it to the floor. A pinprick drop of blood pooled under the nail and ran down his hand. Jake used his thumb to smear the blood across the top of the canvas.

He picked up the room phone, dialed the front desk, and waited. The phone felt like an icicle against his ear.

"Can I help you with something, Mr. Varmette?"

Jake didn't recognize the voice of the man on the other end of the line. So, it wasn't the blue-haired kid.

"Who was in my room last night?"

"Pardon?"

"The painting above my bed . . . someone changed it. Maybe while I was out or . . ."

"I don't understand."

"Dammit, do you know who I am?" As cliché as it sounded, Jake sometimes wondered if *anyone* knew who he was. Including himself. Still, he found the part of the frustrated fame-adjacent artist got results whenever he pulled it out.

"I'm sorry, sir. What's the matter with your room again?" The words were conciliatory, but the undercurrent of disdain flowing beneath them wasn't subtle.

"My father's painting. Someone tampered with it last night."

"Mm-hmm. Someone?"

"Yes. *Someone* came into my room, and either changed or swapped out the painting above my bed with an altered forgery. I trust you understand what a violation that is."

Jake listened to the clerk's fingers sweeping over computer keys. "Let me just look up your room. Ah, here we are. You requested a change of linens?"

"They—some paint spilled. One of my tubes burst."

"Well, regardless, our housekeeping staff works the same shifts all week. Perhaps you can ask the person who changed your sheets about your painting when they come by later today."

"My father's painting."

"Of course. Your father's painting. Will that be all?"

Hanging up without saying "Yes," Jake headed down into a storm cloud of sun hats and travel easels. He put on a rehearsed happy face, pretending to give a damn about the students' "progress."

"Alright, who's ready to paint?"

The painting had been changed again.

This time, Jake's monster was *gone*.

Unsure how anyone could've made the alterations, Jake was nonetheless undeterred. His blood streak had dried from a bright red to a more subdued brick-colored hue. He painted faster than before, building his new monster from that foundational blood-line. He slashed acrylics across his father's painted mountains. He fanned brush bristles, transforming his blood splatter into the discolored sacs bulging under his monster's bottom jaw.

Once he'd finished, a feeling of deflation took over his body. Feverish from the back-and-forth between the heat of artistic fire and the impossible chill of the room itself, Jake fell onto the bed. Slipping under the covers, he glanced over at the clock.

A red *12:00 A.M.* flashed back, blinking and unreliable.

Jake's monster was burning.

The other vandal, that unseen rival engaged in a sort of "Spy vs. Spy" battle of graffiti one-upmanship had somehow repainted the new monster's limbs, flailing and wild. Where Jake's portrayed power, this altered version looked pathetic. Jagged flames shimmered under a painted sunset.

Jake eyed his paints, brushes, and other supplies spread across the floor by the bed like offerings placed on the altar of an ancient temple.

He'd have to try again.

Taking up almost the entire background of the old man's painting, Jake's third monster dwarfed the mountain range, both in height and width. Impossible by real-world metrics, the creature didn't blend in with the scene, but threatened to overtake it.

Jake brushed his thumb across a stray glob of paint that had fallen from the tip of his brush and landed on the monster's teeth.

"Fuck!"

He pulled the thumb back. Fresh blood oozed from irritated skin.

"Housekeeping!"

Jake took in the chaos and disarray of his room, the way a wounded person might assess a broken limb in a brief window of lucidity before shock settles in.

"I'm sorry. Not now!"

The loud atonal beep of a keycard in the door slot marked the housekeeper's arrival. Her cart's wheels squeaked as she pushed them into the room.

"I'll leave soon. If you could come back and clean . . ."

Jake turned around to make sure she was leaving, but found her standing right behind him instead. He looked down at the tiny, brown-skinned woman wearing perfectly-pressed slacks and an ill-fitting cotton Polo. Her black hair sat flat and tight against her head. Her eyes darkened with fear. Jake wondered what exactly it was that had her so afraid.

They stood locked in a battle of "who'll move first?" Jake ended up on the losing side. He looked behind him, following along the housekeeper's line of sight. It led back to the painting—to *his* monster.

Jake didn't think, he acted. He pushed her back, away from the painting. "How'd you do it?"

"Señor?"

"How'd you change my painting? What did you do to my monsters?"

Jake pushed her again. That was enough for the housekeeper. She moved like she knew when to get the hell out of a bad situation.

Jake kept up a rapid-fire litany of questions and accusations all the way to the door.

The housekeeper reached back, fumbling for the handle. Jake made a half-hearted grab for her wrist, but she twisted free. The door opened with a click like a starter pistol.

"Don't!"

Jake's door shut in his face. His fist slammed near a peephole unmoved by his impotent howls of rage.

Later, a small, folded yellow Post-it note was shoved into the room from under the door. Jake picked up and unfolded the note. Fingertips sticky with paint rubbed against the blackened tacky glue on the Post-it's backside.

"Mr. Varmette, several students have already opted for early checkout, citing erratic behavior and insufficient instructional support on your part. We've been instructed by management to place any unresolved charges on your organization's bill."

Jake crumpled up the note and flicked it against the indifferent door.

Jake's arms ached, but he was done.

His latest creature, with moss-green skin and black, abyssal eyes, glimmered with a slapdash layer of gloss. It seemed to vibrate under inspection. But there were also other unwanted changes to consider in the piece. Puncture wounds dotted the body in an almost ritualistic pattern.

Jake retched. Booze had nothing to do with it. The fault belonged to the smell permeating the room's freezing confines. The smell of death had lingered at home for nine whole months while Jake's old man rotted away in the makeshift hospice bed they'd set up in his studio.

Nine months dying. After he was buried, Jake had found some gallows-humor comfort in the notion that his father took as long to die as to be born. But now, two years later, Jake still couldn't evade that foul odor. Like his old man's legacy, it felt inescapable.

Jake climbed on top of the bed. Brush in one hand and a palette pock-marked with sloppy dollops of paint in the other, he stumbled, losing his balance momentarily. Hands gripped the sides of the painting until he'd steadied himself.

Like an out-of-control game of whack-a-mole, for every oozing red wound Jake patched with creamy white, he'd check the expanse of his monster's form and find more red.

Despite the unceasing chill in the room since check-in, Jake suddenly felt an intense heat against his face. Like someone had lit an entire book of matches under his chin. He turned his head from side to side—King Kong dodging bullet-spraying biplanes. His eyes watered as though exposed to smoke.

Paint fumes, maybe. But not smoke.

Then he noticed a new change from his unseen rival. The painted villagers remained where Senior had placed them in his original composition. But each adult-sized figure held a lit wooden torch in their hands.

Jake dropped to the floor. He stared at the illuminated faces. With the trompe l'oeil torchlight added, the red of the faces made sense, giving their features more definition.

No one else was in the room. No one could've made the changes without Jake seeing them. *The painting had changed itself.*

A single word appeared in the painted snow. Deep grooves cut through layers of paint to spell:

"STOP."

Jake stood and drove his shoulder against the side of the bed's headboard, moving the bed aside. He pushed as hard as he could, his muscles on fire. He bit his tongue. Hot, wet, coppery blood filled his mouth. He stopped only after he'd successfully moved the bed clear of the painting. With nothing in the way, he reared back and spat at the canvas. The bloody wad slid down into the snow.

The real-world impact of the old man's winter landscape seemed to increase every time Jake touched his brush to the canvas. Head pounding,

Jake pinched the bridge of his nose with raw, aching fingers. Though he'd never experienced frostbite, Jake was pretty damn sure he had it. He reached for the room phone, hoping he'd be able to hold onto it.

The front desk answered on the third ring.

Jake didn't give them time to speak. "Help! I need—there's something wrong . . . with my room. With my dad's painting!"

"Mr. Varmette?" The blue-haired kid cut through Jake's panic.

Jake felt relief smoothing his brow, stirring up a relaxed smile. The words came easier, slower. "Something is wrong with the painting."

"Mr. Varmette, I must inform you that we've received numerous noise complaints from guests and staff. Not to mention reports of disruptive, potentially abusive behavior. While we appreciate your father's past patronage, we cannot abide by an unsafe environment for others. If it persists, our policy is . . ."

Jake switched tacks. "Kid, look, I like you. I get *they* want you to say that. But you're a free spirit. An individual. Like me. What do *you* want to say to me?"

The silence on the other end of the line landed like a gut punch. The ache traveled from Jake's stomach and pressed against his ribs. And the tiny click as the kid hung up, grew to a roar as blood rushed to Jake's head.

The alarm clock lay in pieces, ruined beyond any manufacturer's warranty. Its destruction came after the painting had destroyed another of Jake's monsters, right in front of his eyes.

Jake had stripped to his underwear. He'd pulled the duvet off the bed and draped it across his shoulders to hide his nearly naked body. Intermingling layers of paint and sweat gave his exposed skin a rainbow sheen.

He regretted that the duvet didn't provide enough warmth to protect him from the cold wind blowing from the painting and filling his room. The curtains fluttered, revealing late afternoon shadows transitioning to a heavier coating of darkness.

Jake understood what was happening was impossible. But faced with his father's painting and his own monsters, he chose to believe in that impossibility and in doing so, had to fight back, using every last droplet of paint he could squeeze out, rubbing and scratching brush bristles across the canvas in bigger, bolder, more obscene strokes.

At some point, he pressed down too hard on his last brush and snapped it right in two. He let it fall to the carpet, alongside the other broken brushes, splintered palettes, and used-up tubes of paint like shed cicada shells.

But Jake didn't stop. Multicolored fingerprints left identifying hoops and whorls across the painted sky. A paint-drenched index finger extended a line up from his new monster's chin. With a swooping, elegant curve, more natural and relaxed than anything he'd ever achieved, Jake brought the line up to the top edge of the canvas. There was nowhere else for his monster to go. Within the confines of the painting at least.

But Jake took his line past limits his old man had set. The gray and black sludge from the remaining paint marred the empty white wall-space above the canvas.

Neon-green discharge dripped from the monster's eyes and mixed with yellow, foaming drool leaking from its mouth. Otherwise a gray and ugly thing, Jake's final monster extended to the surrounding wall, where it seemed to wrap the canvas up in its veiny arms.

Jake flashed on the source of his inspiration, an old photograph he'd found tucked away in one of the many boxes cluttering his late father's studio. A candid shot taken in L&D on the day Jake was born. Senior holding Junior. The not-so-old man in the photograph looked like he'd taken that exact moment to decide the fate of the fragile being in his arms. Would he love it or would he destroy it?

So, what did you decide, Dad?

Jake's monster licked its lips.

Its long, yellow, and gnarled claws released their hold on the painting and burst from the wall, leaving the canvas hanging behind on nail and wire.

It pinched the corners of the duvet draped over Jake's shoulders. With a push like a caress, the blanket fell to the floor. Exposed, Jake shivered again.

Jake didn't run or even stumble back. He waited. After all, he'd made the monster. He felt entitled to see what it would do next.

Then, the claws pushed down deep into bare skin. The thin barrier split easily, like the peel of a rotten banana. Jake looked from shoulder to shoulder, and saw twin pools of blood bubbling out.

The shocking sight of crimson brought Jake screaming back to reality. He raised stained hands to cover his face. His fingertips brushed the underside of the creature's lengthy, writhing tongue. The fleshy, forked protuberance wrapped around his wrists, pulling his hands together. The monster dragged its creator forward. Blood ran down Jake's back, mingling with the paint already soaked into the carpet.

Jake screamed again.

The beast leaned out from the wall even farther, like a demented pop-up book illustration. Its tongue, still binding Jake's hands, vibrated in a rhythm suggestive of laughter. Jake's arms felt heavy and numb.

Pulling its claws out of Jake's shoulders, the monster kept up the attack. It scratched and tore, ripping away Jake's skin like wrapping paper at a child's birthday party: a bothersome task to be dispatched with as soon as possible.

So cold . . .

I can't feel . . .

Like sawblades, the monster's fangs shredded the flesh connecting Jake's right ear to his head. The ruined wrinkled flesh fell to the carpet.

One more hard tug and flesh-and-blood man and paint-and-pigment monster would become one. Jake strained against the sinuous binding of his monster's tongue. He pulled his frozen hands toward his chest, pulling as hard as he could, trying to use the monster's bulk to his advantage.

His knuckles brushed along the bottom edge of the canvas and came back blackened with the still-drying paint from which his monster was formed.

He pulled again, freeing enough space to pry his hands apart, reaching for the wall.

The painted villagers swayed from side to side. Like the tempting figures of a desert mirage, waving weary travelers closer.

Jake didn't scream again. But he did whisper. This time, his words were simple, inevitable. Saying them aloud felt like cutting out his own heart.

"I'm sorry."

He took the painting off the wall. The rusted wire dug into his palm, cutting through layers of paint and blood.

Jake brought the painting up to his face. He held it, not like a parent cradling a child, but like a warrior hoisting a shield for protection against the onslaught of some incomprehensible beast, some living night terror dredged up from the darkest corners of imagination.

Those darkest corners belonged to Jake. The monster belonged to Jake. But it still wouldn't let him go. It'd met its maker and found him wanting.

Jake stopped pulling and instead pushed forward, driving the painting back into the open mouth of his creation.

Hot breath, reeking of dyes and chemicals, melted layers of paint from the canvas. One layer after another, all the changes Jake made and all the countermeasures in response, disappeared from sight, like birthday cake frosting pressure-washed down an open sewer drain, the swirling primary colors intermingling with darkness and shadows. This continued until all that remained was what Jacob Varmette Sr. had painted: the tiny, rustic village, sitting beneath snow-capped mountains.

Jake fell forward. He refused to relinquish his iron grip on his father's painting. The dimpled canvas surface felt like his father's artisan fingers, wrapped around Jake's tiny child hands and guiding his first marks with crayons, pencils, and paintbrushes all those years before. That memory had been supplanted by the frustrations, the feelings of falling short of expectations that Jake himself had piled on, like all those layers of paint, over and over again. It felt like the old man had let his son create this nightmare narrative.

Or maybe he'd tried a more collaborative approach all along.

Jake remembered being a kid, falling asleep outside his father's studio with pencil in hand and graphite smears on both cheeks. He'd drawn faces on the studio door. Faces that the old man never washed from the surface. They'd stayed there until he died. It had been Jake who'd finally made the cleaners wipe them away.

He kept falling, hearing the winter winds stirred into a frenzied, shrieking chorus. He didn't land on carpet, but on snow. His touchdown was soft, but the cold air against his bare, bleeding skin drove the breath from his body.

He sat up with tears frozen to his face. Looking over he saw the lights of the village waiting for him.

Grinning like a fool, Jake whispered to no one, "My father made this place for me."

Still weak from blood loss and the cold, Jake rose to his feet. He turned from the village and took in the familiar snow-covered scene from his new point of view. Jake started walking forward, wincing with every agonizing step. He thought he heard voices calling him back and wanted to listen to them. But he couldn't. Not yet.

He walked until he reached the barrier, the line separating this "sky" from the world he'd left behind.

The monster's shadow, cast by a creature now living on the other side of the canvas, fell back on Jake inside the painting. Muted tones spread over snow. Jake whispered the name of the horror left behind on the other side. Then, as though signing off on his own work, with blue-and-black fingertips, he traced the curves and lines of his father's signature hovering there in the snow.

And why not? It was his name too, after all.

CASUAL

Of course, I'd never killed *with* someone before. I stood outside the pub, checking my phone again and again, rereading her old texts between drags on my cigarette. It was just my luck we picked a night where New York City was gripped by that kind of "eff you, buddy" cold that sets your teeth chattering so hard you're amazed the next day if you find your tongue intact. With no new messages coming, I let my nervous energy keep me warm. I wiggled my fingers, raw-red from the wind, just to make sure they were still working. (They were.)

But if I'd left my leather gloves on, I would have had a hell of a time ashing my Camel. So, I had to make do with boiled-lobster fingers.

For the moment, I was the sole inhabitant of the chained-off designated smokers' area. I liked the spot—not just because of the nasty habit that I swear I'm gonna quit someday soon—but also because it provided a clear line of sight back through the pub's open doorway. "Silver Bells" bled out onto the sidewalk, smacking me in the face like a melting musical snowball. Never mind that it was already January . . .

Above the door, cradled on top of a stiff metal arm jutting out from the brick façade, the security camera stared back with electronic nonchalance. Encased in the camera's hard shell, the black lens peeked out like the shy head of a turtle. As I neared the filter on my smoke, I thought about that camera peering over the shoulders of all the incoming and outgoing patrons. Getting just the briefest of glimpses into so many passing lives. What secrets, what whispered confidences, what bad decisions had that little camera been privy to up there on its isolated perch?

I held the yellowed end of the Camel between blistered thumb and forefinger. Then, I cocked my index finger back. Paused. And released. My fingernail launched the spongy layer of the filter on contact. I watched the arc of the departing cigarette butt. Up, up, up . . . and then a crash right back down at my boots. I raised one foot and brought a ridged-rubber sole down on the butt. I finished with a grind and a twist, leaving it for some street cleaner to deal with when the black sludge we all call "snow" finally melted away.

I heard the CD playing from an old boombox behind the bar skip on "Jingle Bells," producing a constant loop of "Dashing through the snow, Dashing through the snow, Dashing through the snow . . ."

I looked down at my phone again. I'll be honest, I wondered if she was actually going to show. I also wondered if maybe—just maybe—I'd misread the emails, if the code words I saw in her postings and texts were really just the friendly, if slightly esoteric banter they appeared to be at first glance.

But then, "One thing at a time."

That's how I'd gotten by so long with no notice, no trail, no suspicions, and no end to my fun. It all came back to "one thing at a time."

This wasn't even the first time I'd tried to set up something like this only to have it all fall apart.

The first time, I chickened out. I stood leaning against the stairway railing at the top of the subway entrance, tapping out a last-minute "Sorry. Too hungover to do it tonight. Some other time?" But then I deleted that number and ditched the phone.

The second time, I got stood up. That was fine. Only fair, really.

And so, I did what I always do, I planned my escape, my retreat back to another night of flying solo. I imagined it'd go something like this: (1) Close tab, (1A*) but maybe have another drink though . . . (*) Do they have a limit if you're paying with a credit card? I didn't have any more cash, so . . . (But don't worry, the credit card wasn't in *my* name.)

Lost in mounting minutiae, I missed hearing the squeak of her suitcase wheels as she rolled them across the icy sidewalk in front of the pub. It was only after "Lizzie" (that was the name we agreed on—she was *Lizzie* and I was *Jack*—and we didn't want to waste our originality on codenames) cleared her throat that I looked up. On impulse, I felt a smile twitch out at the corners of my mouth. It cracked my wind-chapped lips and hurt like a sunuvabitch, but I didn't care.

There she was.

She wasn't a fading-filter hipster Polaroid recreated via blurry iPhone photo snapped midexclamation. She was real. And she was really standing in front of me.

One mitten-clad hand gripped the handle of her large floral-patterned suitcase, and she extended the other hand to me. She kept a small black clutch jammed against the armpit of her coat. "Jack?"

I liked the way my name, even though it wasn't *really* my name, sounded coming from her mouth. It sounded cool. It made me sound cool.

In that moment, I wished I had a breath mint, a piece of gum, or something. Because I sure could taste that burnt tobacco at the back of my mouth, and I couldn't remember if she'd told me if she was a smoker or not.

"Lizzie?"

"Yes, that's me."

I couldn't help myself. I found myself studying her—looking her over just like I would if she had been "one of them." I shook off the inherent misogyny of the act, though, reasoning that she was probably doing the same thing to me.

She was shorter than I'd expected. You didn't have to take a very long trip from her purple knit wool cap to her black curls to the brown faux fur coat cinched around a black dress, all of it ending on the final punctuation of gray leggings and black boots. And then? The sidewalk.

I brought my eyes back up to find her waiting for me to make the next move, to say something. I smiled. "You wanna go in?"

"Sure," she said, "Beats the cold."

As we walked inside, I caught her looking up at the lone camera. "Place got robbed a few times in the '80s . . . '90s maybe. Before gentrification," I said, punctuating my "explanation" with a shrug.

"Yeah, I passed two yoga studios and a Starbucks on my walk from the train. This seems like a real rough hood."

I laughed, caught off guard by her deadpan delivery. But I shouldn't have been. Detachment's kind of *our* thing, right?

Her suitcase's wheels rattled on the maroon-painted cement floor. *Rattle, rattle, rattle,* and stop.

A string of red lights stretched across the front of the bar, making the pub look like the type of place that catered to high-class call girls and their johns, instead of its actual clientele of trust-fund kids who could still afford the rent and the muse-seeking artists who refused to admit they couldn't. The bartender, an indie rock wannabe with a caveman beard, came over from drying pint glasses. He stopped in front of Lizzie and asked, "What can I get for ya?"

I couldn't help but smirk. "Be right with ya, bud," Beardy the Bartender had said when I first walked in and tried to order. Never mind that I was the only one trying to do so at the time.

"What were you drinking before?" she asked me.

"Just a pilsner." I nodded over to an empty barstool and the near-empty pint glass in front of it. I'd placed a cardboard coaster on top, backwash and beer foam webbing the insides. Further down, at the end of the bar, the pub's only other patron, a red-faced businessman, held his head up on wobbly elbows, trying to forget his troubles with the help of a seventh— or maybe a seventeenth—Guinness.

"Oh."

"But I could go for something stronger."

"What do you recommend?" Lizzie asked Beardy. She unclasped her coat, slipped it off her shoulders, and held it back for me to take. I took it without question. As I did, I caught Beardy's eyes dipping down the plunging neckline of Lizzie's dress. "I'm partial to our take on the old-fashioned," he said, "I call it the 'Before It Was Cool.'"

"Oh, so you came up with it?"

She waved her palm just above the bar. Close enough that you might assume she was touching it at first glance.

"I did."

"We'll have two." My words sounded harsh and bleating. A jackass's lament.

"You got it."

Beardy turned his back to us and started pulling bottles from bar shelves. "You want to add this to your tab?" he asked without turning around.

"Actually, we're gonna go sit over there."

I pointed past the red lights of the bar. In the late evening bar-room haze, worn-down leather booths held together with duct tape and rusting furniture staples radiated out like little islands. "Is that gonna be okay?"

Plopping a spherical ice cube into one of the glasses, Beardy sighed.

"Technically you're supposed to place those orders with the waitress, if you're gonna sit over there," he said.

"But you can let it slide when it's this late, yeah?" Lizzie asked.

I watched her fingertip brush across Beardy's exposed arm hair. I thought I saw him wince as she snagged one hair out. But then again, I might have been getting ahead of myself.

"Yeah, yeah, I'll call ya when they're ready," he said.

"C'mon." Her fingers intertwined with mine as she led the way to a booth on the far side of the open barroom.

On the way, I nodded toward the previously mentioned waitress. She sat in a chair back in the darkness. She twisted a finger around a stray lock of hair as she gazed down at her phone screen. Like she'd never even known we were there.

The bulb of a nearby wall sconce was burned out, so the lighting at our booth was especially low. Lizzie released the handle of the floral-print suitcase and slid into the booth. She looked up at me and patted the spot beside her.

I didn't have to be told twice. I grabbed the handle of the suitcase to move it aside. To my surprise, it came right up off the ground light as a feather pillow. "There's nothing in here," I said, taking my seat beside Lizzie.

"No. There isn't," she said, "I found it out on the street on my way over."

"Aren't you worried about bedbugs?"

"Are *you* worried about bedbugs?"

I stopped the sure-to-be-flustered response about to stumble from my lips when I saw her smile. She put a hand on my shoulder. Then, she laid her head down against that hand on my shoulder. "I'm glad you suggested meeting like this," I said.

I wished I had a drink right there and then. I don't know how people go through these ritualistic bearings of the soul and only expect . . . sex at the end of it all!

"You're sure you don't mind it being so last minute?" she asked, raising her head up from her hand—the hand on my shoulder.

I shrugged, and smiled back. I figured if she could get away with it, then why not me?

"You come here a lot or what?"

Before I could explain that this was my first time, before I could tell her about the open mic show I sat through earlier in the evening—the one capped off with Beardy stepping out from behind the bar to sit up on the pub's "stage" (actually the chair that the waitress inhabited) and tune his guitar strings for ten minutes before warbling some Iron & Wine, the bartender balladeer waved at us from across the pub. "Your drinks are ready!"

"Mind if I get 'em?" Lizzie asked.

It was a little awkward having to scoot from the booth first to let her out. As I stepped aside, I asked, "You sure you don't need me to—"

She cut me off with a wave. "Nah, I got this."

After I plopped back into the booth, I looked out, following Lizzie on her journey to recover our retitled old-fashioneds. I watched as Beardy made an elaborate show of dunking orange peels inside the caramel-colored liquid of our lowball glasses.

Even with the pub as empty as it was, the acoustics made it so I couldn't hear a word Beardy was saying to Lizzie over at the bar. I watched her lean in close. She gestured over at the doorway. Beardy said something back. Then, Lizzie turned and made a beeline back to me, with the two not-quite-old-fashioneds in hand.

My eyes dropped to my phone's lock screen. I didn't want her to think I'd been sitting there the whole time watching her like some sort of creep. I wanted to seem busy, to play it cool. The lock screen faded away to reveal the last part of our text exchange.

Hope we can do it soon.

Y not now? Tonight?

Tonight?

Ya. U scared? ;)

A drop of water splashed my screen. It had fallen from one of the glasses Lizzie was holding. "Geez, stalk much?" she asked with a smile.

She slithered into the booth, this time taking the spot across from me. She reached across the table. I put my phone back in my pocket. Then, she took my hands in hers. "Relax. I'm kidding," she said.

"Sure, sure."

I reached for the old-fashioned (let's be honest, that's all it was), and tilted it up to my lips. The ice sphere smacked against my bottom lip and some liquid made its grand escape, running down my chin. Wiping it away, I gave my best exaggerated "Ahhh" to mask the fact I'd lost about half my drink. I used my shirt sleeve to clear the drink splatter from my cheeks, red now from embarrassment rather than the cold outdoors.

Lizzie left her glass sitting on the table. "You ever done *this* before?" she asked.

I set my glass down beside hers. I told her everything—*everything*. She listened, nodded, and even laughed when appropriate. "One time my old roommate walked in on me . . . um . . . when I was, uh, cleaning up."

Her quick staccato laugh made for the perfect response.

"That must have been awkward," she said.

"I did have to look for a new roommate after. What about you?" I asked her.

Her list followed. It mirrored mine in so many ways, but strayed from my narrative at just the right points to keep things interesting: an abusive stepfather instead of a neglectful mother, a playmate left by an old creek instead of out at the small-town dump.

After she was done, she turned her head from side to side, taking everything in. "Silver Bells" played again. By the bar, Beardy traced the outline of the mermaid tattoo on his bicep with an obvious coke nail. The businessman had his head down, snoring into the sticky spot where he'd spilled his last beer. The waitress sat in the dark, wiping away fresh tears. "How's your drink?" Lizzie asked.

Before I could answer, she turned hers up. I heard the ice sphere clink against her teeth. I watched the liquid spill out the sides of her mouth and run down her chin, droplets racing down her pale neck.

Then, she was up and on her feet. Rocking on her heels, she stood there waiting for me to join her. "Maybe we could go outside and have one of your cigarettes," she said.

Even though she phrased it like a suggestion, she spoke it like a command. The waitress rose from her perch in the dark, having finally noticed us. She floated behind us, our overly perfumed shadow. Lizzie stepped out into the cold. Before I could follow, the waitress grabbed my arm. "You two still working on your drinks over there?"

From the doorway, I watched Lizzie rummaging through her clutch.

"Because it's dead here and we're probably gonna close soon, soooo . . ."

"Yeah, yeah, we're just gonna go have a cigarette," Lizzie said.

"Whatever!"

The waitress pulled the door shut just as soon as I was all the way outside. Through the thick wood, I could hear Gene Autry explaining what Santa had said to Rudolph one foggy Christmas Eve. At least she didn't lock us out.

"So, we gonna do this or what?"

Lizzie punctuated her question by running a finger up and down the icepick she'd pulled from her clutch. I grabbed her shoulder—the first time I'd initiated physical contact—and pulled her over to the snow-sludge-covered smokers' corner. "Be careful," I said, nodding up at the camera sitting sentry over the doorway.

She pushed me away. She walked over and stood right in front of the door. She waved at the camera. She licked the icepick. No cold temperatures were needed to freeze me in place at that moment.

"Relax. Mr. Bartender told me that thing's been outta service for at least a month."

I still wanted that cigarette, but I figured it would have to wait. Especially as Lizzie's free hand snaked into my front pocket. "I've been admiring this thing all night," she said.

I didn't mind. I let her pull out the stainless steel butterfly knife I kept there. "Why don't you show me how you use it?"

Again, her suggestion was a command.

I flipped open the blade with a flick of my wrist—just the way the tweaker at the flea market had shown me. I made him show me so many things I could do with that knife. I watched Lizzie's eyes land on the rust-colored spot at the tip of the blade. Not quite as stainless as originally advertised. Her smile was equal parts approval and anticipation.

I felt overcome by relief. This time, it was me stepping in front of her. I grabbed the door handle. "Shall we?"

She nodded. I yanked open the door. Bing Crosby and his "White Christmas" were there to greet us. Lizzie made sure the door was shut behind us. Locked too.

I hit "STOP" on the boombox. Christmas was officially over. I looked out from the bar and saw Lizzie stepping through the reopened front door and out onto the sidewalk. I sprinted after her.

On my way out, I grabbed the handle of her suitcase. It was much heavier now. I grunted, as its weight slowed me down mid-stride. A new red blossom—courtesy of Beardy's hacked-up bits—appeared amid the suit-case's original bouquet. We hadn't discussed it or anything, but I figured she'd want to dump the suitcase a few blocks away. At least that's what I'd have done.

We stood there in the dark, in the silence. Each breath sent falling snowflakes swirling off in new, unexpected directions. Lizzie smiled and it made my night. I shut my eyes, hoping to lock that image away. I'd done the same thing earlier, watching Lizzie stab her icepick deep into the wait-ress's eye socket.

When I opened my eyes again, I saw Lizzie making circles in the snow with the toe of her boot. The blood trails her circles left reminded me of fresh berries in powdered sugar.

"Would you—would you maybe want to—"

I was off script. Operating without a plan, like when I had to chase down the surprisingly agile businessman and drown him in the piss-filled urinal trough of the men's room. "Would you want to do it agai—"

Lizzie cut me off with a mitten-covered hand to my lips. "Shhh."

Her shushing blended with the whistling chorus of the wind. She turned away. "That wasn't the deal, remember?"

"We do this together. One time. To share it with someone . . . for once. Then we go our separate ways. Nothing serious, just casual," she said.

She stepped into the smokers' circle.

There was a lot I wanted to say. *"But what if someone finds out about us? What if they ask me about you? What if I see you later—years later—on the street with your co-workers? Or on the subway, your arms filled with grocery bags? Or at some gas station convenience store in a shit-hole town with a too-baggy tank top purchased from Daytona Beach with your overly-straightened hair, looking dull and lifeless? What then?"*

But I didn't.

She stood there waiting for me to say . . . something, though. "Yeah, you're right."

Lizzie nudged me as I joined her in the smokers' enclosure. "How 'bout that cigarette?"

I slapped gloved hands against my jacket pockets. I reached into one for my lighter and into the other for my pack of smokes. I held out my cigarettes as a final offering to her. I looked down at my gloves, then back at her. That was enough.

She understood I needed some help fishing out the smokes.

She took the pack, smacked it against the inside of her wrist—once, twice. She opened the pack and pulled out one cigarette. She held the empty pack toward me. "Damn," I said, "Sorry about that. Thought I had two left."

"It's okay."

She flicked her mitten-covered thumb across the flint of my lighter. A flame sparked to life. It felt like the flame had been in dress rehearsals all those other times I'd used it, and now it was finally taking the main stage. Lizzie held the flame to the cigarette that hung between her lips. I watched her suck in and let the orange embers glow at the end.

Blood dripped through the suitcase fabric and onto the snow. Inside the pub, a cellphone, probably the waitress's, rang over and over.

Lizzie tapped me on the shoulder. Practically shoved me to get my attention. She held the cigarette out—her final offering in return. One end glowed orange and the other end was marked by the smear of her lipstick.

I opened my lips and she set the cigarette filter between them. I sucked in the smoke.

It tasted like a kiss.

ROSE FROM THE ASHES

Mindy spread the dead woman's ashes across the prep table. She cut a perfect line with the edge of her credit card. "Let's see what you've got for me . . . Rose," Mindy said, reading the deceased's paperwork.

She leaned over the table with a rolled-up dollar bill and snorted a fat rail of Rose's cremated remains up her left nostril. Mindy inhaled until black spots and exploding stars appeared behind her eyes.

An opening door brought Mindy crashing back to the present. She scrambled to the other side of the table and turned around, blocking the remaining ashes from whomever might be at the door, while her heart beat like Neil Peart was playing a drum solo in her chest.

"Are Mrs. Devere's ashes ready?" Mr. Evergreen, Mindy's boss, asked.

"Oh yeah. Sure thing. Comin' right up."

Rubbing her hand under her nose, Mindy's index finger came back black from the ash she'd missed.

Not like it mattered. Her boss was already gone.

Mindy walked to the open clerestory window on the far wall of the crematorium. She stretched for the sill, feeling along with fingertips until she gripped the ashtray containing the remnants of her clove cigarettes. She'd balanced it out of sight from nearsighted old Mr. Evergreen.

She dumped the fragrant tobacco ash and the stray damp chocolate-brown butts into the gold-plated urn provided by the dead woman's family. She'd make sure to seal it tight in case any grieving family members got too weepy and curious about the state of the dearly departed. "Shame they couldn't spring for *actual* gold though," Mindy said to the remaining pile of ashes on the table. She kept a Tupperware in her bag for the leftovers.

Mindy's eyes twitched. First left, then right. Then both together.

Knowing she needed to move fast, she set the urn down and pictured the deceased Rose Devere as she'd looked before cremation.

"What're you doing here?" The old woman's voice was sharper than the others, aimed right at Mindy.

The young woman watched as Rose's spectral form unfolded into the material plane like some demented Magic Eye image.

What're you doing here?

Mindy smiled as she considered the query. It was new, she'd give it that. Most summoned spirits—especially fresh ones—asked the same question. *"Where am I?"*

What're you doing here? A smarter question. Because who the hell was Mindy to this dead lady anyway?

Still, she'd performed the ritual enough times. The dead, no matter how perceptive, couldn't phase her.

"Where'd you hide the money, Rose?" Mindy asked.

Pursing blue-black corpse lips, the ghost scowled. Before she spoke, Evergreen pounded on the door again.

"Come on, Mindy. Mrs. Devere's children can't wait all day."

Mindy covered the distance to the door in record time, pulled it open, and shoved the clove-ash-and-cigarette-butt-filled urn into her boss's waiting hands.

He accepted it with a dumb grin on his face, oblivious to the spirit peering over Mindy's shoulder from within the crematorium.

When the door shut again, Mindy spun around to confront the ghost.

"Listen, bitch. I overheard your kids whining about money being missing. Tell me where you hid the cash. I'll grab the urn from my boss before he hands it off to your family and put the rest of your ashes in there so you can rest. Understand?"

"Pardon me, Miss . . . Mindy," Rose started. "I don't know what you're referring to."

The dead woman's features settled into a cold, impassive stare.

Mindy rolled her eyes, making the specter flicker like a deteriorating film reel. "Suit yourself," she said. "It's your funeral."

She moved to exit.

"Wait!"

Her hand hovering above the doorknob, Mindy smirked and faced her latest ghost. "Yes?"

"Where will I go if I don't tell?"

Mindy's smile widened.

"You'll stay here." She tapped the side of her head. "Most ghosts come around. But sometimes, y'all think you can resist. Tell you what, why don't you take some time and ask the others?"

Mindy closed her eyes in concentration, drawing ghost Rose into the firing synapses of her brain. When she opened them again, the old woman reappeared—paler than before, a shade of white radiating resignation.

"Okay. I'll tell."

Mindy clapped her hands. "Good, good."

She walked to the control panel by the furnace. There, she pressed the round red button, opening the burnished metal doors and letting the flames jump to life, roaring like a yawning dragon. The digital temperature read-out ticked upward.

Mindy had another body to burn and figured, *no harm in multi-tasking.* "So, now that you've had a chance to gossip with the others, tell me, where'd you hide it?"

Rose kept her eyes on the ground, avoiding Mindy's insistent, inquiring gaze. When she spoke again, her voice was quiet, a trembling whisper. "You have so many in there. How long have you been doing this?"

Mindy laughed. "Not long enough, since I'm still working here, burning you stiffs. Lost my damn sense of smell and still haven't paid back all my student loans. But you'll change that, won't you, Rose?"

The dead woman flickered. Resisting. Her voice grew in volume as she spoke. Her eyes met Mindy's and the younger, living woman released an involuntary gasp. "They told me about you. Those other ghosts inside your head. You're strong. You defeated them all—one after the other."

"Uh-huh." Mindy pulled the sheet from her next body, playing at nonchalance and letting Rose chatter on.

The slabbed corpse belonged to a younger man. Twenty-something. College boy. None of Rose's wrinkled skin and varicose veins. Alive, Mindy would've plied him with shots at a seedy bar and taken him home for her terrible pleasures.

But not now.

Something tickled the hairs in her nostrils—more ash stuck there thanks to Evergreen's interruption.

She snorted, attempting to pull the last stray bits of the dead woman inside her sinus cavity.

Instead, the ash went the wrong way. Mindy coughed as the gritty remnants traveled down her throat.

Wet, phlegmy explosions rocketed past her lips. A muddy green mucus wad dredged from her chest fell onto the lips of the handsome dead man.

Mindy wasn't pleased. She wiped the tears from her eyes. Then, she rubbed her sleeve across her nose and mouth, leaving silver circles behind on the fabric. She let a low frustrated growl escape.

"Okay, tell me where the goddamn money is!"

But Rose was gone.

That wasn't supposed to happen. For the other encounters, the ghosts were so cowed by the one-two punch of being dead and being imprisoned in Mindy's head that they remained frozen in place. Obedient to the crematorium operator's commands.

"They told me you defeated them one by one . . ."

This time, the old woman's voice sounded muffled as though it came from behind layers of padding.

Mindy froze, as Rose's location became apparent.

The handsome dead man took his handsome dead hand and pulled open the stitches from his handsome dead mouth. Rose's voice came through clearer then.

". . . so I convinced them we'd stand a better chance working together."

Sitting up, the corpse swung its legs to the floor. Mindy no longer heard

Rose alone. Instead, a ghostly chorus addressed her, consisting of all the dead she'd consumed and never released. Trembling fingers rose to her lips, her nose. Mindy swallowed, thinking she might hold back any of the other spirits from escaping.

She knew it was too late though.

Mindy ran for the door, but there wasn't time. Filled with stolen souls, the handsome corpse pulled her into their embrace.

They dragged her toward the open maw of the furnace.

In the front, Mr. Evergreen met a grieving husband to discuss tombstone options for his deceased wife. A variety of funeral bouquets drooped down from the lip of a shelf along the wall. Lilies, daisies, orchids, and blush roses. Reaching for the light shining through the front windows of the parlor and waiting a spritz from the plastic spray bottle sitting beside the flowers.

Evergreen shouted his condolences over the roar and rattle of bodies burning in the back.

HAVE YOU SEEN MY MISSING PET?

While the Old Man waits outside Sally's awning, rain sluices down his scalp, falling past his eyes, so it looks like he's crying. The steady, hammering raindrops roll through the labyrinthine indentations of his wrinkled cheeks.

Sally doesn't say a word as the Old Man's brown leather dress shoes squelch and squish, then twist and tap against her discarded jacket and Baby's diaper bag, the one she's sure she hung on the hooks by the front door, all puddled on the floor. She ignores the rainwater leaking from the Old Man's gray trench coat. The water soaks into the brand-new hardwood her father-in-law—*soon-to-be ex-father-in-law*—installed when her in-laws bought the place for Sally and Val. "You know, I paid a lot of money to get the floor replaced, young lady," he used to love to remind her.

But now Sally doesn't give a damn what happens to the floor. There's a not-so-small part of her hoping the dripping Old Man ruins it forever. As they stand a moment past awkward in the foyer, Sally breathes in the lingering scents of her hoity-toity Park Slope neighborhood at night—humid late-summer downpour and the sidewalk offerings of trash day. "Thank you for letting me in," the Old Man says with a smile more genuine than his tears, "I was asking if you'd seen my missing pet."

How long's it been since I hosted guests? Since Val lived here? Even in those times, it was always *his* friends, *his* family. She holds a hand out to the Old Man. But when she notices Baby's pink pacifier gripped between her thumb and forefinger, she pulls her hand and the unexpected pacifier back into the shadows.

If the Old Man notices, he doesn't give her any indication.

As if he's just become aware of his leaking presence in a stranger's home, the Old Man wipes a pale hand across the top of his head. The simple act sends water, scented by his Old Man hair tonic, splattering onto Sally's coat and the diaper bag and the brand-new hardwood floor.

"My apologies for the mess," the Old Man says. His voice reminds Sally of lozenges—smooth, sweet, but also antiseptic, clinical. "It's raining cats and dogs out there, as they say."

Let's take another look at Sally—Sally from before. The Sally from before worries she's about to pull her arm out of its socket as she yanks Baby's car seat out of the back of the Uber. It's the same Uber she waited forty-five minutes for—because navigating the subway stairs was out of the question given the bulk of the car seat, and there wasn't a single cab in Manhattan willing to stop for her.

None who'd go to Brooklyn. And they don't care when you tell them they're legally obligated to do so either.

Assholes.

Of course, the jostling of the car seat wakes Baby. He opens his mouth to scream and gets a mouthful of rain for his troubles. He sputters, coughs, and then finds his screeching wail, beseeching the heavens for God knows what.

Sally wishes for another hand—to stroke Baby's chubby cheeks, to offer her finger to his always eager mouth, giving him something to drool on. She'd let him grind his one jagged popcorn kernel of a tooth, freshly popped past his gum line, along her knuckle. Instead, she's got one hand on the carrier handle and the other is filled with Baby's overstuffed diaper bag. Her laptop bag—with its frayed, broken shoulder strap—was clutched between her arm and ribs.

"You know, you oughta get a stroller, one you can put your car seat in. You're living in such a nice neighborhood for walking," the Uber driver says. He makes no move to unbuckle his seatbelt, get out of the car, and help Sally.

"Yeah, I know," she says, pushing her hip against the car door, hoping she's swung it hard enough to click shut but not hard enough so she ends up with another bruise.

It's not like I planned for my husband—my almost ex-husband—to call me at four in the afternoon, and say, "Sorry, babe. Change of plans. Can't take the baby this weekend. Come and get him? And hurry, okay."

He left the stroller back at his parents' house and then handed this baby to me—this capital-B Baby we'd made together back when he still said he loved me and I still half believed him (because we made a capital-B Baby together, ya know?). And then he left without giving me a word of excuse or apology. But he kissed me on my cheek, and when he did, I smelled his special "time to get laid" cologne. So good for him, right?

The Old Man sits in one of the seafoam-green-dyed wicker chairs Sally's using around the breakfast nook. Its seat creaks as his jagged-glass angular hips settle into it. Sally stands between the Old Man and a view of her sink, overflowing with unwashed dishes caked in reheated Sara Lee detritus and half-dissolved remnants of powdered formula.

"My pet," the Old Man says, continuing the conversation they'd started in the foyer, "he got loose around here. Right near your home."

"Oh," Sally says. "Do you live around here, then?"

Before he answers, Sally runs through the lookbook of her day-to-day: flipping past the faces, voices, hands, and all those walking, walking, forever-walking legs she's encountered, from the coffee shop at the end of the block to the subway platform one avenue over, and up and down, winding through the sidewalks of her memories.

The Old Man waves a liver-spotted hand like he's got more important business to attend to. "With the weather like it is, it makes him so upset. And, well, you know how it goes with pets and thunderstorms."

Sally nods. She doesn't know much about pets. *My last pet was a hermit crab in middle school. I begged Ma to buy me one from the Shore. It took a week until my whole room smelled like someone pissed seawater and died. I never even got around to naming it before I got stuck with an empty shell and the nauseating odor of dead and dying things.*

What Sally does know is how weather like this affects babies—affects *her* baby. On cue, thunder rolls, lightning smacks the sky—storm clouds moving closer. Another lightning strike hits the cable antenna of a nearby building with a crackle and pop. A sizzle follows, instead of a snap. Sally's grateful the noise doesn't wake Baby. The last thing she wants is for him to scream so loud he blows out the speakers on the monitor. Again.

Dammit, the monitor.

Sally pivots from her position blocking the sink. She stretches across the kitchen countertop and flicks the switch on the tiny white baby monitor resting on the corner. The worn device is covered in scuffs and scratches like a boxer past his prime. An orange spot glows in the lower right of the hard plastic shell, like a lit match head in the darkness—a sign of life.

He's quiet. *Of course he is.*

"I'm sorry," Sally says, as her knuckles brush over a stack of unopened bills she keeps by the stove, daring herself to someday set them ablaze, "My baby's sleeping upstairs."

"It's good you're able to get him to sleep in weather like this," the Old Man says. He places both hands flat against the table. His knuckles jut out, swollen like twin mountain ranges, blue veins exploded across them.

The rain from before unleashes itself in rapid-fire machine-gun bursts. It strafes Sally's hair, the sidewalk, and, of course, the crying, crying (*when'll he stop crying?*) Baby.

After getting herself adjusted for the walk to her brownstone, Sally tunes out the cries, focusing instead on the slap-slap-slap of the Baby Carriage Lady's cheap rubber flip-flops. The noise comes from behind mother and child. The Baby Carriage Lady makes her evening rounds circling the puddled end of Sally's block.

Sally pictures the disheveled woman in her dark gray hoodie with the hood pulled over wispy, silver hair. The Baby Carriage Lady's face is pale—cottage cheese complexion revealed in part by the moonlight and the streetlamps reflecting off her dark garments resembling a starless sky. Sally can't recall how long it's been since the Baby Carriage Lady appeared on the block. *Six weeks?*

That's how long it's been since Val told me about Tina—or TeeAnna or whatever the hell her name is . . .

Is that how long it's been since I worked up the nerve to tell him to get the fuck out? He punched the window in Baby's nursery, and I screamed and Baby screamed and Val cried and cried. Of course, I ended up calming Val down and calling an Uber to drive him to the hospital. I tried to get in the back of the car with him, but he grabbed my wrist and squeezed tight. He held it there for a moment, before saying, "No, Sally, you've gotta stay with the baby, remember?"

Sally imagines how Val would handle the Baby Carriage Lady if he was still around. She sees his nostrils wrinkling after getting a whiff of the woman's heady, au naturel perfume—*like cabbage shits and boiled tires.*

But there's no Val. So, the Baby Carriage Lady keeps to her circular path, pushing an empty stroller. No words, no screams, no spitting. It's why Sally's neighbors let the disheveled bag lady stick around.

Of course, she does stink like a dead dog.

"Get you anything to eat? To drink?" Sally asks the Old Man. "Coffee? Tea?"

The monitor chirps like a startled baby bird. Sally's eyes fall to it fast. But no sob, scream, or whimper follows from upstairs in the nursery.

"Oh, a *hot* cup of tea is just the thing."

"I don't remember any Lost or Missing Pet posters around the neighborhood," Sally says, filling her dented silver teapot, the one she got from *her* mother. She flings open the cabinets by the stove, trying to remember where she put her last box of Darjeeling.

"He's *just* run away tonight. But I worry about him out all alone. I guess he's like my child . . ."

The Old Man nods when Sally holds out the box of teabags for his inspection. "My wife and I worry about him, out in the rain like this. We fear he'll catch a cold . . . or act out without our supervision. Don't misunderstand, we trained him well. But we never sought—to domesticate him."

"Uh-huh, is that so?"

Sally's on autopilot. She turns a knob on the stove. The flame leaps up, licking at the sides of her teapot.

"We've kept him inside our house, down in his cage, since the day we brought him home. Fifteen years ago now."

The teapot rattles as the water inside grows more and more agitated. Sally presses on the silver knob at the top of the pot to fix the seal. Already, the metal's hot enough to burn her palm before she pulls it back.

Across the table, the Old Man sits with his legs spread wide, like an old friend come a-calling for gossip and giggles. "Fifteen years? Quite a life for a dog. He must be a good boy," Sally says.

"Good . . . boy, yes. But not a dog." The Old Man stands. The kettle shrieks.

Baby joins the chorus, his screams come filtered through the monitor, like a middle school principal's announcement from a cafeteria loudspeaker. *Attention, Mommy, please report to Baby . . .*

Sally moves for the stairs. But she finds the Old Man blocking her way. Standing there, in the area between the kitchen and the living room, he fills more space than she expected. Baby cries in stereo—the garbled electronic shrieks of the monitor and the bellowing, tumble-down "real" ones from upstairs. She pictures him there—*one chubby, red-splotchy arm burst free from his cloth swaddle, pounding his fist against his chest. Tears, salty with rainwater, cover his cheeks. Baby watches the Yankee Doodle mobile his Mommy bought him at the flea market.*

The Old Man puts his hand on Sally's arm. His skin is soft to the touch. It reminds her of marshmallow fluff.

Sally made it down the block and into the townhouse. She trudged up the stairs to the second floor. At least Baby wasn't crying anymore. Instead, he sucked loudly on two fingers. Later, she'd pull those same fingers from his mouth and find he'd left them wrinkled and white. Thin, pale sticks like leftover happy hour pretzels.

Like they used to serve for free (with the purchase of a beer) at the bar where she first met Val. They'd set a 5:00 p.m. date, right after work, so no funny business could happen. But then it was nine o'clock, and Sally had forgotten to eat dinner. Then Val said, "Let's do shots." He'd kissed her by the jukebox after letting her pick The Breeders. He'd told her he didn't care who saw them. And she'd wanted to believe it because he'd kissed her like he didn't care about anything.

Even me.

All alone with Baby, Sally let herself fall back into the nursing chair. She kept Baby's head level to her chest as she descended. With the practiced precision shared by long-range snipers and exhausted nursing mothers, she performed a one-handed Houdini, partially shedding her work shirt and undoing the nursing bra below before her ass even touched the cushioned seat.

Baby's pebble of a tooth ground against her nipple as he fed. But Sally refused to cry out until he drew blood. When she did, he pulled away from her breast to look at her—scared, confused. "It's okay, Baby. Mama's here."

"I'm sorry," Sally says, "It's my baby, I need to . . ."

The Old Man removes his pillowcase-soft fingers from her arm. He places one finger against his lips, shushing her. They stand there in silence at the bottom of the stairs.

There it is—the silence.

Relief radiating from every pore, Sally tiptoes back to the kitchen. She's giddy as she pulls down the mugs and pours the piping hot water from the kettle over the teabags slung inside. The Old Man's returned to his chair. "How'd you know he'd go back to sleep?" she asks, placing Val's unclaimed "Just Like Daddy" mug in front of her guest.

The Old Man holds up two fingers. "Two things I use with my pet. The first is patience," he says.

Sally leans in, placing elbows on the table, not caring if her cleavage shows. *It's some Old Man looking for his lost pet, after all.*

"When my wife and I brought our pet home . . . oh, how he cried and cried. Didn't matter what bed we let him sleep in or the treats we'd give him. He cried even more. But I told him, 'You cry, but I wait. And I've far more *waiting* in me than any tears you hope to shed.'"

Sally blows across her tea. Her breath sends the teabag pinwheeling around inside the mug. Her eyes grow wide as the Old Man takes his second finger and sticks it right inside the steaming hot contents of his mug. Red welts pop out on doughy white skin. Without skipping a beat, he stirs and continues to speak. "The second is through discipline. There's a pain for the pet, punishment—verbal, physical, or mental. But there is also a pain for the master. You must endure, stand firm."

He pulls his red finger from the mug. The orange-brown liquid drips onto the tabletop. Sally checks the orange dot on the monitor. *So quiet again.* "Do you understand what I'm saying?" the Old Man asks her.

Sally pulls her attention from the monitor and back to the Old Man. She shakes her head with a bemused grin. "I'm afraid not," she says.

The Old Man sips his tea. He doesn't offer any filler for the awkward silence.

It's not until Sally's third attempt to place Baby in the crib and pull her arms away that she gets it right. Baby coughs for a moment, his eyelids fluttering. Sally whispers a quick and foul-mouthed prayer, hoping God excuses the salty content of her language and grants her wish to *please let this fucking baby go to fucking sleep.*

His eyelids fall. He gives her one last squirm, and . . . he's asleep.

Sally shuffles back, away from the crib. Each step is taken with care. The last thing Sally wants is to step on some squeaking, squawking rubber monster or some singing teddy bear. Below the crib, a night-light plugged into the corner socket pulses red—off, on, off, on—like a heartbeat. Street light from the block behind the townhouse shines into the nursery, distorted by the repair tape applied to the broken glass of the window.

Val was supposed to send someone the week before to replace the pane. But, of course, he forgot. At least there's enough tape to hold the broken pieces in place. But it's not enough to stop the whistling of the wind from seeping indoors.

The Old Man sips his tea, not saying a word about his strange and violent stirring method. Sally does the talking. "Our landlord won't let us keep pets," she says.

The Old Man turns to look at the stairs. "What is it?" Sally asks.

"My pet, he likes to climb," the Old Man says. "We found him swinging by his hands across the monkey bars at the park."

"Paws . . ." Sally whispers her correction. Now she can't take her eyes off the stairs either.

Why is it so quiet up there?

The Old Man bangs his mug against the tabletop as he sets it down. The last splash of tea sloshes out and springs across to hit Sally's hand. *Ouch!* It's still so hot.

"He's a rescue. The pack he ran with—soft, weak. They couldn't care for him as he needed caring for."

Sally's mug sits untouched. She's listening to the Old Man, but she's also listening for something else—something unheard, an absence she can't name.

"The problem is, we got him too old. Too old to become the pet we wanted him to be. He came with so many bad habits. We did what we could to turn him into a serviceable creature. Obedient, fiercely obedient."

It's the wind.

The wind's changed. The whistling, thumping sound of the storm against the taped-up glass is gone.

The window's open.

Sally stands again. This time, the Old Man remains seated. His eyes follow her. And then, his words: "He made me stop here. You sang to your whelp on the fire escape. He pulled at the leash, dragging me closer and closer. His instincts growing sharper and sharper. And I *did* promise him a treat."

Sally stumbles, her hurrying feet caught under the hem of her dressing gown. Fight-or-flight triggers all defenses. She's ready to spin around and yell at the Old Man, tell him to get the hell out of her house. But he's an Old Man—an Old Man's who's lost . . . *what breed of dog again? One with hands, found on a playground, kept in his house for fifteen years . . .*

"What kind of dog?" she asks.

"Young lady. I never said he was a dog."

There's a creaking at the top of the stairs, right by the nursery door. "Ah, there," the Old Man says, rising from his seat at last, "I told you he got lost around here."

The Pet paces at the top of the stairs. It's a man, but *not* a man. Something once intended for manhood but brought up . . . *wrong*. It crawls down the steps, hairy arms and legs outstretched. It scrambles for purchase against the padded carpet and the finish of the hardwood floor.

Its hair hangs, oil-slick, dripping strands over unkempt brows. A beard flops against a bone-white chest. The Old Man's Pet tilts its head at the sound of Sally's whimpering gasp. Bloodshot eyes move from Sally to the Old Man.

Sally's hands tremble like a junkie inside a withdrawal. She's certain she's the one grinding her teeth until she figures out the sawing sound comes from the stairs. The Pet growls at her, showing yellowed teeth and blackened gums. Long, chipped fingernails scratch into the carpet, ripping and tearing out strands.

The Old Man stands behind Sally while she's frozen at the bottom of the stairs. He holds a hand up, steadying his Pet with silent commands.

Breaking free from her trance of fear, Sally clutches the railing for lack of better support. *Breathe in, breathe out. Like labor. Concentrate on breathing, babe. The baby's . . .*

"Why can't I hear my baby?" Sally spins and grabs the Old Man by the collar of his shirt. Slight relief washes over her when she turns from the stairs. She can't stand the sight of the Pet, resting on its haunches, with its tongue lolling out from between blistered lips. She escapes into this more manageable panic.

She pulls the Old Man's face close to hers, her nose against his. Spittle flies from her lips. "What did it do to my baby?"

The Old Man pushes her back, shoving her against the steps. She lands hard on her ass, hitting the bottom step. "Attack!"

There's no time for Sally to think. She throws up a hand, a last-ditch defense. The Pet stumble-crawls down the remaining steps to its prey. Then, it's on top of her.

Its hair, hands, and feet cover Sally. Its rotten teeth sink into the flesh of her arm. Blood sprays and she screams. The tangy, copper liquid hits her mouth. It tastes like hot pennies on a summer sidewalk after an evening's rain. She pulls her arm away. Still, her flesh relents to the Pet's hungry mouth and tears like soggy cardboard.

More teeth—more biting. Next, the Pet's claw-like fingernails pierce her nose and cheeks. She moves her hands, desperate to cover her eyes. *Can't let him bite me there.* Mama bear strength comes in the form of an adrenaline-fueled shove.

The Pet tumbles over her, headed for the floor. The Old Man continues watching, studying the attack.

Sally pulls herself up, crawling, sliding back, trying her best to move up the stairs.

Can't slow down. Baby. Baby.

What did it do to Baby?

She stops at the landing. At the top of the stairs, the nursery's door is open. Her eyes fall on the gangrenous wound of baby blue wallpaper illuminated by the moon and lightning strikes outside the busted-open window.

Sally pushes herself onto shredded arms, flesh dangling and blood ooz-ing out onto the ruined carpet.

From her resting place, Sally strains to see the crib, to see Baby still bundled tight, shivering. But she's not close enough. "Go on, boy," the Old Man commands, without urgency, without anger.

His Pet obeys. Because he's a Good Boy. Teeth—broken and reset, chis-eled to fangs, fed on a diet of meat—penetrate the skin on Sally's feet. She cries, but she doesn't fall. She kicks.

One, two. One, two. Faster now.

Her heel crunches through the Pet's nostrils. There's another dull, throbbing ache in her foot as she breaks its nose. Blood gushes into its mustache hairs—thick steel wool, wire cable strands clotted with red and green snot.

Sally dives for the open door of the nursery. But even a broken nose won't stop the Pet. It's got her scent. It's coming for her. Panicked calcula-tions rush through Sally's head.

The bathroom door's closer. The bathroom door's got a lock.

Sally finishes her leap, spinning her broken and torn body as she goes. Once she's inside, she shoves her body back against the bathroom door. It clicks shut, just as the Pet slams into it from the other side.

The door's made of "old" wood. "Strong wood," as Val's dad loved to remind her, while he walked through the house, knocking on every damn door to prove their permanence.

Sally's crying as she reaches for the lock.

I'm sorry, Baby.

The scratching follows. Quick urgent scramblings peeling off the door's painted and lacquered surface. When Sally closes her eyes to try and keep the tears at bay, she pictures the Pet's nails snapping off while strips of off-white paint tear away. Its blood turns the whole mixture into a foam-ing, pink gruel like melted cotton candy insulation.

Sally pulls herself away from the door, streaking blood and bits of skin across the black-and-white checkerboard tile floor. Vomit explodes from her lips and between her fingers, a heady mix of hot tea, blood, and Sally's breaking point. It splatters into the toilet bowl.

When she's finished, Sally sits back, cold tile on her legs and ass. The

Pet's still on the other side of the bathroom door—panting, whining. She dry heaves, but she's got nothing more to give the porcelain gods.

Sally wants her phone. She needs her phone.

Jesus, my phone.

She could call Val. He'd kill the son of a bitch. But she remembers leaving the phone in the nursery, playing ocean sounds to help Baby sleep.

Sally wonders where the Old Man's gone. With a sobbing, exhausted breath, she turns and faces the door. She expects she'll find the Old Man on the other side, waiting with his Pet.

Instead, she hears Baby.

First, there's an inquisitive, high-pitched gurgle. The scratching against the door slows. Then, Baby unleashes a shriek to match the rage of the storm outside. Black spots float before Sally's eyes, but she still sees him—forehead wrinkled, cheeks wobbling. His tongue presses against the bottom of his mouth, giving whoever dares look inside his crib a full view of the black and pink of his insides.

My baby. He's crying for me.

Sally presses her ear hard against the bottom of the door, desperate for more. Baby becomes her anchor keeping her moored to this hellish reality. Each colicky, coughing exclamation keeps her fighting—to breathe, to live.

She shakes her head. Bangs slick with blood and sweat flick across heavy-lidded eyes.

No, no, no.

The scratching's stopped.

The *slap-slap-slap* of palms and callused foot pads moving along the hallway hardwood follows. The Old Man's next command drifts in under the bathroom door, like cursed words from a nightmare's ending, before you wake soaked in fear all alone. "What're you waiting for? Bring me the new pet."

Looking to pull attention away from the Baby, Sally pounds bloody fists against the door, streaking crimson across the old, reliable wood.

Fuck your property value, Ken. Fuck you and your son and this stupid house.

The Pet stops in its tracks. The pounding does the trick.

Sally drops to the floor, pressing a cheek against the cold tile. One eye is all she can manage, looking through the slight gap between the bottom of the door and the floor.

Out in the hallway, the Pet twitches in place, waiting.
Baby's still crying.

"What do you think about this mobile for his crib?" Sally asks Val, picking
it up from a flea market table. Val's eyes remain fixed on his phone screen.

By now, Sally's already read the first of the texts. She can't help it. He
keeps his damn screen so bright, it's impossible not to read every "I miss
you" and "XOXO" flashing by whenever he leaves his phone unattended.

You'd think he'd try a tad more fucking discretion.

But none of it matters. All she wants is for him to tell her he likes the mobile
she's selected for Baby's crib. "What the hell is it?" he asks, already walking five
steps ahead before she can answer. Already moving, always moving.

It's a piece of macaroni in a tri-corner hat with some smaller stars
around it. And when you turn it, it plays . . .

You know what, never mind.

Sally hands the woman behind the table the money marked on the
price tag and shoves her purchase deep into her purse. The heels Val insists
she wears when they go out in public *click-clack* against the asphalt of the
basketball court turned flea market.

"Yankee Doodle went to town . . ."

Sally sings, her rasping and barky voice caked in blood and phlegm. But
she keeps going, watching the hallway through the sliver under the door.
She watches the Pet—stuck between the bathroom and the nursery.

"Riding on a pony . . ."

Baby's crying slows. The Pet turns away from the nursery. The stairs
creak, this time from the bottom.

Here comes the Old Man.

"Stuck a feather in his . . ."

The Pet scratches at the bathroom door again. But not like before. There's an urgency, yes. But missing the violence from before.

"... cap. And called it ..."

The tears come. Sally lets her breaths out in rapid succession.

And one and two and ... c'mon ... there's the head ...

Sally doesn't want to know if she heard the Pet say "Macaroni" when the knob turns and she pulls the door open to rush from the bathroom. She can't take it if it's true.

Baby's not crying anymore.

But it's not enough. She's at the top of the stairs again. The Pet moves, more ape-like than canine now. He's coming to tear her face off. The Old Man stands on the landing, wearing a nightmarish mile-wide smile between his sunken cheeks. She won't let him win.

Sally throws herself down the stairs—into the arms of the Old Man.

The Pet follows. Bloody fingernails and teeth serve as claws and fangs. Doing what comes "natural" after years of conditioning and training.

Sally's outside of herself. She watches her body tumble, bouncing off step after step. The Old Man won't stop her. A limb snaps—not Sally's. A howl of pain—not her own. More black spots appear, deeper and darker.

"Bad! Bad! Not me, you stupid animal!"

Screaming, gibbering curses echo off the townhouse walls.

So, this is what it sounds like when someone dies ...

Looking up from the bottom of the stairs, Sally watches the Pet dragging the Old Man into her living room.

The Old Man's face is gone. No false tears, no wicked smiles.

Everything goes black.

Then, there's light again.

Who's crying?

The front door's open. Sally doesn't remember dragging herself there, but she peers through the open doorway nevertheless. A delivery truck speeds too fast down the wet road. Its horn screams out a warning—too late for a naked young man who runs past Sally and out of the townhouse, not looking where he's going.

No one's around to yell "Heel!"

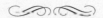

Sally sits on her front stoop. She's shivering, pulling herself back from the dark. They've got their flashlight beams dancing across her eyes. But they've given her a thick emergency blanket to cover the ragged remnants of her nightgown at least. Blue lights swirl, making the last of the rain look like laundry detergent—washing nightmares away. Plastic poncho-clad, black-hat-wearing wannabe tough guys—like Val, but with badges—yell at Sally's neighbors, telling everyone to go home.

But they won't stop. They stand on their stoops and lean out their windows.

Where'd you rich bastards hide when I needed you, huh?

Sally can't shake the sudden feeling something's missing. She ignores the EMTs' questions about how many fingers they're holding up, the offered hands ready to take her to the waiting ambulance she can't afford.

She leans forward to get a better view of the street. There's a black bag, zipped shut. The truck's pulled off to the side of the too-tight thoroughfare. There's a similar black bag inside the house.

But someone's missing.

Sally cranes her neck, blood-caked fingertips push away offered help. She stands on wobbling, ragdoll legs. Sally checks the end of the block. Nobody's there. Behind Sally, someone steps out and ducks under the yellow tape stretched across the entrance to the townhouse. "All clear upstairs. There's no one else in the house."

Sally listens for but doesn't hear the *slap-slap-slap* of cheap rubber flip flops against the wet sidewalk. She misses the gray-hooded figure with her pale white, pillowcase-soft fingers wrapped tight around the ornate handle of a baby carriage. She misses the squeaking wheels, the cradle rattling in its frame.

I wonder what she hides under those baggy clothes. I wonder how fast she'd climb the fire escape behind the house . . .

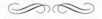

If only Sally could stop screaming, then she'd pick out those squeaking stroller wheels and the *slap-slap-slap* of flip flops splashing along the wet sidewalk, moving away from the flashing lights.

A block or so away, the Baby Carriage Lady beams at her new Pet. She hadn't needed to tell it to be quiet.

It'll be easier to train. Much easier than the last one.

She'd raise this new Pet fine all by herself. After all, hadn't she done a good job finding it—waiting for the right moment to snatch it, separating it before it became too attached, too dependent on its mother?

One thing's certain, this new Pet has the makings of a *Very* Good Boy.

AND OUR NEXT GUEST . . .

The gun goes off outside the green room.

And now I'm awake.

The smell of sand in my nostrils reminds me of the worst parts of summer. It's all the heat—muggy, overwhelming, relentless to boot—and none of the fun. Before I know it, I'm blowing sand-covered snot rockets onto the carpet. Not like it's the worst thing ever spilled on this floor, I'd bet.

There's ringing in my ears. I wonder who's messing around with the prop firearms as I slap around for my cellphone.

I can't find it.

Typical.

Someone's laughing. Several someones by the sound of it.

Who's laughing?

I rub knuckles under my eyelids. I blink once, twice, three times. I find my center (or what passes for it these days). I shake my head from side to side. I'm still not used to the long, dirty blonde locks I'm sporting for the untitled *SWORD & SORCERY PROJECT* shooting next month—next week? I can't remember. The hair slaps across my forehead, dragging against my eyelids, all of me dusted with sand.

I tuck the hair back behind my ears. There's a TV screen bolted to the wall on the other side of the room, and I take a moment to watch the action on-screen.

The red curtains part. Tad Thompson, the host of *The Late Evening Conversation* steps onto the stage. (Of course, I remember when Tad opened for me back when I used to do a few stand-up gigs in New York. Funny kid, even back then. Harmless, but funny.) Even on this tiny backstage TV, his cheeks appear redder than the curtains. The studio audience loves him, though.

"Stop, stop, you're killing me with all this applause!" Tad mock-strangles himself. His hands drop (I see him using eye blinks to count the beats), and then he winks. The camera zooms in tight.

I stand. My body aches as I get off the green room couch. I guess I was napping (but I don't remember falling asleep). A lap's worth of sand spills to the floor.

Good luck to whoever's gotta vacuum all this up.

I look down and watch grains of sand shift and slide between strands of carpet fibers.

"We've got a great show for you all tonight . . ."

Tad rattles off his guest list. I'm in the last spot, his final guest for the taping. Sure as hell beats being the first guest. I think it's the French horror director—Jean-Marc, Luc-Jean, or whatever.

God, I hate that guy.

But "last guest" is the spot you want. No one can show up the last guest.

I look back at the TV as I hear my name, spending far too long analyzing and dissecting the rise, rise, rise and sudden fall of the audience's applause accompanying it. I can't help it. Even after all the premieres, the award shows, the trips to Cannes, and promotional appearances like this one, it's still uplifting to hear someone say my name.

"Mr. McQuade, are you taking these proceedings seriously?"

That's not the show I'm on. That's a different show, several years old now. I look up at the screen and there's the judge, staring down at me the way I remember him—all wrinkled, pale white neck flaps like uncooked chicken sagging down to the black of his robe.

The courtroom camera zooms in on another me, a *bad* me. There's bad-me, looking like death in an oversized olive-colored suit.

"Is this a joke?" I ask, but there's no one else in the green room to answer.

The audience groans.

And we're back to normal.

Tad sits behind the desk, its lacquered wooden surface sparkling under the studio lights. Someone told me it's a replica of the original desk from the show's 1960s incarnation. Good for whoever they got working in the props department for investing so much in faithful re-creation.

Silence.

I realize I'm not used to the silence. And if it's not silent here, it's at least quiet.

There're no noises except the banter onscreen, my breathing, and the slow but steady hiss of falling sand. I check my Rolex—black patent leather, gold fastener, diamond-encrusted face. A gift from the head of the studio after *Commander Man* broke the billion-dollar mark at the box of-fice. ("A SUPER-RECORD!" the *Variety* headline said, making it official.)

I see bits of sand stuck inside the smashed watch face, blocking the exposed gears.

"Jonathan!" I release my PA's name as a question, a command, and an exclamation all in one.

I'm cotton-mouthed as a son of a bitch. My eyes move in their sockets, darting around with the energy and lack of focus of a methed-up street puppy.

"Jonathan! Hey! Anybody listening out there?"

The studio audience laughs some more. I half listen as Tad works his way through some strained bit about superheroes. It's not the most orig-inal material, but his audience doesn't strike me as one made up of com-edy sophisticates. More like a combination of L.A. wannabes working as seat-fillers and Midwest rubes ready to gobble up any half-baked pun com-ing their way.

Without warning, like in the old days, blood rushes to my head, and my lunch rushes out and all over the couch. My lips slick with sick, I stumble to the makeup table and vanity mirror they keep in one corner of the green room. Perfect for those last-minute touch-ups! As I go, I'm praying (or as close as I come to it) I won't miss a step and go crashing through the table.

I sure as hell know this feeling. I know every piece of it: the rush of blood, the sick, the withdrawal, and the aching feeling moving under my skin. I'm well-acquainted with the sagging pull on the eyelids that make them feel like they're going to droop right off your face.

I also know there's no way in hell I should feel like this.

I reach into my pocket. I jam my fingers down as far as they'll go. I wrap a tight fist around my chip, squeezing it for good measure. I let my fingertips brush against the raised "5 Years" imprinted on its surface.

On the TV, Tad introduces his first guest, the French director Pierre-Claude promoting another of his bloody torture-porn horror flicks. Meanwhile, there I am, grinding away at my teeth. And that's causing the ringing in my ears. An incisor rubs hard against a molar, then slips forward and I bite down hard on my tongue. The blood tastes sweet and metallic all at once, like the buzz from the whirling electric drill hitting a nerve at the dentist's office.

I need to think back and figure out what the hell happened to me. It's what I'm supposed to do, right? I'm an actor. I'm told how to feel. Then it's up to me to sort out why.

"Jonathan!"

There's blood in my mouth. And my voice sounds strange. I feel something pulling inside my chest. I worry I'm going to barf again. My eyes feel swollen inside their sockets, like two grapes about to pop.

The audience laughs as pre-taped footage plays. *Look, there's Tad Thompson, your host of hosts, green-screened into my Commander Man trailer.*

"In a world without control, it's time for a hero to take command."

In the edited trailer, Tad sits on a whoopee cushion, right when my

Commander Man delivers a pointed line of "rile-up-the-fanboys" dialogue. The subsequent long, drawn out fart from the TV syncs with my fumbling efforts to get the green room door open.

The movie trailer footage fades, replaced by an old home video. A little boy, wearing Superman Underoos and sporting one of those cone-shaped party hats on his head, runs like his life depends on it. A man, with a face I can't recall, clad in Bermuda shorts and a Lacoste polo gives chase. He sprays the kid's legs with a water hose. The kid yelps with laughter after each spray.

I watch entranced. The boy on the TV looks familiar. For a moment, I see myself.

I let go of the green room door. It's barely budged anyway. It feels like something's blocking it from the other side. I wonder if it's one of my bodyguards, their backs pressed up against the door, crappy European dance music playing in their earpieces, drowning out my cries for help.

I give the door a good kick hoping whoever's on the other side feels it. The door bends but doesn't break. Doors shouldn't act that way. Doors should open.

I look down at my broken watch. It's still broken, of course.

Rituals repeat themselves in times of crisis. So I rub my thumb across my chip, still safe in the clothed enclosure of my pocket. I give it another squeeze. I run my tongue up across my gums behind my teeth. When its bloodied tip touches a small deposit of white powder, my toes curl.

I yank the chip from my pocket and hurl it across the room, sending every cuss word I can think of along with it.

And I know a few.

Of course, in my movies, the chip would sail over to the makeup table, strike the mirror, and smash the glass to pieces. It'd explode in a brilliant lens-flare flash of jagged glass and light.

But my chip makes it about halfway across the room before dropping like a wet turd and falling into another pile of sand.

I don't think Jonathan's coming.

Tad's back at the desk. He holds up a *Commander Man* action figure. It looks nothing like me, with its angular jaw wider than its chest.

"They say this thing's anatomically correct," Tad says, his finger drifting down to the smooth plastic crotch. The audience moans, then howls with laughter.

"He's the star of the blockbuster film *Commander Man* in theaters now. Please welcome, Lance McQuade!"

I'm still here—still stuck in this green room. But then on the TV, I'm also *there*. I stand frozen in place, watching as a bad-me walks through the red curtains. I watch myself turn and wave to the audience. I still hear their screams.

The bad-me takes off at a near full sprint across the stage, headed straight for Tad's desk. I watch the herky-jerky, new-foal gallop of this unknown bad-me. I see his wide-eyed desperation.

The bad-me lurches closer and closer to the desk. I watch him throw his arms out wide and make a spread-eagle dive, belly flopping across the desk's hardwood surface. The sound of skin on unforgiving wood echoes here in the green room.

I pull up my shirt to find a bruise I don't recognize stretched across the curve of my stomach. It lines up with the spot where the bad-me's stomach hit the desk.

Back on the TV, the bad-me's head collides with Tad's chest. I wince at the sound of feedback as he makes contact with Tad's mic pack.

For his part, Tad unleashes a string of cusses putting my recent offerings to shame. I guess he's learned a thing or two since our stand-up days. The feed drops away, of course, replaced by a test pattern.

Over and over, I drive my shoulder into the green room door. But it still won't open.

I'm the star of the biggest goddamn movie in the world, never mind in the good old US of A. I'm supposed to be backstage at a taping of one of the country's biggest late-night talk shows, a cultural icon on a cultural institution. I expect at least twenty people waiting for me on the other side of the door, if not a hundred, each at my beck and call.

I step back and pull at my hair. Long strands come out in my fingers. I retreat to putting the pieces of what came before back together.

First, the drive over. Jonathan was there. (Of course Jonathan was there. Good, loyal, put-up-with-a-ton-of-crap Jonathan. I wonder where he's gone.) And my bodyguards too.

I close my eyes, pinch the bridge of my nose, and I'm back there again.

They're ushering us from the limo. We're already running late. We're always running late: "C'mon, c'mon, c'mon."

Paparazzi flashes explode like artillery fire around us. All of it focused on me.

Autograph-seeking fanboys hang like barnacles along the security railing. They reach for me with their greasy fingers, gripping 8 x 10 glossies, movie ticket stubs, and collector's edition photo-cover movie-tie-in edition graphic novels. They make their offerings with hooted pleas for recognition by their one true god—me.

I break away from the path and grace the masses with my presence. I'm nothing if not a benevolent god, after all. I reach across the barrier but still look above their heads. Always remembering to smile, smile ("Yeah thanks"), smile ("No, you're the best"). I even shake a few hands.

I do it with ease, knowing Jonathan's nearby with special hand sanitizer (the brand he swears by), ready to wash the stink and stain away. I swipe at the sugar cookie dusting of sand on my palms. I could use some of Jonathan's sanitizer.

I'm still here in the green room. The test pattern screams back at me with its silence. I close my eyes, and I listen—for something. I try to remember more.

I see us all marching down the studio corridors. A PA pops up, or maybe she was always there. Cute girl with the reddest of red hair. I tell her, "Oh, we're gonna find your pot o' gold."

She doesn't smile.

We make it to the green room. The room I'm in now. The redhead PA asks if I need any water.

Things start to speed up, someone hitting fast-forward on my memory tape.

I've got a water bottle in my hand. That was fast. Who cares, though? I'm thirsty. *Really* thirsty. I hear the green room door shut.

"Where's Jonathan?"

I gulp down the water. It stings at the end. I cough. Water's not supposed to sting.

Then, black. Scene deleted, I guess.

Hands—whose hands?—lead me to the couch. I'm outside myself, not in control.

The redhead PA smiles at me. Finally. Funny, it's never me who asks: "Hey, don't I know you from some . . ."

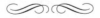

It's getting hotter and hotter inside this green room. My shirt's soaked through. I'm shivering, I'm so hot. *Some hero, huh?*

I wish I had more water. Must've drunk it all.

"Help!"

I peel my shirt off. It slaps against the carpet, sending particles of sand into the air, making me cough again. The sand sticks to my damp shirt.

Cue another memory montage.

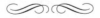

The redhead PA straddles me. I wonder what my wife would say if she saw her. She's—my wife's—young too. *Someone without baggage, you've got enough to go around.*

But Helena's not young like this girl's young. *This girl—I know this girl. I know her eyes.*

I always forget faces. You see so many of them, they tend to blend into one universal "face." But those eyes—I know those eyes. I know I know those eyes. I want to know *how* I know those eyes.

"Do I know you?"

I hear myself ask the question, not only inside my head but on TV as well. She's on top of me. My words come out slurred: "Durrrr I knurrr yurrrr?"

The footage cuts away before her answer. Loud music—a fanfare of horns—tests the limits of the TV's speakers. A news title graphic sweeps across the screen and explodes.

I'm back on-screen. This time, I'm reduced to a still photograph inset at the upper right-hand corner of the TV, above a bleached-blonde talking head. "Looks like former Hollywood Bad Boy turned Box Office Super-hero Lance McQuade got back to his old tricks again yesterday when he appeared on . . ."

What am I waiting here for?

Yesterday?

This place I'm in looks like the green room. (Well, except for all the sand.)

I see it now pouring through ceiling tiles, falling like the first rain after a decades-long drought. It's unrelenting. Like living inside an hourglass.

After a running start, I slam my body against the door. I want it to fly open. I want to burst through the doorway and fall face first into the studio hall-way. What I wouldn't give to find some B-roll camera crew waiting on the other side for me. "Surprise! You've been pranked!"

But it doesn't feel like a prank.

The door doesn't open. It cracks, though, splitting down its center. Whatever's jammed against it on the other side sure isn't moving. The collision sends me flying back to the center of the room, knocking the wind out of me for good measure.

I fall on the carpet. My lips kiss its woolen surface and I come up with sand on my tongue.

Slick with sweat, my hair curls at its ends. I haven't let my curls show since before I came out to L.A. I changed my name before the move too. Brushing those resurrected ringlets away from my eyes, I feel another bad-me returning from the dead. Lawrence "Little Larry" Muchnick, the name my old man gave me.

I used to daydream about reaching across our kitchen table, grabbing the bottle of Jack he always kept close at hand for every meal and bashing it across his big, dumb face. I used to sit there waiting for him to piss himself and pass out at the table (not always in that order). Then I'd steal a few sips from the bottle and cry myself to sleep, watching old black-and-white movies on the pull-out couch in the living room.

I'd watch with the volume turned down real low. I studied the mouths—and the eyes—of the actors on TV, watching to see *how* they said what they said and not just *what* they said.

My hands tremble as I wipe the sand from my lips and scratch it away from my tongue. I pick my chip up from the floor. A few more layers of sand and I'd never find it again.

I sit back down in the sand and pull my knees to my chest. I rock back and forth and back and forth. Over and over again, I repeat my mantra: "Remember me remembering me."

That's what my guru gave me during my last rehab stint. Strung-out, desperate, and ready to kill off another bad-me, I gave into those words she made me say over and over. When I woke up, before every meal, in those quiet moments where thoughts and memories threatened to overwhelm me, and then once again before going to sleep, I said the words. "Remember me remembering me."

I hated the words for the majority of my treatment. But then, near the end of my stint, they became my salvation.

I lean into them now, clinging to them for all they're worth.

The air sits on top of me, thick and hot inside this wherever-I-am. I'm mumbling now. "Remember me *remembering* me."

I'm driving. I'm *actually* driving.

Driving fast.

Driving too fast.

My upper body presses hard against the steering wheel. I feel like it's going to penetrate my skin and cut me in half.

I pull up the bottom of my shirt. Again, another unexpected bruise, this one the mark of the pistol someone jammed into my side. I can't remember who held it against me, though.

I hear a voice. Someone broken. "My son, my son . . ."

Dad's been dead for years. Plus, he never called me *son*.

Sand falls on my face. The ceiling sags lower over my head. I wonder when it'll break open.

I feel sand under my eyelids. If not for my delirium, I'd scream.

"Mr. Sandman, bring me a dream . . ."

There he is. Dear old Dad.

I remember Dad. Lurching from side to side, standing in the doorway to my childhood bedroom. Singing the song with a smile on his face, while tears rolled down his cheeks.

I hated those nights.

"Remember!"

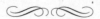

The command is clear and overwhelming. I crawl to the TV screen. Reduced to arms and legs.

I sound like Dad at his most pathetic. "Pleasehelpme, pleasehelpme, helpmeplease . . ."

The digitized green rectangles of the TV's volume bar appear on the screen. I watch their number increase. No sound comes from the TV, though. *Yet.*

I stand in ankle-deep sand. The shush of falling sand roars closer to silence, reminding me of a night standing on the beach, waiting for heavy waves to fall.

Home video footage on the TV now: someone operating a handheld video camera, except they've tilted the camera too far down. I see skinny, mosquito-bitten knees, shins, ankles, and feet.

"Hold on," the camera operator says. Her voice is young and high-pitched, but already self-assured from the sound of her. She swings the camera up into position.

Upper-middle-class suburban bliss—it's the best description I have for what I'm seeing. A cherry-red Mustang convertible (with the dealer tags still on it) sits parked in a concrete driveway right under the basketball hoop bolted above the garage doors. A large blue ribbon sits on the car's hood.

A teenage boy—a kid, all long limbs and loose-fitting clothing—rushes into view. "Cool!"

With the volume so high, the kid's exclamation forces me to clutch my hands over my ears.

His joy, my pain.

The TV's my oracle, showing me what's been, what is, and what will be. So I watch the boy—Jordan Griffin—as he hugs his smiling parents (both caught in the camera operator's firing line). "We knew about you saving up to buy Uncle Rod's old beater. But, I mean, it's not every day your oldest kid gets his driver's license."

The last time I watched this footage, they played it during my civil trial. His family's attorneys showed it over and over. I watched once and no more. Every time after, I sat in my uncomfortable wooden chair in the courtroom and studied the faces of the jurors. I watched them watch the tape. All of them, every last face, changed. They wept, they averted gazes, and some locked eyes with me, staring daggers of hate so sharp I thought they'd leave scars.

"Never Forget Jordan Griffin."

The words appear across the frozen image of the smiling boy as he dangles new car keys in front of the camera. It's the last footage of him recorded from before the accident.

Remember me remembering me.

"You're a murderer, *Lance McQuade*."

There it is. I grab the TV by its sides, trying to rip it off the wall, not caring if I bring the whole damn ceiling down with it.

I'm too close to the freeze-framed image of young, dead Jordan. He's looking right at me.

I close my eyes and see him again—but different. Burst guts splattered under the thick black tires of my SUV. I see this Jordan choking on bubbles of black-red blood, spitting his life out onto my dashboard. I see him looking up at me. "Dad?" he asks.

I laughed at his question. Imagine someone thinking of *me* as their father. I wish he hadn't died listening to my laughter.

On TV: Jordan blinks out of freeze-frame. He drops the hand holding his new car keys. The camera operator speaks again. "When I turn sixteen, I'm getting a new car too, right?"

Jordan laughs. "I dunno, Jana. I know Uncle Rod's beater's available!"

A skinny, freckle-spotted arm flies into view, reaching out to playfully slap at Jordan. "You ass!"

It makes him laugh all the harder. He feints left, then right. Then lunges forward, coming right for the camera. His hands fill the frame. A struggle follows, punctuated by teenage giggles. The camera swings around, as the camera operator and Jordan vie for control.

Jordan wins. The camera swings up, catching the blue sky overhead framed by Jordan's fingers. Then, he swings the camera back to Earth. He focuses on a brace-faced, redhead girl—the camera operator. He zooms in close on her face.

It's the eyes.

I'm looking into the eyes of the redhead PA—Jana Griffin, Jordan's sister.

"They assured me you wouldn't remember. They cleared all the paperwork. Helped train me, coach me. They set everything up for a new identity under Mom's maiden name."

This Jana (the one I met backstage earlier—though, *how much earlier?*) narrates at me over the footage. I feel lightheaded. Every breath I take tastes of heat and grit.

"I know. I know. You served your time. Well, they counted it as time served, didn't they? But the settlement money made everything possible. In a way, *you* paid for this. Thank you."

A snippet from a local news program plays on the TV: "The father of sixteen-year-old Jordan Griffin, the young man who lost his life in an automobile accident involving beloved screen actor Lance McQuade,

Mr. Griffin was found dead Tuesday outside Ajax Pool Hall and Bar. Authorities say . . ."

She continues narrating over the footage. "Dad took drinking back up after Jordan di—after you killed my brother. Mom made him give it up when they got married. But as it turned out, he was barely holding on. And then, he decided not to hold on anymore."

If I could talk back to the recorded voice, I'd say, "I know the feeling! I *am* the feeling!"

"Mom, well, what else could she do? *Not* die of a broken heart?"

Inside this green room death trap, the sand's up to my knees.

"So, that left me. A girl with an inheritance close enough to your 'pot o' gold' and a head full of dreams of revenge. Not the whitewashed 'it was a complete accident, this is a real wake-up call for me' redemption story you peddled to the tabloids. I knew what we lost because of you. And what did *you* lose? A couple of months in rehab? Then you're back—a new man. I watch you taking those critically-acclaimed bit parts to build your image back up, waiting until you get the chance to play a big-time superhero. What kind of a hero are you?"

I can't answer.

She's crying.

I swear I hear the ticking of my broken watch. But it's the sand falling, more and more now, faster and faster.

I'm no hero. But I know how to play one when the story calls for it.

"The money came to me after Mom died. Not much to you, maybe, but it was a damn fortune for me. But how could I spend your blood money? I decided blood money should buy more blood."

"Remember me remembering me."

There she is. On the screen—*live and in person*. She leans forward. She picks up the camera from wherever she'd set it, and I'm greeted with an extreme close-up of her face. She's dirty and dusty. I wonder if I look the same.

She spins the camera around, away from her face. She points it at the door.

"GREEN ROOM"

There's the placard. There's my door.

"Like the accommodations? The money couldn't cover everything. But it let me get in touch with the right people. Turns out I'm not the only one who hates you. You're apparently a real treat to work for. Didn't take much convincing to dose your hand sanitizer with hallucinogens . . ."

Jonathan.

Son of a bitch.

"They helped me get a job on Tad's show. Then, I waited until the paths of fame and fortune lead you right to this room. Though I guess there's also something to say for jamming a pistol into the rib of a functioning addict and forcing him to drive while blasted out of his skull."

I rub my bruised side. Knowing where it came from doesn't make it ache any less.

"Pierre-Claude worked with *their* prop team to replicate the green room. He does such wonderful, innovative, and immersive work, doesn't he? You know he told me he'd *kill* to have you in one of his movies?"

I look above the TV and notice the mini camera placed above it, just out of sight. I wonder who's out there watching me.

Jana picks up a handful of sand. She lets it run through her fingers.

"You being the big-time celebrity and all, I was surprised you could drive all the way out here. To your gravesite. Took a lot of work to bury you inside this room—under all this desert."

It's almost impossible to walk through waist-deep sand. But I have to. I slam against the door. I dig toes deep into it, trying to touch the carpet below.

Jana laughs a bitter, tired cackle.

I run full steam ahead. Head down, I let my shoulder go through the wood, sending splinters flying. Blood trickles down my chest, as tiny chunks of plywood stab into my skin.

I feel whatever strength I've got left fading. But I can't stop. I dig through scraps of wood and grains of sand—so much sand. More of it waits for me on the other side of the busted-down door.

Fingers sift through the wreckage, looking for a way forward—and a way out. Fingertips touch someone else's skin.

The TV keeps playing inside the green room. I can't see it, but I can *see* it. Jana lifts the gun to her temple. Her finger hesitates on the trigger, grains of sand falling from her like dead skin. She's down here with me now. I know how it ends.

The speakers blow out as the gun goes off.

I come close to gagging. My fingers come back slick with blood. Wet sand sticks to blackened fingertips.

There's a muted groan and the ceiling collapses. Sand falls, not one grain at a time, ticking away the seconds of life, but as a crashing wave, dark and final.

I crawl ahead, not giving a damn what or who I crawl over. I need to keep digging.

I pull out my chip one last time and give it a final squeeze. Sand fills my nostrils and leaks into the corners of my mouth with each rasping, rattling breath I try to take. But I keep digging.

I dig and crawl forward. I dig and crawl forward.

Dig. Crawl.

Dig. Crawl.

The sand's everywhere. It's everything. It's inside me. I feel it flowing across my eyes. As I dig and crawl, I don't even know if I'm heading up or heading down.

I hear Tad's announcer in my ear. "And our next guest . . ."

I hear the roar of the crowd, primed for my entrance.

A rescue worker pulls me up and out of the sand. Sunlight stings my eyes and I feel my body already fading back to unconsciousness. Before I fade out, I hear her shout. "Got him!"

Hands slap down on my shoulders. I look up into her face. Her expression is a mix of relief and awe. I blink and remember who I am. Not just anyone, I'm *Someone*. "We almost couldn't pinpoint the signal on your GPS tracker."

With the last of my strength, I hold up my sobriety chip. The red glow of the high-tech tracking device implanted in it by my security detail is hard to see under the harsh natural desert light and heavy sand cover, but trust me—it's there.

Vultures circle over our heads.

What follows?

Flashing lights, shouted commands, and questions—reserved until they think I'm ready for them.

When they come back later with the excavation equipment, they'll find the trailer Jana and her conspirators mocked up to imitate the green room. They'll find the camera and trace it back to a computer in Pierre-Claude's possession, with all the footage of my time down there saved on a hard drive. They'll also find Jana's body.

Arrests follow. I'm the talk of the town. Again. Everyone's ratings soar. But I stay away. I stay quiet.

I let others talk about me, about what they think happened. I let them call me "brave—a hero!"

Until my press agent gets a call, and she tells me they want me to guest on *The Late Evening Conversation* with Tad Thompson again.

I say yes.

Standing there, waiting backstage, I wonder what I'm going to talk about after I walk through those red curtains and take a seat beside the desk.

I WILL NOT READ YOUR HAUNTED SCRIPT

I *will not read your haunted script.*

Be brief. That's one of the first big lessons you need to absorb if you want to become a screenwriter. Any books you read, classes you take, overpriced workshops from hack gurus you attend, if they don't mention an "economy of words," then ask for your money back. Now.

Producers, actors, directors, all those folks above our pay grade, they barely read anything. So getting to the point in the scripts they do read is essential.

To that end, when I say "I will not read your haunted script," that single declarative sentence should do the heavy lifting of a conversation I don't want to have and you probably don't want to experience.

Then again, you're still here. You're standing in my foyer with a stack of pages bound together with two dull brass brads that resemble the worn-down doorknobs of an antique house. I can smell the heat radiating from paper freshly ejected from a printer, so I'm guessing you stopped at the FedEx Office around the corner.

Look, I'm sorry you drove all the way out here to the Valley. Believe me, I've lived in your shoes, doing the whole desperate neophyte writer thing. I appreciate the initiative and I hope my dogs, wherever they've gotten off to, didn't scare you too bad.

I know why you came here to see me. I know *why* you insist that out of the millions of writers, wannabes, and was-once-and-never-agains in Hollywood, I'm the only screenwriter who can appreciate your script and the fact that it's "haunted."

But now, because you've come out all this way, and because you've got me here alone practically cornered, I have to play the bad guy. Again. Lucky me.

The truth is, you're the asshole here. Yeah, that's right. Let's kick this conversation up to a PG-13 because I need you to understand the seriousness of the offense you're committing. You've already told me again and again that your screenplay's haunted. I see you wiping sweat from your brow, and your right leg's shaking slightly. But I won't offer you a bottled water or a seat, because either one of those actions might be interpreted as an invitation to ask me again about reading your damned haunted script.

And I *won't* read your haunted script.

You think because I wrote the first script for that original movie in "The Franchise," the horror film series so notorious I'm forced to Scottish Play it and leave it unnamed, that I have some insight into scripts, films, et cetera you for some reason believe to be possessed, cursed, haunted, or whatever the hell you want to call them.

But I don't.

I mean, if you *are* the type of person to believe in Hollywood curses and the existence of haunted screenplays, then you already know that almost everyone involved in the first movie has ended up dead as a doornail. Maybe *dead-er* in the case of our director Cam, with that whole experimental-submarine-imploding-from-deep-sea-pressure-on-a-livestream-at-the-Oscars thing.

And if you know all that, then you also know I'm the film's last survivor—crew or cast.

I'm a writer. I'm *the* credited writer on that first film in "The Franchise." We weren't aiming for high art or cult status appeal when we made it. We conceived it as another late 80s "gore, tits and ass, blood and guts" flick. We certainly didn't think we'd jump-start a movie series, with its accompanying clothes, posters, cute little stuffed versions of our masked maniac, and even an ill-advised Saturday morning cartoon series complete with breakfast cereal tie-in. Folks like you think all that success stemmed from *my* screenplay. That's *if* you believe everything you see from the Writer's Guild arbitration committee.

By the look of you, especially the absence of the blue-black bags of sleeplessness around the eyes, I'm guessing you're too young to have seen the first movie when it came out in the theaters. So, I'm thinking you either had a big brother or sister who rented it, and you snuck out of bed to peek at it behind your living room couch. *Or* you waited until later when you could buy a re-released special edition on Blu-Ray.

You don't wanna tell me which one it was? That's fine. But you *have* seen the movie. Of course. Otherwise, you wouldn't be here . . . at my house . . . asking me to read *your* haunted script.

And I won't read your haunted script.

You're probably thinking, *The parts with the 'old woman,' that's where haunting occurs. They're so dialogue-driven that there's no way they didn't originate in the screenplay.*

But let me tell you, if you wanna make it here in Hollywood, prepare yourself for disappointment. Do you know how many scripts—original scripts, ideas from my own brain—I've written since that first produced credit? Hundreds. I used to print them out and keep stacks in my office. But it got hard to maneuver around all those towers of paper. Now I just save them onto flash drives. So I've got drawers full of these rectangular metal things and no clue which scripts are on them.

The point is, I never stopped working on my own ideas. Coming up with characters, conflicts, building these worlds. I love that shit. Now, ask me how many of those hundreds of scripts I've written got made into movies.

Zero. But you knew that, didn't you? Bet you have my whole IMDb profile memorized.

You write a screenplay and everyone thinks it's haunted. *Everyone.* I found out the hard way that no one wanted to buy anything original from me—no comedies, actioners, or Oscar-bait dramas—because they were afraid whatever I wrote might be another haunted script. And I had to go through three agents and five managers before that lesson sunk in.

Of course, the residuals from the first "Franchise" movie and the "story by" credits for the sequels and that remake they tried, all of that drops into my checking account in varying amounts. Plus, I get brought in for punch-ups and last-minute ghostwriting projects for stuff already in the pipelines at the studios. I'm a reliable old hand, especially to rosy-cheeked junior studio execs fresh out of Stanford Business School or wherever.

But I'm never credited. I write, I work, but no one ever knows about it. They make me sign these NDAs. Some people try and guess. My writer friends—the guys I play poker with once a month—they're always trying to pin some new horror cult favorite or superhero blockbuster on me. I'd say they're about 50/50 in terms of accuracy.

Still, with no new credits to my name, it's like I don't exist out here. It's like I might as well be dead, as far as this town is concerned.

Sorry, sorry. I've become a melancholy middle-aged fuck. I either started drinking too early or started too late. I can never tell the difference.

The point is, I'm probably drunk and I *still* will not read your haunted script.

So don't think about leaving it by the front door or slipping it into my mailbox or placing it under the windshield wipers of my car. I've seen it all. If I find it, I'll throw it away. Or burn it.

I've done it before. What? Do you think you're the first person to bring a supposedly haunted screenplay to me? It started with friends passing me their scripts—the ones where they wrote about all the messed-up, weird shit echoing back from whatever past drug trips they'd embarked upon.

"Bro, think I got a haunted script here?"

And I'd smile, take the printout or open the PDF attachment, and read. They're my friends, after all. It's not like I could say no to my friends.

Next, the production companies and even some studios came calling. They were all looking to replicate the success of "The Franchise," which was big enough for most to ignore the unseemly consequences of accompanying curses, assuming they didn't directly affect the bottom line. If a few creatives had to die under mysterious circumstances along the way? Who cares?! UCLA cranks 'em out fresh and palatably edgy every year anyway.

I had an agent who kept a whole separate email folder with requests for me to read this or that allegedly haunted screenplay. She'd say, "I don't think there are even that many dead people around to haunt all these scripts. I bet they're killing folks just to get more ghosts to haunt the damned things."

Starting out, I tried to read everything I got sent. I felt like I had to read my *friend's* scripts out of obligation and the *studio* scripts because I wanted work. But it was a slog. Eventually, the friends stopped calling after I kept telling them I didn't think they had any haunted scripts. They thought I was holding back on them. Like I wanted to be the only "haunted screen-play" guy in town.

It was almost the same story with the work-for-hire "haunted" scripts. I'd head into these meetings with well-tanned development executives seeking the *easy* dollars from the horror diehards, and I'd sit on their comfy leather sofas, sipping from their complimentary water bottles. And I'd start my pitch, saying, "First, I don't think this script is haunted. But I did notice some structural and character motivation issues—"

They'd cut me off around that point and send me on my way. They didn't want *me*. They wanted the assurance of a profitable *haunting*.

But I couldn't—I *can't*—give that to them. I can't even point them in the general vicinity of ghosts. Do you want to know why? Want to know the big secret I've felt compelled to keep all to myself this whole time?

I didn't write the haunted parts of my script.

There you go. Hopefully that juicy tidbit makes the drive out here worth it. I mean, I'm sure you bought a copy of the screenplay book they put out. Real nice binding on that thing, right? I bet you have that haunted scene memorized. That's all everyone ever talks about. We're in the middle of a scene where our masked killer is somehow using a chain-saw underwater to hack off the kicking, flailing limbs of some co-eds, and then *BAM*, we . . .

CUT TO:

EXT. COTTAGE - MAGIC HOUR

A simple gingerbread-style cottage in the woods surrounded by tall pine trees. Like something from a
fairy tale illustration. The sound of WHISTLING pulls
us to the home and through the open FRONT DOOR.

INT. COTTAGE - CONTINUOUS

We move past the modest FOYER and into a sparsely
furnished LIVING ROOM. With urgent strokes, the Old
Woman sweeps dust across the hardwood floor. She
wears a black housedress and a red kerchief tied
haphazardly around gray hair resembling steel wool.

> OLD WOMAN
> He's coming. He's coming.
> We must prepare. He'll be here soon.

God, you've got that hungry but worshipful look in your eyes listening
to me talk about that scene. It's not the first time I've seen it, believe me.
And that's *just* the beginning of the scene. The movie spends some twenty
minutes following the Old Woman, as she's so creatively named, while
she cleans her little grandmotherly cottage in the woods and talks about
this mysterious "He" and his imminent arrival. Twenty minutes of screen
time! In a horror movie!

Any horror flick worth its salt should be 80, 90 minutes *tops*. No
one wants to be scared longer than that or it starts feeling a little too
much like life. So, stop and ask yourself, would I really write a script
that spent nearly a quarter of its length on cryptic, folksy weirdness
that has absolutely nothing to do with the plot of my cheapie cash-in
slasher flick?

```
EXT. COTTAGE - FRONT PORCH - NIGHT

The Old Woman leans against the guardrail enclosing
the front porch. The weathered boards under her feet
are nearly stripped of paint. The MOON hangs full
and low in the sky. So low, it looks like she could
reach up and touch it.
We hear FOOTSTEPS O.C. Someone approaches from the
woods. The rustle of something that sounds like
pages being turned accompanies the arrival of --
```

BANG! They jump cut to the movie's virginal heroine discovering the dead bodies of her fellow camp counselors, all mutilated in various gruesome and creative ways. Most of those death sequences got cut because of the damned cottage scene.

And no one from the production even knew until the first screening. We had a big showing for all our investors, so they could be sure they hadn't wasted their kids' college tuitions or whatever. I couldn't speak when the credits finished rolling. No one could. Don't believe that shit you see in the DVD special features. None of that "spontaneous applause breaking out" B.S. What actually happened is we all stood up and filed out of the theater. One by one. No one saying a goddamn word.

We went over to the bar they'd rented for the after-party. I remember pushing open the double doors at the front and stepping into another world. Like I'd crossed over into another timeline where my screenplay hadn't been completely hijacked by an injection of some random artsy-fartsy crap. The same people who'd stumbled from the theater like Romero's undead were hugging and high-fiving, ten sheets to the wind and only ten minutes into drinking.

"Brilliant."

"Revolutionary."

"Genre-redefining."

I went up to Cam and our editor Elise Joyner, asked them, "What the hell happened?" Cam insisted he'd never shot the cottage footage. And Elise eventually admitted she'd never cut it into the print. Getting that much out of them was tough. They both looked doped up, half-dreaming. Stars in their eyes, you might say. I left them to make my way around the bar, nursing a Jack and Coke and asking everyone from our crew if they had any idea where the scene had come from. No one knew anything about it, but they were sure as hell happy to claim it.

And, yeah, I've read all the fan theories that've come along in the intervening years. There's the group that thinks the Old Woman's supposed to be my masked killer's mother. But, c'mon. I know Sean Cunningham. You think I'm gonna rip off what he did with those Jason movies? No way. And then there's the people who think it's a whole Jesus thing. *Jesus!* Let me tell you, I wish it was. God knows (*heh*) I'd love to have the kind of notoriety that comes with making a movie that pisses off my old Sunday School teachers and their ilk.

Finally, there are the real sad cases who claim the Old Woman is their actual mom or grandma or whomever. But she's never *playing* a part. "Oh no," they insist, "that's her. She's being herself."

I'd get tear-stained fan letters, folks thanking me for including their Mee-Maw or Mama-Lou or Gin-Gin in my screenplay and conjuring her back from the spirit realm along with my fellow filmmakers so she could prepare her loved ones for . . .

Who knows?

When the movie took off and everyone kept talking about the Old Woman scene and my haunted script, the producers dug up an alleged copy of a final draft. Except it wasn't *my* final draft, because someone had added *that* scene. I sure as hell hadn't. But it looked like I had, and we're talking about Hollywood, where, each and every day, the way things look will win out over the way things are.

It became *my* haunted script. I'll carry that with me for the rest of my life, for the rest of whatever I patchwork together into a career. And I hate that. I hate *it*.

So, no, I won't read *your* haunted script.

You know what? We're done here. Let me get this door for you and you can get on your way, and I'll get back to not reading your "haunted" script or anyone else's.

Step right this . . .

What the hell? Where did—There's not supposed to be a . . .

FADE IN:

EXT. FOREST - NIGHT

The moon hangs fat and heavy among the pines. The WRITER, a middle-aged man with a receding hairline wearing sweatpants, flip-flops, and stretched-out Star Wars T-shirt, turns at the sound of a DOOR closing behind him with a CLICK.

                    WRITER
    The hell?

But there's no door. No bungalow. Just trees, trees, and more trees.

Stop it. Stop whatever this is right now. I'm going to . . .

With nowhere else to go, the Writer walks ahead, deeper into the night woods. Pages of the SCREENPLAY

he now holds rustle back and forth along the forest
floor, like tall blades of grass caught by an autumn
wind. He looks down and we ZOOM IN on a SCRIPT PAGE.

                        WRITER
            (reading)
            His lips move with the words as he realizes
            he's the one reading. He's the one speaking the
            scene into --

Existence. This is *real?* How is this real?

And where did you go? Hold on, I think I see something up there. Wait,
is that the . . .

EXT. COTTAGE - MOMENTS LATER

The Writer steps through a break in the trees onto
the land where the Old Woman's cottage sits. Her simple dwelling is lit from within by candlelight and
sparkling clean outside and in.
The FRONT DOOR is already open. The Old Woman stands
in the doorway.

                      OLD WOMAN
            He's here.

The Writer flips through the pages of this haunted
script. The one he refused to read. The one he
wanted nothing to do with.

Now, something compels him to keep reading, to keep going. Leaves CRUNCH under his feet. He's desperate for a way out, some MacGuffin or Chekhov's gun set up for the final pay off. But he's the only writer here, and he has no idea what happens next.

He's on the bottom step. Three more steps to go and he'll be on the porch. The Old Woman holds out a hand for him to take.

The Writer can't look into her eyes. He won't look into her eyes. He looks down and flips to the last page.

Nothing. There's nothing here. It's not even finished! You brought me a work-in-progress.

CLOSE-UP: He's wrong. There is something, right at the top of the last page.

FADE OUT.

THE END.

THE OTHER HALF
OF THE BATTLE

When the "soldiers" came for us, we weren't standing anywhere near that old freezer, with its rusted-out hinges and cobweb-draped interior. I dropped the joint I'd taken from my big brother Marc's room the second I saw these strange-looking dudes crashing through the piles of useless shit sprinkled like cow pats around the Ryerson Junkyard. The two men marched in lockstep, waving their hands as if we wouldn't have noticed them otherwise. One of them called out to the three of us—Dexter (that's me), Carlos, and Noah.

"Get away from there, kids!"

Trying to look as casual as possible, I got the J under the heel of my Converse and ground the thin Zig-Zag paper and shag weed into the gritty dirt.

No great loss, considering Marc would constantly roll and forget joints around the house.

But it was the principle of the thing.

"Yo, should we run or . . ."

Typical Noah question. Dude was so naturally paranoid he didn't *need* mind-altering substances. Carlos and I loved to get him riled up, call him "Just Say Noah."

It was always so funny to see Noah sputter and stutter, trying to list off every time he'd gotten high. Like both me and Carlos hadn't been there for all of them.

"Fuck no!"

Leave it to Carlos to respond exactly how you'd expect him to.

He answered just loud enough that I worried the two jacked-up "sol-diers" had heard him. My eyes kept dipping to their twin shadows falling across us, a trio of eighth-grade stoners playing hooky.

I can't pinpoint why my brain immediately pegged the duo as some kind of military. God knows I'd seen enough guys take the underachiever-to-soldier pipeline growing up in our nowhere town. Especially kids from our neighborhood. Lots of Marc's friends. Guys would join up and get free rides to college, plus the chance to "kick some commie ass" for Reagan. Minus the college part, it seemed like a dream come true for most of them.

Of course, too many of them came back home on their first leave with a look in their eyes that was . . . off. One of the soldiers heading our way had that look. He wore his blond hair in a high-and-tight crewcut, and there were more American flags sewn onto his outfit than you'd see in a boardwalk beach-towel shop on the Fourth of July.

At the same time, there was nothing *uniform* about what High-and-Tight and his partner had on. I certainly didn't think Dad would recognize their outfits from any of the John Wayne flicks he loved to tell us about over dinner. High-and-Tight wore a skintight neon green top with shoul-der pads straight out of a Saturday afternoon sci-fi flick. The "gun" hol-stered to his leg had a rounded design and glowing lights along the barrel. It was more like a prop than an actual weapon with actual bullets in its chambers. The cuffs of High-and-Tight's camo pants were tucked into his thick-soled silver combat boots.

Even Prince couldn't pull off that look.

"Whoa! What are you boys doing out here?"

His voice was too loud. Not like he was yelling or screaming, but deeper—amplified somehow. Like it came from speakers. And worse, it didn't line up with the movement of his lips. Everything was just a half-syllable off.

I started wondering what the hell my brother could've sprinkled in the ruined joint under my sneaker. At least Carlos didn't seem bothered. He'd always been the stubborn one and today was no exception as he engaged High-and-Tight in a little impromptu staring contest. He shaded his eyes with his hand, trying to avoid the sunlight's glare reflecting off the soldier's sparkling nonuniform. Carlos squinted and smiled that big shit-eating grin of his, the one that dimpled his cheeks. He had that kind of look that made me think he was either destined for greatness or great trouble.

But that smile of his was cut off before its full bloom. The Black-Masked Man, High-and-Tight's companion, dropped his hand down onto Carlos's shoulder, his dark leather glove landing like a nightfall in the winter. He moved too fast, like he hid in the seconds when we blinked our eyes, waiting for the right time to strike. Lean and muscled, the mystery man wore black from head to toe. His spandex bodysuit and thigh-high combat boots made him look like an aerobics instructor who listened to too much Cure. But the gloves, the ebony-handled sword strapped to his back, and his featureless black mask gave an entirely different, much more intimidating impression.

The mask completely covered his head and wasn't made of any fabric I'd seen before. There was no stitching, no seams. I didn't see the telltale signs of cloth being sucked in and out with his breath. (If he *took* any breaths.) And the color? Blacker than black.

Only other time I'd seen darkness like that was when Dad took me and Marc to Luray Caverns. At one point in our cave tour, the guides cut all the lights to give everyone a sense of how dark it really got down there. The whole stunt probably lasted no more than thirty seconds, but in that pitch-black half-minute, I'd squeezed the hell out of Dad's and Marc's hands. Who cared if they called me a baby the whole car ride home? I came out of that experience feeling like I'd stared Death in the face, and now it looked like Death was back in the form of the Black-Masked Man. I watched his grip tighten on Carlos's shoulder.

That mask wasn't made *from* something; it *was* something. Emptiness. Absence. Noah and I stared into that abyss as the Black-Masked Man used his free hand to waggle a long black finger in Carlos's face, the glove twitching at the knuckles like the leg of a tarantula.

"Remember, boys, it might seem 'cool' to play around with this old stuff, but they can be a real danger. Like that fridge. What would happen if one of you got stuck in there?" High-and-Tight's strange question might've been the only thing to pull me back from oblivion.

"My friends would get me out, suh-suh-sir."

I don't think any of us would have expected Noah to be the one to answer.

"Uh, yeah," I added, wanting to at least say *something*.

Noah working up the courage to respond to these weapons-toting strangers, standing in front of us with their hulking pro wrestler physiques, shocked me more than the soldiers' initial appearance.

Of course, once Noah *had* spoken up, it was clear he regretted it. The Black-Masked Man lifted his hand from Carlos's shoulder, Carlos sagging in response like some heavy burden had been removed from him. He shuffled away, putting as much distance between himself and the Black-Masked Man as he could. I had a sense that things—bizarre as they were at the moment—were shaping up pretty bad for us, but seeing Carlos drained of his bluster helped the realization really sink in.

"No way, Jose! Your friends won't always be there when you make bad decisions, like deciding to climb inside an abandoned freezer in a junk-yard." I read the nametag that High-and-Tight had sewn across his pecto-ral: CLIFF. No last name. Just *CLIFF*.

Cliff and the Black-Masked Man swept Noah up between them before Carlos or I could react. It felt like I'd been thrown into a real-life episode of junk food TV—one of the cheap after-school cartoons we'd binge while putting off our prealgebra homework. All those shows meant to sell action figures and accessories, where they'd skimp on the animation costs and pepper a bunch of jittery jump cuts into the action. One second, they were going to grab Noah. The next, they were already carrying him away. One held him by his wrists and the other by his ankles, stretching him like a dead buck across the hood of a redneck's truck during hunting season.

Noah tried to fight back. I'll give the guy that. Even though it was al-ready too late, he kicked and writhed. He screamed for help until his voice cracked like he was a kid again, somehow simultaneously the slapstick star of the cartoon and the kid watching from the living room floor. His high-pitched cries echoed off the rusted fenders of the junkers Old Man Ryerson kept around for scrap metal. The way the two soldiers held Noah, I worried if he squirmed the wrong way he'd snap both wrists and ankles.

But what were Carlos and me supposed to even do? We were two eighth-grade boys watching their friend get manhandled by two freaks. We weren't even in high school yet. Ninth grade was our shitty consolation prize at the end of another drawn out summer in our piece of shit town. This town where, moments before, Noah had cracked our shit up with his not-half-bad Bill Murray *Ghostbusters* impression, and now look at him. Shrieking, dangling.

At least we didn't run. That was the best we could offer Noah. I reached for Carlos's hand, not even thinking about what I was doing. He flinched at first, but then he squeezed my hand so hard my fingers started to tingle. Together, we followed Noah and his abductors, keeping a good distance from Cliff, the Black-Masked Man, and our captive friend.

We all headed for that old freezer.

The abandoned appliance's rectangular lid gaped open on hinges bleeding rust along its black rubber sealant. It gave the freezer the appearance of a monster slobbering blood around stained lips. The orange power light dull and dimmed around the rim became the freezer-monster's dead, still-open eye.

Never blinking, never looking away from the approaching offering.

They dropped Noah into the freezer's waiting gullet without pause or ceremony. One second, we could still see him, and the next he was gone.

I looked around the junkyard, hoping to see Old Man Ryerson or someone, anyone, who could help us. But there was no one. And that was by our own design. We'd picked this exact place and time to hang out and get stoned, knowing Ryerson never missed his afternoon nap in his shed/workspace/home.

It was up to us.

"Hey! Hey! Hey!" I ran toward the strangers as they stared into the open freezer that held my friend.

Carlos followed a half-second behind me. "Hey, assholes! Show us your badges!" With the addition of a voice cracking similar to Noah's, Carlos's words echoed the slurred cries of his dad during one of his Saturday night benders—the ones that usually lead to Carlos, his mom, and little sister Pam sleeping over at my family's house until things "cooled down."

But for all our shouting, it was like we didn't exist to these two strange soldiers. Standing with their backs to us, the indifferent duo ignored our cries. They had their hands on the freezer's lid, tipping it back dangerously on its hinges. Someone—or something—groaned; I couldn't tell if the sound came from the old machine itself or from Noah inside of it.

Soon we were close enough for either Carlos or I to reach out and grab Noah's abductors. We could've tried to give our friend a chance. Maybe if we drew their attention away long enough, Noah could make a break for it. But the TV-inspired memories buzzing in my head kept flickering back to those weapons: a sword, guns, and I could've sworn I saw some grenades strapped to the both of them. That was enough to keep us in check.

"Help!"

Carlos and I shouted together, united in desperation. Noah might have cried out too, but I can't say for sure. The soldiers finally slammed the lid down, trapping Noah inside and sending up a mini-mushroom cloud of dust.

The two costumed men positioned themselves on either side of the closed-up freezer like a couple of grunts ready to have a smoke and complain about their commander. That left a direct path for me and Carlos. We barreled toward the freezer, and when we skidded up to it, I heard the muted pounding of Noah's small-for-our-age fists against the appliance's interior. I tilted my head, pressed my ear against the lid, listening for anything Noah might be yelling up at us. But I didn't hear any words, just an undercurrent of sobs beneath a droning hum.

I didn't have to ask Carlos if he heard the same sounds. He jammed his index fingers into both ears and wriggled them with frantic intensity before shaking out his shoulders and reaching down. He wedged his fingers under the lip of the lid, grasping at its edge, his palms pressing up to the sky. I did the same. We pushed as hard as we could, trying together at first and then in separate, individual efforts, but the seal around the freezer lid was tight. It wouldn't budge an inch.

Seconds felt like minutes and those minutes cascaded on for what felt like an agonizing lifetime. Something wet and pungent rolled down the bridge of my nose, leaving a bitter aftertaste as it passed my lips. Tears or sweat? I couldn't tell. Combined with the piss stench rising out of the freezer's insulated membrane, we were all three of us experiencing things our previous fourteen years of life could never have prepared us for.

"See what we mean, kids? You can never be too careful."

"What the hell, man?" Carlos spun around the second he heard those meaningless after-school-special words. Right before he turned, I caught a glimpse of his bloodshot eyes. They popped out like they might hop right off his face. He looked just like his old man, like he wanted a fight. But that's not what he got.

No, nothing like a fight. Cliff and the Black-Masked Man brushed us aside like indifferent tomcats swatting away mewling kittens. I felt my knees buckle at the touch of a black glove against my chest. I held it together, and so did Carlos, but we got out of their way all the same.

They opened the freezer's lid like it was nothing at all. Noah sprung up like an over-cranked jack-in-the-box. His tangle of dirty-blond hair looked like a bird's nest in a sweatbox.

"Th-th-th-thanks."

Was Noah thanking me and Carlos, or had he gotten so mixed up that he would thank the two strangers who'd trapped him in the first place? The smile on Cliff's face, like some cheeseball politician posing for a photo, made it clear he'd taken Noah's gratitude as intended for him and his partner. I wondered if the Black-Masked Man had a smile stretching beneath the dark cover of nowhere and nothingness that hid his features.

"I hope you've learned a valuable lesson. Hanging out in abandoned freezers is *not* cool," Cliff said.

Carlos's elbow dug into my side. Our eyes met. "What's going on? Are we too high?" he whispered.

Before I could answer, the laughter started.

It crept up on us and made itself known without warning, like cold hands to the backs of our necks. At the freezer, Cliff had his head tilted back at a sharp angle, his throbbing Adam's apple exposed. His "laugh" sounded more like the static at the wrong end of the AM dial. A staccato "Ha. Ha. Ha. Ha. Ha. Ha." faded in and out between roaring white noise. On the other side of the freezer, the Black-Masked Man mirrored his compatriot's mannerisms, though no sound emerged from the darkness covering his face.

"Heh. Heh. Heh."

Then there was Noah.

Carlos and I'd heard Noah's nervous chuckling plenty throughout our friendship. Like when he hadn't quite gotten one of the dirty jokes Carlos retold from his old man. I could tell Noah wanted to fit in so badly that he wouldn't dare do anything to risk possible alienation. He never wanted to be the outsider, even among us, his fellow outsiders.

Hence, that laugh of his. Whenever he laughed like that, I wanted to look him in the eyes and tell him that he didn't need to try so hard. Maybe that would've made a difference.

But instead of saying anything, I watched Noah chuckle nervously, and then I noticed the blood. Forcing his laughter out in time with the strangers', Noah coughed between strained guffaws. With each cough, a fine mist of cranberry red exploded from his lips, like popped, splattered bubble gum. I gasped, inhaling the copper scent of Noah's blood intermingled with the heat radiating from the Black-Masked Man's unsheathed ebony-dyed sword blade.

Once again, the masked man's movements had been too fast. One moment, he was pantomiming laughter. The next, he stood stiff and angular like some Rock 'Em Sock 'Em sci-fi robot. He'd shoved his sword through Noah's chest and back out the other side. The saturated razor-sharp tip scratched against the interior of the freezer lid, splitting a dangling strand of cobwebs.

I looked over at Carlos. His face was as white as the Black-Masked Man's was its opposite. I looked back at Noah, still standing up in the freezer, blade in his body. Still laughing too. His brain was struggling more than mine to catch up. "Noah . . ."

I couldn't finish. Whatever words my fourteen-year-old mind could grasp seemed hopelessly inadequate.

Luckily, I didn't have to torture myself composing those final comforting words. Why worry about *one* inexplicable action of violence when more was fast approaching? A beam as red as the letters of the EXIT sign on our middle school's back door fell over me and then moved across to Carlos's chest. Then the light returned, drifting between us from the nose of Cliff's gun. As he aimed his weapon at us, I couldn't stop looking at the beam flashing its way through the dust kicked up by all the movement. The red was a shade lighter than the crimson covering the front of Noah's shirt.

I heard a sound like a skewer pulled from raw meat. Noah followed with a tiny, insignificant-sounding grunt. His last word was nothing more than a confused and dream-like "Huh?"

"Move!"

Cliff didn't have to order us twice. (And I don't think he would have.) I threw myself one way and Carlos went the other. I landed facedown on the ground, my arms and legs sprawled like a crash test dummy. Debris strafed my elbows as I crawled away, trying to get clear of Cliff's line of fire. I scrambled over rocks, screws, twigs, cat shit, and God only knows what else.

The mistake I made was looking back at the freezer.

With my arms bleeding into the dirt, I watched the Black-Masked Man resheath his sword and draw his own laser blaster that looked like it'd come straight out of *Star Wars*. Noah was already out of sight, crumpled back down into the death-trap interior of the freezer. The lid came down again. But my eyes stayed open. On the other side of the freezer, Carlos hadn't stopped to look like I had. He kept moving.

Raising their guns, letting the beam fan out with an adjustment of the knobs on the sides of the weapons, the soldiers bathed the dirty white exterior of the appliance in that cherry red. Then, they fired.

Blasts tore out of their shiny high-tech barrels, screaming like the souls of the damned. Red-hot energy crackled in rapid-fire volleys one after another after another.

Chunks of plastic and metal flew backward, forward, and to the sides. The old freezer was dismantled in seconds. Next came blood, bones, skin, and hair: one of my best friends in the world reduced to meat in seconds. Noah rained down on us all, sizzling. His blood boiled and hissed when it splashed my face.

I scrambled backward on all fours. I shouted for Carlos over the chaos of the soldier's volley. I wanted him to be there for me.

For Noah too.

But he didn't answer.

He was already gone.

I blacked out.

Next thing I knew, colors flooded in on top of me like overeager pets greeting their owners who've left them home alone too long. A steady beam of white light pierced through the multicolored chaos. Someone held open one of my eyes and aimed a penlight into it, then switched eyes.

I heard a voice just past the light. I struggled to move. I felt so out of it. I couldn't remember if I should run to the voice or get away from it. From behind me, a second set of hands, clad in black leather gloves, held me up by my arms.

The person holding open my eyelids pulled their hand back from my face. Seconds later, the penlight's beam winked out. When my eyes adjusted, I saw the soldier named Cliff standing in front of me. There wasn't any malice in his eyes. No murderous intent. I swear what I saw looked more like compassion, or at least some tough-love variation of it.

"Easy there, recruit."

I assumed he was talking to the Black-Masked Man, who was holding me upright from behind. But when Cliff's steel-blue eyes locked on mine, I knew his words were meant for me.

"First time in the field?"

It was the sort of question I'd heard in Dad's war movies. Unsure how to respond, I licked my lips, swallowed a couple of times. I took these great gulping breaths and something that smelled like meat left out in the sun filled my nostrils.

Noah.

I gagged. Tried to hold back the rising tide pushing out from inside me, but I wasn't strong enough.

The Black-Masked Man held me so tight I couldn't even bend over to direct the spray away from my body. Chunks of fast-food burger gushed down my chin and covered the front of my shirt. Some drips hit the Black-Masked Man's gloves. The rest landed in the junkyard dirt.

Cliff laughed. "Never gets better, how bad they smell, does it?" he said. "Night Sky and I were sure impressed by the way you led us to those two DRAGON soldiers, though."

"I don't . . ."

And I *really* didn't.

Night Sky, or the Black-Masked Man if you prefer, finally released me. Two things followed, both of which surprised me. First, I was able to remain standing, and second, I didn't immediately run. Looking down at the blood-and-gore-soaked ground, I caught sight of the trail left by Carlos's escape. He'd dragged himself through muck and entrails to the cyclone fencing separating Old Man Ryerson's junkyard fiefdom from the rest of the overgrown, left-to-rot part of town.

I was alone with two strange killers who acted like they knew me.

"Please don't hurt me."

I'd never had the quips or one-liners Carlos always spouted off to our teachers and the asshole prep school kids from the other side of the tracks. (Never saw him mouth off to his old man, of course. That was one line even *he'd* never cross.)

"Hurt you? Soldier, why would we hurt one of our own? Sheesh!"

There it was. That s-word. Me and my brother Marc, we'd made a vow to never be soldiers. Mostly to spite Dad and his hard-on for war, I think. At least for me. I didn't give a shit about the rest of it.

"I'm not a soldier." I wanted to forcefully reject any lingering doubts about who the hell I was supposed to be that these two psychopaths had instilled in me. "I'm not even in high school."

I was speaking truth, but I checked myself over all the same. I studied my concave, bird-like chest covered by a t-shirt two sizes too big. ("So you'll grow into it," Gram-Gram would say when she sent our clothes at Christmas time.) My right hand still had the yellow blisters on my thumb from where I'd smoked one of Marc's old joints down too far.

I reached for an explanation to make sense of this whole encounter. I started to suspect maybe Nancy Reagan had been right after all.

"Drugs . . ."

Cliff and Night Sky had stepped away from me. Like I wasn't a threat. Like they weren't at all worried I might run. Their boots kicked rocks and dirt and crunched through freezer remnants and whatever was left of Noah.

Cliff carried on a one-sided conversation with his silent companion.

"You hear that Night Sky, old buddy? Sure you do. That vow of silence you took when you donned that black mask of yours didn't come with a vow of not listening. Recruit said 'drugs.' Sounds like those DRAGON creeps are up to their old mind-altering, brainwashing tricks again."

"Please. I just wanna go home." But they weren't listening.

I don't know why I didn't run. I don't know why I didn't follow Carlos. That had always been the easiest thing to do in the past. It got me through three shitty years of middle school.

Hot, slick tears streamed down my face before I registered Night Sky's black-gloved hand slapping me across my cheek. The sting of his strike seemed to travel back in time to reach me. The crack of tough treated leather against the soft fat of my face came at the very end. An explanation provided too late. Through watery eyes, I gazed into that black mask of his. I still saw nothing, but I felt *everything*. Every terrible emotion, every bad dream, and every unwanted thought, all of them sewn together in a patchwork wrapped around my shoulders like a quilt of depression.

"Don't think, soldier. Thinkin'll get you killed out here on the battle-field," Cliff said.

"This isn't a battlefield. It's a junkyard."

"Any battlefield is a junkyard when those scumbags from DRAGON are involved."

The sharp teeth of the pine tree tops on the west side of town had nearly devoured the setting sun. All I could think was, *How long do I have to wait until someone comes for me? How long until someone even notices I'm gone?*

"What does D-R-A-G-O-N stand for?" Cliff asked me.

They had guns and swords. What was I supposed to do? Not respond? I had no idea what the hell Cliff was talking about, but I followed his orders when I tried to answer. I didn't think.

"Diabolical Renegade Armed Guerilla Occupying Nation!" I shouted my words up to a sky slashed with bloody reds and burnt oranges, all fad-ing into bruised and battered purples. "Sir."

I threw the "sir" in at the end.

Cliff and Night Sky nodded approvingly. Once I'd said the words, I ex-pected *something* to happen. I waited for it. But they stood there. We *all* stood there. I looked up, down, and off to the sides, like that kid at the PTA Night school play who hadn't known about rehearsals or that he'd have *lines*.

"What the hell's going on here?"

Old Man Ryerson's voice, thick with an electric can-opener gravel, cut through the strange, dream-like tension. All three of us turned our heads to the sound of him stomping through the debris. Ryerson reeked of Old Crow sweats and he had what I hoped were gravy splatters visible on his overalls.

The junkman stopped suddenly, swaying forward and back. Somehow, he managed to stay balanced on the balls of his dirty socked feet. I thought he'd topple over or at least spew like I had. But then he righted himself at the last second, pinching the small of his own back with a gnarly, liver-spotted hand. Air blew out of his mouth like he was trying to spit. The old-timer seemed all dried up inside, though. Nothing more than a walking, talking mummy.

His bloodshot eyes looked ready to burn holes into Cliff and Night Sky. "Well, hold up now. What in the hell's goin' on here? Y'all boys ain't getting up to any nasty business here in my junkyard I hope."

Cliff marched forward, his hand extended for a no doubt firm, all-American shake. His movements were stiff, overly deliberate, rehearsed.

"No worries at all, sir. We're securing the perimeter and we'll have that last DRAGON agent apprehended ASAP."

Refusing the handshake, Ryerson wiped the back of his hand across his wrinkled, sunburn-scarred forehead. "What the hell are you talkin' about, son?"

The old man pivoted and pointed a trembling finger at me. "You. I remember you now. Remember that brother of yours coming 'round here smoking reefer too. What kinda trouble you getting into, boy? Y'all doing acid like those hippies give to kids on Halloween? That what this is?"

"They're . . . soldiers."

I wanted to call them *killers*, *psychopaths*, *murderers*. But those words wouldn't come. They stayed buried deep down inside. And I didn't know or understand why.

"Ha!" Old Man Ryerson laughed once—a long, loud screech. An owl or hawk or some other bird of prey looking for an early dinner cried out in solidarity.

"I assure you, citizen. Night Sky and I are part of an elite fighting force dedicated to protecting America from the evil machinations of DRAGON, the Diabolical Renegade Armed Guerilla Occupying Nation!"

"Son, you ain't served. That smile on your face? It's too damn big. You ever hold your buddy's hand in some fucking backward commie country while you sing him his favorite Hank Williams and try'n make him forget that his guts are all laid out on his lap? You ever done that, huh?"

Ryerson almost sounded eloquent, but I just wanted to scream the whole time he spoke. I couldn't take my eyes off the bloodstains and brain matter splattered at the junkman's feet. I wanted to warn him, make him see how *wrong* the situation was. The words still wouldn't come.

Much to my surprise, I didn't have to say anything. Night Sky pulled his sword out and pointed the blade down at a sizeable chunk of what had once been Noah.

"Jesus Christ! Where the hell'd ya get that pigsticker from, son?"

Ryerson followed the blade down, down, down. The splotchy-red coloring slid from his cheeks like his face was a draining bottle of ketchup. He looked up at me like there were too many things he wanted to say all trying to bubble out at once. Finally, he managed to ask, "Son? You okay there, son?"

I shook my head, trying to keep the motion small, indistinct. *Subtle.* I hoped the sight of Noah's blood and guts had sobered the old man enough to get it. I mean, he *was* a grown-up after all. An adult. There had to be something he could do to fix this and put everything right.

Ryerson put his hands up. He kept on talking while taking a cautious step closer to me. "Well, look here, fellas. I don't want any kinda trouble here, okay? This here's my place of business and my home. And, sure, it's a bit like me in that it ain't much to look at, but it's the best I got. So, if y'all don't mind . . ."

Night Sky hadn't resheathed his sword.

For all of his drunken buffoonery, Ryerson managed to move forward until he stood inches away from me. He rose on slight tiptoes and gazed over my shoulders at the strange-looking soldiers or whatever the hell they were supposed to be. "What I mean to say, fellas, is I don't want any trouble. So, uh, why don't you let the boy go, okay?"

Cliff laughed again. I watched the sound of it hit Old Man Ryerson in the same sickening way it had hit me.

"Let him go? Why this is what he signed up for, old-timer. If you served like you say, you should know we can't let this young recruit go AWOL."

"Goddammit! That ain't no recruit. He's a damned boy."

"Aren't we all?"

Everyone turned at that last question. Even Cliff. He hadn't asked it. We all looked into the black void of Night Sky's mask.

"You're crazy is what you are," Ryerson said. "All of ya. Boy, come to me!"

He held out a trembling hand, but before I could take it, before I could speak, before I could even think, Cliff's voice blasted in my ears. "Hey kid, watch out for oncoming traffic. You never know when a distracted driver might be out joyriding while you're running after your favorite ball."

Something oval-shaped bounced in the dirt between me and Mr. Ryerson. We stared down at this new something, trying to make sense of the object as it landed in the dust and grit between us. The old man's eyes widened, connecting to a past he'd been trying to drink away for years. "Grenade!"

I don't know how much strength he usually carried around in those shriveled limbs of his, but, at that moment, adrenaline turned Old Man Ryerson into a superhuman. He shoved me and I flew back, my feet leaving the ground, arms windmilling. I slammed into something hard, unmoving. Soon enough, I realized I'd returned to the side of Cliff and Night Sky.

Ryerson stood over the grenade. He looked like he'd given away all he had left inside. I saw that familiar look of defeated acceptance, the same one I'd seen in Marc's friends when college wasn't in the cards and they knew they'd have to drive to the recruiter's office over in the strip mall. That look, but different—more permanent.

Marc had given me that same look when he'd left at the start of the week, skipping out on the start of boot camp and stealing the revolver Dad kept under his bed as he slept. He hadn't come back to get his weed like I'd thought he would. Here in this moment, surrounded by death, I started to realize he wouldn't be coming back at all.

The growling in my stomach grew louder.

Ryerson kept staring at the grenade. It almost looked like he wanted to pick it up and make sure it was what it seemed to be. Part of me didn't blame him. The other part wanted to yell, "Run! Get the hell out of here while you still have a chance!"

Instead, I just watched as he looked up at the three of us. His mouth moved but I couldn't hear what he was saying. The growls had reached a crescendo. The soldiers held me by the arms. They dragged me backward.

The black and red tank crashed through the junkyard's cyclone fencing. It exploded toward us, its treads grinding over metal, plastic, rocks, and dirt. The ebony paint job on the body reminded me of a black hole swallowing up matter and crushing it into something less than nothingness.

Old Man Ryerson didn't have a chance to turn around and face the fast-approaching death wagon. He didn't get to see the ending of his tour of duty on planet Earth. The orange bloom of the grenade's delayed explosion flared at his feet, spreading fast to consume him as the large predatory tank took him from behind, its grinding, growling treads swallowing up man and fire alike.

Guns out, Cliff and Night Sky held onto me with their free hands. Laser blasts rippled through the narrowing space between us and the tank—like psychedelic black light poster effects. *Ping-ping-ping.* The tank deflected their blasts like pennies bouncing off the bottom of an empty fountain. Unanswered wishes flew left and right, and the death machine kept moving forward, forward, forward.

"Don't worry, recruit. We won't let these DRAGON bastards win."

I nodded like I knew what the hell he was talking about. Faced with everything I'd seen, it was easier to just believe. I had to accept that he—that *they*—really were fighting some war against invaders on American soil. I accepted it all. Including the tank with blood-colored, black-veined dragon's wings extending from its turret. One thing I *couldn't* accept: getting ground up by some damned tank. I shrugged one of my arms free and the soldiers let me go. The tank rolled closer. *Closer.* I reached behind me and grabbed the top of Night Sky's mask. My fingers felt cold. Colder than they'd felt before.

But I held on. I wouldn't let go.

"Give me a gun."

The tank stopped. I turned as its top panel popped open.

I should've known it'd be Carlos rising from the hatch. Popping up the same way Noah had from the old freezer.

For a second, I thought I saw the Carlos I remembered. The one who'd drawn me and Noah into his orbit. There was the smile that radiated so much confidence, bravado, and sheer, unbridled fuck-the-world energy. But it was gone just as quickly.

Carlos held his hands up. He looked down and studied the three of us: Cliff, Night Sky, and me, the seasoned veterans and their newest recruit. He started talking once he saw I had a gun.

"Dex, c'mon man, we gotta get out of here. These guys—whatever the fuck they are—they're everywhere. All across this side of town. Fighting. Killing. It doesn't make any sense, man. There's no war here. War's out there." He swept his arms across the sky in these widening arcs, like he could never capture the sense of scale for what he'd experienced.

I realized why that look of his had failed to impress me earlier in the junkyard. With him sitting up in that tank, I finally saw his smile for what it was. He was just a kid pretending to be tough but missing the mark when it came time to be a man.

From a distance, I heard other sounds—explosions, laser blasts, rallying cries shouted into the night. I smelled our town burning. Inhaled the slick scents of spilled oil and blood.

"Come on, Dexter. Quit pointing that gun at me, man. You *know* me."

"Why are you in the tank?"

My new companions flanked me and nodded, approving of my question.

"I dunno, man. I thought it'd be safe. It was easier to drive than I thought. Like driving Dad's truck back from the bar. Figured I could come back and get you. I know—"

I didn't let him finish. The single blast from my gun turned his head into a rose-red blossom graffitied on the underside of the hatch.

"Good shooting, recruit."

I wanted to tell Cliff, "Thanks." Or maybe say, "He said he knew . . . but knowing's only half of it."

But it didn't matter. I was just another recruit pulled into the never-ending war machine. Soviets, Viet Cong, or whatever the hell DRAGON was—there'd always be somebody to fight. One way or another, I think I always knew I'd end up here. Either I could accept it or end up dead and rotting. Like Noah. Like Carlos. And, yeah, probably like Marc.

Having survived the Battle of the Junkyard, what else was I supposed to say?

"Let's roll out, troops."

I sounded like someone had pulled a string on my back to trigger the perfect catchphrase.

PRE-APPROVED FOR HAUNTING

❝ Someday, at some indeterminate point in the future, this house may become a *real* haunted house, one inhabited by the restless remnants of the deceased. But not yet—not today."

That's the last line of the first report I filed for the house at 410 Lilac Lane. Back then, 410 L.L. wasn't even a house yet, just a frame of cheaper-than-it-needed-to-be lumber and a foundation of well-poured cement on a cleared lot.

There was nothing buried under the grounds of 410 L.L. either—no persons, pets, or things more peculiar. I double-checked county records and did my own off-the-record inquiring with the older folks in town who might know better than what was written down, to be sure.

Still, the couple who bought the lot and had grandiose visions of the fortune they'd make flipping 410 L.L. insisted they had ghosts on the premises. So, they contacted me.

They'd got the lot cheap. The factory that provided the lifeline for the town in its earlier incarnation had closed about four years prior, and reality had finally caught up with that sad fact. All those living souls nearby determined to stick it out until "the end" had decided that their current situation was as close to "the end" as they were comfortable letting things get. Empty lots like 410 L.L.'s went for a song in those days, with people willing to take anything to get themselves free of the town and whatever obligations they might have to it.

Of course, it didn't take too long before those same lots would go for a million "songs" or more. New houses, like the one at 410 L.L., helped kick-start the eventual, inevitable turnaround.

"But it's haunted. We're told all the workers say they've heard noises," said one of the house-flippers, the one with movie-star-nice hair.

I let him talk. I let him get all worked up until his partner, the other one with even nicer hair, whispered something into the agitated man's ear. I couldn't hear what he said, but I caught the words "the investment, though."

The only way I could've changed my answer would have been to stand there and make myself a liar. But I was and remain a professional, so that option was not something I'd entertain. Instead, I asked for a full accounting of everyone who'd set foot on the lot since it had come into their possession. I asked for the names and addresses of everyone their foremen had used—all the carpenters, plumbers, electricians, ditch-diggers, dirt-haulers, and bricklayers. They obliged, providing the names and even addresses of everyone they had a paper trail for. After I checked those names, I pressed harder and got the names of everyone working off the books too.

They were all alive. To a man. No on-site deaths or after-work traffic crashes among the lot. I even checked on their families, most of them living crammed into the RV park out past the abandoned factory. They were all alive as well.

Alive, but I wouldn't say they were all healthy and happy. Unmarked white vans driven by large men with faces flat and pudgy like thumbs—the kind of men who'd never willingly tell you who they worked for unless they thought you were on *their* side—rolled slow past the work site and past their trailer homes. Those thumb-men did their own kind of haunting, scaring children and getting spoken about exclusively in whispers. But theirs wasn't the kind of haunting I was hired to investigate. I set it aside for someone else.

In my initial investigation, I went out to where they were building 410 L.L. and talked to the foreman. He was a guy who looked like a "Hank." He squeezed my hand so hard when he shook it, practically guaranteeing

I'd never care to remember if I was right or wrong about his name. Getting down to business, I asked him to describe the haunting. "Tell me what exactly it is your men are hearing."

"Well, first off, do you actually believe this shit? Seems a bit ridiculous, right?"

I didn't give him the reassurance that a response—positive or negative—would provide. I didn't tell him that my interest was not in what I believed or in how things seemed. I didn't stand there, with that pungent smell of hot churned-up gravel filling our nostrils, and explain that my role as a *paranormal investigator* was based upon evidentiary study and real, though admittedly highly theoretical, science rather than supernatural hokum.

I gave him nothing. And I waited.

He wasn't as strong as his grip led me to believe; he didn't make it thirty seconds before he started talking again. "They hear hammering and drilling. There's some of 'em, heading out to the trucks on their lunch breaks, who say they hear, like, this big boom box radio blasting all that mariachi shit. You know, with the horns?"

I nodded. I did know what mariachi music was. "But this is a construction site, right? What else would those men be doing except hammering, drilling, and listening to 'that mariachi shit'?" I asked. "I mean, are they hearing those noises after hours? Is the music coming when they've got their radios off? Something like that, maybe?"

He shook his head. Suddenly, he wouldn't look at me. He stood there, leaning against his mud-splattered Bronco and staring at his hands. I guess he thought if he looked hard enough, he'd find the answers in the calluses and wrinkles etched across his palms.

His hands must not have given him what he was looking for, though, because he finally stopped and shook his head again. "They say it's like an echo. But not. Because the sounds don't match up with the noises they're making. Like they hear themselves working, but on things they haven't worked on yet. Things they're about to work on. It's stupid . . ."

I thanked him for his time and wished him luck on the project. He smiled at my last comment. "You bet your ass. Do you know how many folks we got coming here looking to build big houses like this one? I'll tell ya, it's a goldmine, bud. I don't even know who the heck they're gonna get to come live in 'em. King of England, maybe?"

I asked if he still lived in town. "What?" he said, already forgetting about me and any discomfort my earlier questions had given him. "You kidding? I got my kids to think about. We got a place next town over. Schools are better there."

I walked through the skeleton of the soon-to-be 410 L.L. I counted its beams, its studs, its nails. When I finished my circuit, I looked over at the few ancient clapboards eyeing this potential new monstrosity from across the street. Those smaller homes appeared to huddle together with their boarded-up shutters like downcast gazes. The winds were picking up, and, as they roared past my ears, I could almost fool myself into thinking I heard those old houses whispering, gossiping. "It's the end for us. Ain't it, just?"

Sure enough, within a year or two, those same houses were torn down, bulldozed, and replaced. None of those replacements held a candle to 410 L.L., though. At best, you might call them its acolytes.

No one called me to investigate those houses. Not even once. And why would they?

If the next client from 410 L.L. had asked me to deliver a report, I would have filed the exact same one I'd made back during construction. As far as I could tell, just because I returned to a finished house with walls, ceilings, state of the art kitchen appliances, a two-car garage, and that to-die-for open-concept living room/ dining room space, that didn't change a damn thing when it came to my assessment of a potential haunting.

Or lack thereof.

I walked through the front door, having already wiped my feet free of dew-wet grass on a WELCOME HOME mat placed just so on the porch. I stepped into a foyer where a dog's food and water bowls sat sentry near a leash hung beside the human occupants' coats and umbrellas.

The glowing hum of suburban domestic tranquility always frightened me more than any fog-filled cemetery ever could. With cemeteries, you'd pull away the vines, read the names on the grave markers, and know all there was to know about its inhabitants. They lived, they died, and here they are forever.

Simple.

But when you're taking off your boots because the client's wife asked you to, and you're trying to hold onto your equipment you carted in from your old beater station wagon—the sonar devices, infrared goggles, Geiger counters, etc.—you learn to forgive yourself for thinking maybe David Byrne was a prophet and onto something when he sang that eternal question: "How *did* I get here?"

I nearly tripped over the dog bowls when little hands came out of no-where, each set paired with a couple of overeager little feet. All those limbs attached to little children with inquiring eyes and giggling mouths. They moved fast even when standing still. I couldn't nail down their number. They came for my equipment with a singsong offer to "Let us help you with your stuff, Mister," and they were gone before I could insist that they "Please be careful with those!"

I followed them, taking a more direct path than their own winding, weaving, and bobbing course. We moved down the front hall and across the main room. I watched them deposit each item, with as close to rever-ence as chocolate- and grass-stained fingers could hope to provide, onto a dining room table. I'd later learn the table had been repurposed from "a piece of the old dock." I'm not certain which dock exactly, but I like to think it was one where kids had fished—not these particular children, of course, but certainly someone's children at some point in time. I still think about those hypothetical fishing children, dropping their lines into murky black water from the ends of makeshift poles.

"Kids, why don't you go watch some TV or play on your computers while the grown-ups talk, okay?"

At their mother's command, the children obeyed. Not necessarily out of deference or fear, though. I got the sense they had been wait-ing for that signal, for the call to return to whatever sanctuary they'd claimed for themselves inside the walls of 410 L.L. Quick as they'd come, as though they'd emerged from and returned inside the very walls, they were gone.

I accepted the offer of a slushy frozen margarita from the Mister and Missus of 410 L.L. I watched tequila-infused slush dribble down an over-worked and sweaty blender pitcher. The Missus poured it into a faux-fancy novelty glass with an etched inscription revealing its origins in *Destin, Florida!* The Mister—a real Man of the House type, or at least someone who wore the face and clothes of a Man of the House—watched from over her shoulder. He flashed a Cheshire-Cat-moonlighting-as-a-used-car-salesman smile in my direction.

At least he didn't offer a handshake.

Instead, he slammed both his hands down on the table, smacking the surface so hard that he rattled my equipment and sloshed icy lime-green liquid into the crevices of the tabletop. I watched the melting booze race through the cracks like dull metal balls rolling inside one of those wooden Labyrinth boxes. "Give it to us straight, pal. We got ghosts here or what?"

In my line of work, it's hard to use "or what" as a professional answer over and over again. "You don't have ghosts," is never what people who think they *do* have ghosts want to hear. But when you have a reputation to uphold and you refuse to join the hucksters and con artists who fill the field, that's the unfortunate (and much less lucrative) choice you often have to make. It was especially hard to do with a house I'd visited before. A house like 410 L.L.

When I spoke, I directed all my inquiries to the Missus. She had some celebrity gossip magazine spread across her lap, but her eyes were on me. I glanced under the table and saw her index finger tracing across the head-lines above paparazzi pics of cheating superstars and crash-dieting has-beens, like she was divining answers from whatever words her acrylic nails touched.

"What have you heard? What have you seen?" I asked.

I expected to hear the same as before—the hammering, the buzz-saw-ing, the sounds of 88.9 El Hombre Radio. At the very least, that would have given me some context, a proper starting point for investigation. *Establish a pattern.* That's rule number one in the book about my work I'll never have time to write.

In that moment, I dared to imagine that fresh research would reveal one of the workers *had* died in some ghastly on-site accident after my original report was filed. Or maybe there'd been someone killed by a jealous lover in the house, brains splattered into what everyone had assumed would be the last coat of paint, the finishing touch before 410 L.L. went on the market.

I wasn't that lucky. The workers were all still accounted for, every last one. Most still worked on houses, filling every gap of green the town once possessed or remaking older homes whose original occupants had held out as long as they could. Yes, those men were still haunted. But their dread specters didn't come from beyond the grave. They came with a fear held at bay (*perhaps*) by papers clutched tight in hands and made worse (*certainly*) by the sounds of cleared throats or hard-handed knocks against the door of an overcrowded Airstream at three in the morning.

The Mister and Missus shook their heads in response to my queries. She spoke first, and I thought maybe I'd misjudged them. "It's the children who told me about it. It took a while to get them to talk. They're always so absorbed in their screens, you know?"

All at once, all three of us took our hands off our phones and slid them onto our laps like they'd been slapped by a nun's ruler in Catholic school.

At least I had my phone out for work. I reminded myself of that fact and reached back to turn on the Voice Memo app to record the interview. I motioned for the Missus to continue.

"Finally, I got sick of all the whispering, the nasty looks I saw 'em giving out of the corner of my eye. I saw them do it. They thought I couldn't see. But I saw . . ."

She gulped down the rest of her frozen margarita, drinking it so fast I got brain freeze just watching her. But God bless the alcohol tolerance of the suburban housewife in the wild. Her story continued without so much as a citrus-scented hiccup.

"I took away all their devices," she said. "All of 'em. Of course, they cried and cried. 'What'd we do? What'd we do?' All I wanted to say back was, 'You know what you did.'"

The Mister nodded as punctuation. One of those full, neck-stretching, affirmative nods guys who brag about how few books they've read like to give.

"But then, I looked at their faces. I could tell, you know. Like, mother's intuition, right? I knew they were telling the truth. The whispers, dirty looks, those faces I'd seen with all that spite and hatred on 'em? Those weren't my kids. They couldn't be."

No other children had lived in 410 L.L., except those spawned from the loins of the margarita-buzz-sharing Mister and Missus seated across the table from me. But I wasn't about to interrupt and share that information. I simply followed with a thoughtful and professional "Mm-hmm."

"That wasn't the end of it," she said.

It never is.

She pulled the magazine up from her lap and slapped it down on the table, covering a stack of unopened mail. I caught a glimpse of a long white envelope with a cellophane window announcing the imprint of some banking or credit institution. The red *URGENT* stamped across the front was replaced by a triptych of "The Best Beverly Hills Beach Bods."

"My youngest wouldn't stop crying. She just cried and cried. I swear to you, she'd been the happiest little baby you ever saw. Even teethed with a smile on her face. But the tears . . ."

"Tell him what she said she saw," the Mister interrupted, putting a hand on his wife's elbow and squeezing a little too hard for my liking. But that may have just been my second frozen margarita talking.

A short while later, I sat in a too-small wooden play chair and spoke with the children about their "ghost." Would you believe that the kids—not just that youngest one, but all of them—claimed to have seen a woman reflected in the electronic glow of their screens? If it doesn't surprise you, then maybe you've got a future in my line of work.

"The Woman in the Screen looks like Mommy. But it isn't her," one of them told me after a little coaxing from the parents. The Mister and Missus peered in from the hallway, glassy-eyed but trying their best to remain laser-focused on my every move, every question.

"Why can't it be your Mama?" I asked, letting my accent slip back in a little so the *can't* became more of a *cain't*.

Filtered through several small, rapid-fire voices, I sewed together a patchwork answer. The Woman was always crying. Sure, Mama cried sometimes, but not like the Woman cried. Mama hung photographs and set up papier-mâché Santas on the mantel at Christmastime. The Woman tore everything down, boxed it all up inside her Mirror World.

She drank too, but not like Mama did. The Woman drank alone, no umbrellas in her cups. And, *worst of all*, the Woman was always alone.

As the children finished, I looked up from my tiny perch. For the split second, between Missus's eyes meeting mine and her pulling a smile up from her databank of expressions, I could see her as the Woman in the Screen. I pictured her—alone, crying, packing everything up for a bitter-sweet new beginning.

Back in reality, the Missus's hands snaked around her husband's midsection, and she pulled herself into his orbit, a hunk of meteorite so tiny its impact wouldn't be felt on the planet's surface where it crashed. Her lashes fluttered, and the shields were up again. The ghost had left the Missus's eyes.

"Let me show you one more thing, before you run off."

That's what the Mister said after I'd extracted myself from the children's chair and we'd left the bedtime routines to the Missus. For lack of nothing else except more billable hours, I followed him back through the labyrinthine hallways of the finished 410 L.L.

We trudged past picture frames crammed with smiling faces. Weddings, births, birthdays, and summer vacations immortalized because nothing's real until there's a photograph of it. Of course, no one ever takes photographs at funerals, and we still trust that the dead are dead.

The Mister stopped in front of two closed double doors at the end of a hallway. Someone had mounted a novelty placard up onto one of the doors: WARNING! MAN CAVE! ENTER WITH CAUTION!

I couldn't help but smile, thinking how the couple who'd built 410 L.L. had expected the room to get used as a dining space, somewhere people could hold salon-like parties and pontificate about the decline of civility and the importance of journalism. The Mister took my laughter for either endorsement or pandering. I don't think he cared which.

We walked into his sacred space, guarded by a shiny leather recliner, big-screen TV, surround-sound stereo, and a beer-filled mini fridge. I felt like I'd walked into the lair of a boy who'd never grown up. The Mister cracked open two beers. He passed a third to me. Then, he cranked the volume on his stereo.

"You like it?" he asked. "I come in here to think."

I felt a sense of profound relief that he hadn't waited for me to answer his question. I hated having to lie to clients, even ones like the Mister, who swayed in front of me, a great oak of a man afflicted with unreliable roots.

A Fender-shredding guitar solo reached its crescendo, and the Mister grabbed for my arm. Fingertips that smelled like rubber golf club grips pinched the skin at my elbow. He leaned in close. I cursed myself for feeling as helpless as I'd earlier judged the Missus to be.

"I see him," he said. As he tensed, my own body relaxed. I was only there to take confession.

"When I'm in here, after work, after the kids go down—whenever, I keep the door shut. It's my escape. But . . . it's not. I know he's out there. I can hear him breathing—*heh-heh-heh*—like that, you hear me? I feel his hand resting against the other side of the door, out in the hallway. At first, I thought he wanted to come in. I looked once, with the door cracked. I saw him wearing one of my suits. Custom-made, Italian, real nice. But it didn't fit him. It was like seeing a kid play dress-up. I don't think he wanted to come in. I'll tell you, I think he was trying to say goodbye."

His beers were finished; mine wasn't. I hadn't touched it. I still had to drive home. "Why won't he stop saying goodbye?" the Mister asked me.

I had theories, but it wasn't the time or place or client for articulating them. So I said, "Maybe, it's because it's not his time yet."

I left him there, probably cursing my name. On my way out of 410 L.L., I slipped the Missus a business card: my friend Jessica, a divorce attorney in the next town over. I figured she could squeeze one more client in as a favor for a friend.

Standing at the edge of their yard, I looked up into the front façade of the house. I studied its doors and windows, especially the ones where the curtains were open and the blinds raised. I looked for faces looking back at me.

And I saw them.

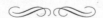

By the time of my third visit to 410 L.L., they'd relegated the mail— envelopes, packages, election mailers with smiling, diverse faces—to the porch. I had to nudge aside a mini mountain of paper and cardboard before ringing the doorbell. When I didn't hear the echo of chimes, I went ahead and knocked as well. One, two, three quick taps with just enough knuckle against the peeling paint to make them count.

I turned away from the front door as though I risked staring into an abyss and worried what cliché might meet my gaze. The acolyte houses across the street—those reborn in 410 L.L.'s image—appeared to have reverted to their old huddling, gossiping ways.

They were empty again. Overgrown grass in their yards threatened to overtake long-abandoned *FOR SALE* signs. They didn't look like the old, forgotten, empty houses you used to see on the edge of the bad part of town. Those houses looked gray, with warped wooden siding puckered like the buildings themselves were disgusted by what they'd become, their busted windows like jagged-glass smiles. They were the houses you could walk by and scare yourself to death by asking, *What if?*

But, even in decline, the acolyte houses of 410 L.L. looked perfect. Empty, but perfect.

The front door of 410 L.L. opened, and it was time to work.

Terrence Daughtry didn't look at me like he was going to pretend he didn't know why I was there. He looked relieved. This time, I offered *my* hand. We shook, exchanging initial pleasantries. "Thanks for coming to see us on such short notice," he said.

I didn't tell him he was my first client in three weeks. I didn't tell him that the calls weren't coming, and not because people didn't believe they had ghosts anymore. I didn't tell him I thought it was because those would-be clients had looked at my fees and decided that maybe it was better to allow for a noisy poltergeist tenant or two. At least that would mean they had somewhere to live and someone to share the space with.

What I told him was, "It's not a problem at all."

The inside of 410 L.L. was the same as before, and yet different. It's like when you see an old acquaintance outside of the social circle that first brought you together. Terrence introduced me to his wife Sherice and their two kids, T.J. and Laila. The Daughtry family huddled tight across a sofa that looked to have survived a few moves in its time. I wondered about its point of origin, guessing it might be a relic from someone's college dorm room. The family stared at a flickering TV propped up on old milk carton crates across the room.

When Terrence joined them, crouching down to rest his elbow on one arm of the sofa, rubbing his fingers up and down the length of Sherice's arm, I swear the scene looked as close to whatever imagined vision of modern American bliss I held in my head, as any scene of tranquility could ever hope to reach.

I wasn't sure how 410 L.L. took to that scene, though. The house appeared to sag with the presence of a new family. Its walls, floors, and ceiling like loose skin. The Daughtrys took up so little space relative to what I'd seen inside the house the last time I'd been there.

"Go on, go play in your rooms," Terrence said to his kids after making the introductions and shooing them off the couch. After they wandered off, Terrence offered me a seat. Right there on their family couch.

"Sorry, we don't have more seats in here," he said. "We've been meaning to get more furniture for the place. But, I mean, you know how it is."

I nodded. On the TV, local news ran NBA highlights. "Who's your favorite?" I asked. For some reason, I wanted to avoid the topic that had brought me, over and over again, to 410 L.L.

"What, you think just 'cause I'm Black I like basketball?"

I tensed up quick before my eyes had time to drift from the TV screen to the laughing faces of Terrence and Sherice. "I'm just messing with you, man. I'm from Chicago, so I gotta support my Bulls. Miss Buckeye over here though's the LeBron James fan, pulling for those Lakers these days."

Sherice gave her husband a light tap, pushing his hand away. "Psh! I'm no Lakers fan. I'm a King James fan, babe. And don't you forget it."

More laughter echoed off the walls of 410 L.L. I joined in, and it felt good. It felt real. When the laughter stopped and their eyes settled on me, I took a deep breath and said, "Well, I'm a Knicks fan. So, there's no fucking hope for me."

The laughter returned, intensified. But I didn't let it reach its crescendo. I knew if I did, then I wouldn't be able to get the job done. "So, tell me," I said, "Where in the house have you been seeing these ghosts?"

That did it. That killed the laughter dead.

Terrence stood. Sherice followed. Both of them moving like clockwork automatons. I had this awful feeling in my guts, like we were back to going through the motions.

Terrence shook his head and Sherice echoed her husband. "We haven't seen or heard any ghosts *inside* the house," he said.

They walked back to the front.

I followed, because that's what I'd always done when it came to 410 L.L. I followed, waiting to see what the house would show me. When we got to the front door, Terrence and Sherice looked from side to side, then back the way we'd come. It took me a moment to realize they were looking for the kids. "They got enough to worry about," Terrence said when he saw the realization settling on my face.

When the coast was deemed clear enough, he pulled open the door and stepped onto the porch. Sherice followed, and I brought up the rear. I reached back to shut the door behind us, but Sherice stopped me. Her touch was gentle but firm.

Terrence pointed to the family car, a sedan with scratches across its left back passenger door. For a moment, under the starlight, it looked like someone had left the car's lights on. But I looked again, and the lights were off, like they were supposed to be.

"There," Sherice said. In her excitement, she grabbed my hand and squeezed tight. "Did you see it there?"

I had to be honest. For this family especially, I thought I owed them that much. So, I shook my head, *no.*

"We see them sitting in our car. Sometimes they turn the lights on. Sometimes we hear tires rolling backward, like they're pulling out of the driveway. I can usually feel the one behind the wheel. Like I know what he wants. He wants to stay, but he has to go . . ."

"But he can't leave?" I asked, finishing the hard part for him.

He nodded, wiping away tears. Behind us, Sherice picked through the pile of mail beside the door. I heard her mutter an apology for "the state of things."

I told them I'd waive my fee. There wasn't much else to say after that. I took the porch steps down to the walkway as fast as I could. I didn't look back to see the Daughtrys' retreat inside 410 L.L., but I did hear the door slam closed. I stepped off the walkway and headed for my car parked by the curb. I looked up into a black and starless sky.

Even then, I had my suspicions about what the Daughtrys and everyone else around 410 L.L. had seen. Hell, more than suspicions, I think I already knew. I think I'd always known.

I knew they were seeing their own ghosts. Not even dead yet, but already haunting. Like they'd put so much of themselves—mind, body, and soul—into the house, their restless spirits had no time to wait for pesky things like living and dying. That was the power of 410 L.L. I knew it well. I knew it as well as it knew me.

That night, like all the times before, I saw the other-me. Another ghost of what's yet to be. I watched him get out of my car, ready to pick up where I left off.

The first time walking through the bones of 410 L.L., I saw him enter a finished room filled with loud rock music and whispered confessions. I caught a whiff of lime and tequila when he passed.

Next, unsteady from two margaritas and cursing myself for letting it come to that, I watched him leaning against the front porch rail, looking out at something in the empty driveway. That ghost-me looked skinnier, but not in a good "Oh, you've lost weight" kind of way. His clothes looked threadbare, a little too familiar.

The last time I saw him, he reeked of all-nighters and bad decisions. I pegged the smell for booze at first. But I took a deep breath, my hand on the driver's side car door, and realized it was gasoline I smelled, along with the scent of match-head sulfur from those big ready-strike matches.

I smelled intention. A final reckoning to come for my ghost-to-be and the house at 410 Lilac Lane.

I haven't had any clients in a long time. No one's calling, either. Of course, the cell reception's pretty spotty out here in the RV park, near the vine-covered remnants of what was once a factory and the beating heart of the town. That's meant no new calls to investigate 410 L.L. But I still check the real estate listings every day, waiting to see it there again. I'm waiting for the time when it's empty. When it's ready for me and for what comes next.

I already know what I'll do when it's time and the bill comes due. Same as everyone else. We'll pay the cost, no matter what, to stay in our forever home.

THE CRACK IN THE CEILING

A t the end of every week, our town hangs burning bodies from the Ceiling so we'll remember what stars looked like. Born after the Ceiling descended and cut us off from outer space, my sister Callie's never seen the sun, the moon, or *real* stars. For her, the immolation of friends, neighbors, and family is the closest she gets to the cosmos.

"Im-mo-la-tion. It's a sacrifice. With fire."

Callie's got one eyebrow cocked and her left foot taps against the pie-crust-flaky dirt on the kitchen floor. Like somehow I'm keeping *her* from something important. Like she's not the one who ran upstairs with a torn scrap of Word-a-Day calendar, asking "What's this mean?" before I even said "Good mornin'."

I deliver some noogies across her straw-pale strands of blonde hair. She slaps her hand across mine, not interested in big-brotherly teasing.

"What makes our stars im—imo—"

"Immolations?"

"Yeah. I mean, we only use people who're already dead. How's that a sacrifice?"

I don't mention how Neighborhood Watches gather "bodies" to meet Town Council quotas, making sure there're enough "stars" to provide a light show that makes everyone "ooh" and "ahh" on the ground, even as we ignore the barbecue-scented ashes falling like dirty snowflakes onto our heads.

"Go get ready so we can snag a good spot. All right, girl?"

"Sure thing. *Boy.*"

She sticks her tongue out and gives me her best smile, showing yellow- and brown-speckled teeth like bird's eggs. I can see both Mom and Dad in her face.

Our parents didn't wait for natural causes or a Neighborhood Watch Patrol. I guess they volunteered themselves, considering they snuck off into the garage one night while Callie and I were sleeping. Exhaust spilled out like a breath held too long in cold weather when our neighbors pried open the garage door. "Don't look at 'em, boy," I remember somebody saying.

But no one stopped me from looking when they hauled up Mom and Dad and flames gnawed through clothes, skin, muscles, and bones. When Mom's harness snapped and her cigarette-ash remains crashed to the ground, I kissed Callie's forehead to distract her.

"Mom's a falling star, Callie. Make a wish."

My sister waits on our porch, pacing on bare feet. She never wears shoes or sandals. Her soles must be hard as rocks, and I hope they are for her sake. Otherwise, she'll catch a splinter in her heel, or worse, one of these days.

"C'mon!"

Grabbing my hand, Callie launches herself off the porch. For a moment, she's flying.

I step down quickly so her arm doesn't get pulled from its socket.

Mr. Donaldson, wearing pressed khakis and a short-sleeved navy-blue collared shirt, waits for us on the ruined sidewalk. He holds a clipboard between his hands, the metallic clasp covering up the "Grove Street Neighborhood Watch" logo above his pocket. He's always looking down. A guy like Donaldson, with his bald head and lips that droop like a wormy pink mustache, isn't interested in looking at the Ceiling.

I walk up with my head held high. "Evening, Mr. Donaldson. What can I do for ya?"

Callie hangs back, teetering on a chunk of cracked cement. I snap my fingers to get her attention and point down the block.

"Run ahead. Save me a spot for the stars."

She wants to argue. But she can tell by the look I'm giving her that it's not the time.

"Go on without arguing and I'll break out those last three months of the Word-a-Day calendar I'm sitting on."

"Promise?"

"Cross my heart."

I do it so she knows I'm serious.

Callie takes off down the block. No "goodbye" or "I love you." No hugs or kisses. Soon, she's at the corner play-fighting with the O'Reilly boys. Donaldson clears his throat and I finally give him my attention.

"Our neighborhood's up, Devon. We thought Ms. Bansford would pass, but the old girl's hanging on. We had the morning drawing and your name got selected."

It's not worth fighting, but I try. "What about Callie? She'll be alone and—"

"Neighborhood'll look out for her until she's eighteen. She won't be our first Starchild."

I hate the term. Have since Mom and Dad became stars, leaving us on our own.

"What happens after?"

Donaldson shrugs. Alabaster skin peeks through his collar. "She can stay in town or she can go someplace else. *They* didn't put more walls down. We're the ones who do that."

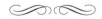

This is what it's like to become a star.

I'm burning. Flames hover over my head like a halo. That's before they pull me up to the Ceiling. Inside my charbroiled skin, blood boils.

I should be dead. Donaldson gave me pills, promised they'd do the job. He watched me to make sure I swallowed 'em.

Now I'm wondering why I'm still awake and aware, pressed up against the Ceiling. I can see everybody from town down below. They point at me and the other stars like we mean something.

My eyes pop like marshmallows microwaved too long. Gooey remnants turn to ash in seconds.

So why can I still see?

This is Callie's first time seeing the stars by herself. I pray she can't find me up here.

A cool breeze on the back of what I suppose is my neck is the last thing I expect to feel. I don't so much move as shift my awareness, inspecting the Ceiling that's inches away. I see a crack, jagged like a lightning bolt, running across the smooth, polished surface. It's a deep wound. I look up through it, expecting to see stars—real ones.

Instead, I see rocks. Dirt. Layers of sediment. I look up through the crack in the Ceiling, past grass, past asphalt and cement. I see people walking, running, smiling, fighting and killing, learning and loving.

Those people up there still look at the stars. And down here?

Down here, we're left to burn.

RETURN TO VOODOO VILLAGE

I nudge the gas pedal on the tiny airport rental car and steer onto the tight one-way lane leading to Voodoo Village. Tires spin, chewing up gravel, twigs, and the past twenty years.

Tall leafless trees, like sun-bleached skeletons, hide me from a fading sun. I glance at the passenger seat, sneaking a quick peek at the map I printed and marked up back at my hotel on Beale Street. No bars on my phone, and Wi-Fi's a pipe dream out here. I'm glad I came prepared.

But my fleeting sense of accomplishment can't erase the screaming urge deep down inside, the tiny voice telling me to *find a place to turn the car around and get out. Go back to the hotel. Pack and catch the next flight home. Kiss Becky and hug the girls. Read them a bedtime story about princesses and dragons and old wizards. Forget about whatever you've convinced yourself you'll find at the end of this dead-end gravel road. Forget about Voodoo Village and the dreams you're still having after all this time.*

I look back at the road after my quick study of the map. Another slight bend beckons, so I miss the wielder of the aluminum baseball bat, its hefty cylinder speckled with red at the tip, a black rubber grip unraveling from the bottom. The bat connects with my driver's side mirror, smashing it off the car. By the time I realize what's happened, the assailant's gone and I've missed their face.

I jerk the steering wheel to the right like I'm in the wrong lane dodging oncoming traffic. I slam my foot on the brake before I careen off the road and crash into one of those beckoning skeletal trees. The car stops too close to one for my comfort.

I shove it into park and check my rearview. No one's there.

Not surprising. After all, my car got a message requiring no follow-up.

I reach into the center console cupholder and extract the silver flask I brought from home "in case" and later filled with minis snuck off the airplane. I unscrew the top and take a long guzzle from the flask's tiny hole. Sobriety and I take another of our all-too-frequent "breaks."

"I need this," I say to no one except my guilty conscience.

I'm not about to let a baseball bat stop me from finishing what I came out here to do. After all, I made a five-plus-hour flight from California (with transfers), cashed in on sabbatical time from work, and left Becky alone with the girls for this trip back *home*. I'm not about to get scared away, not when I'm close to the answers I need.

I take another swig from the flask. The mix of brown liquors rockets down my throat, hot and fast. I choke and booze goes up my nose. It gets me coughing, like a two-pack-a-day smoker. I wipe the back of one hand across my lips and grab the door handle with the other.

Now or never.

I unfold myself from the car's cramped confines and slide out into a face full of mosquitoes. The humidity's thick out here, like getting slapped in the face with a soggy two-by-four. My glasses fog up, obscuring the tiny winged bloodsuckers flying around and pricking at my pale white arms. Soon my skin'll look like the underside of an uncooked turkey.

The booze starts getting to me. I rub my thumbs across the undersides of my glasses' lenses, smearing them as a result.

The broken mirror is a goner.

I reach back into the car from the open driver's side door and pull the keys from the ignition. With the engine off, the weight of silence in the middle of nowhere presses down, heavier than the late afternoon Memphis weather.

I tiptoe around shards of mirror glass glittering between cracked asphalt chunks and gravel. Each piece casts my tiny distorted reflection back at me. I keep my head on a swivel, looking for danger. With my Bay Area mortgage, two kids, frequent flyer miles, and family Zoom calls, I'm an enemy-outsider encroaching on sovereign territory here.

"But I've got to finish it."

I speak the words out loud, figuring I've got a fifty-fifty chance of listening to myself.

On the left side of the road, a few dirt driveways in even worse shape than the "road" I'm standing on snake down to ramshackle single-story homes. Paint peels off screened porch doors. Old Cadillacs sit on concrete blocks. A long heavy-looking chain is attached to a rust-speckled stake hammered deep into the browning grass, and, on the other end, it connects to . . . something unseen.

The last time I came this way, back in undergrad, I missed the houses. I learned about them a few months before my current excursion. Thanks to the internet, I was able to study satellite photos of those acolyte houses, the ones waiting along the way to Voodoo Village proper.

Something clicks, seeing them in person. They're sentinels. They protect the Temple from outside threats. Threats like drunk and stoned high school or college kids coming to indulge in the timeless pursuit of property damage.

Standing in a silence where even the smallest sound's amplified, my ears pick up something. Whether it's the whine of an opening screen door or the jingle and rattle of some unseen animal's chain, the sudden noise floats up from one of the lesser homes. I don't wait to find out what it is or where it came from. I leave the rental car and take off walking down the dusty derelict road to Voodoo Village.

I don't run. I walk. Like it's the most natural thing in the world to do.

There's more road, more trees ahead. Trees and the road. The repetition lulls me into a state of uneasy calm. But not the kind where I'm safe or protected. More like the calm of an unsettling dream, where part of your subconscious remains awake enough to know everything's about to go wrong and toss you into the deep end of the nightmare pool.

Then, in the distance through the next batch of trees, triplet gold- and bronze-plated suns peer down at me. The battered metal stars regard my progress with cold indifference. Two of the disc-like objects sit below a third larger, more distinct star shape. They remind me of the eyes of a giant with a third all-knowing, all-seeing orb in the middle of its forehead. I stumble. Whether from booze or fear, I can't say.

I close my eyes for a moment, remembering the shadows of the three suns stretched by the light of a heavy moon in early May all those years before.

The metal suns crown the makeshift steeples above the main building of Saint Peter's Spiritual Temple. Otherwise known as Voodoo Village.

I take a few more steps, heading for a break in the trees. There's a clearing ahead, the woodlands flattened to indicate the sprawling property beyond. On my approach, I force myself to repeat the Village's true name. "Saint Peter's Spiritual Temple. Saint Peter's Spiritual Temple . . ."

I was raised Catholic, but not *that* Catholic. All the repetitive Gospel readings drilled into my ears at Mass after Mass ended up a jumbled, sticky film clinging to obscure corners of my memory. I try to recall everything I know about Saint Peter. He denied Jesus three times before a bird crowed. Or something.

No birds wait in the branches of the last few trees before chain link fencing takes over. Even the mosquitoes and horseflies that have been buzzing and dive-bombing me for most of the walk have dropped away.

I'm tempted to walk off the edge of the road, move closer to the fence, and run my hand along its length, hooking my fingers around one silver-and-rust-colored diamond after the other. But I stick to the road. Better to stay on somewhat familiar territory than risk electric shock or being grabbed by something far worse reaching from the other side of the barrier. Nothing seems to crawl or stalk along the fence line, but I missed that baseball bat-wielder earlier . . .

Caution is my watchword.

Closer and closer to the main gates, more signs and signifiers reassure me I'm heading in the right direction. A yellow-painted pole, about the size of a large trash can in circumference, stretches toward the darkening sky. The pole together with its crossbeam base reminds me of the crucifix hung behind the altar at Sunday Mass. However, the additional pieces extending diagonally from the bottom suggest the da Vinci drawing depicting the man with multiple arms.

Glimpsed through the fence's checkerboard pattern, smaller, metallic, glass, and ceramic folk art objects hang from trees or sit staked to the ground.

For all these strange sights, I know there's more ahead and even more kept hidden from prying eyes like mine. I lick my lips. A tiny bit of liquor dampens the space below my nose.

I turn around, facing the way I came. Of course, nothing waits down the road I've already walked. The same trees and rocks, nothing else.

"Say, son, what you lookin' at back there?"

The unexpected words knock me sillier than any Louisville Slugger. I tense up, limbs locked.

Dented sheet metal rests against the nearby fencing. Barbwire spools crown the top, reminding me of Jesus's crown of thorns.

I guess this place gets me in a biblical mindset.

Somewhere out of sight, a rickety creak and a low wheeze transition into a gasp at the last second. The sequence repeats. I imagine some wizened elder, clad in homespun cloth, rising from a splinter-covered rocking chair, the kind seen on the front porches of sharecroppers' homes in old black-and-white photos from early Jim Crow South. I picture someone twisted tight with gnarled brown skin, unfolding like a crumpled paper bag, as he moves to stand and then, reconsidering, sits back down.

However, when the unseen speaker addresses me again, there's no trace of infirmity or old age in his delivery. "Don't stand there gawkin'. Folks 'round here won't like it."

"S-s-sorry," I say.

"Sorry ain't mean nothing coming from somebody hidin' they face."

The back-and-forth between creaks and groans intensifies.

Was someone outside last time?

Martin said he saw someone. Right?

Or did Antoine or Eduardo say it?

I shake away those memory cobwebs and press ahead. Eyes diverted from the fence, ignoring the unseen speaker, I instead focus on the trinity of metallic suns. They grow larger and larger the closer I get.

A red arch curves over the main gate into Voodoo Village. It consists of multiple industrial ladders, spray-painted red and welded together. Imagine the planning and engineering gone into its creation. I'd studied pictures online, trying to refamiliarize myself with the layout before my return, but seeing it in person makes all the difference. The tacky red paint shines like a flashing emergency light.

So wet, so fresh.

If I climbed up and touched my fingers to it, would they come away crimson?

Did we make it this far twenty years ago?

The word "STOP" suddenly appears in front of my face, interrupting my attempts at remembering.

The red octagonal stop sign flaps from the side of a school bus so graffit-ied its dark mustard-yellow paint job barely shows beneath the graffiti tags. I stumble again, catching my balance at the last second to avoid falling on my ass. With a gasping exhalation, the sign collapses back against the side of the bus.

There's one mystery solved. No old man making noise, but an old ma-chine—one with a restless operator manning its controls.

The spiders' man sits at the end of the road leading to Voodoo Village. When I see him, I wonder where the name comes from. Black jeans and a white t-shirt, dressed up like he's shopped from the donation bin. I feel a twinge of disappointment he's not stranger in his appearance.

The school bus's back bumper sits close to the wrought-iron gate, block-ing the entrance. The spiders' man sits cross-legged, down in the dirt and rocks. His eyes move under closed lids. It's like I've interrupted him in the middle of some engrossing dream. One hand holds a thick rope snaking back to the driver's side window of the bus. He tugs on it intermittently, controlling the stop sign's release.

His skin's dark, but it bears no signs of old age wear and tear. Aside from the tight white curls on top of his head and the mustache hanging from either side of his upper lip like unraveled butterfly cocoons, the man's appearance is youthful. Timeless even. With the vague sense of strangeness emanating from him, the spiders' man looks like he belongs here more than I do.

"Well," he says, his eyes still closed, "what you want?"

I'm parched, throat scratchy like I've got burrs clinging to my esopha-gus and catching my words when they try to escape. "I wan—I wanna . . ."

The spiders' man opens his eyes and I yelp, the sound squeezed out at high pressure. What I first mistake for milky white cataracts over his eyeballs have moved fast to reveal unblemished eyes beneath. Tiny albino arachnids skitter away, dancing down the man's smooth ebony cheeks, producing a parody of milky tears.

Run. Go back to the car. Turn around and eat the cost at the rental agency.

"You gonna tell me why you here trespassin' somewhere you ain't belong?"

"Martin."

I bite my bottom lip. The sweat drenching my forehead runs cool.

Why did I say that name? Why didn't I tell him I came back to Voodoo Village because I'd visited twenty-odd years before and left . . . what? Disappointed? Unfulfilled? Not exactly. The sleepless nights, bad decisions, my long list of personal regrets—where did they stem from, if not that early near summer night on the outskirts of Memphis?

Voodoo Village. Saint Peter's Spiritual Temple. They write about this place in folk art magazines now. The actual owner of the property lets YouTube documentarians come and film the buildings and statues. But that's not the place I'm standing outside of now.

This place is my reason, and my reason is this place.

Martin? Martin Riddick? He was the catalyst. A starter pistol fired without warning, without a chance to stretch and warm up. I believed I'd left him behind in the swirling dust.

"Who Martin?" the spiders' man asks.

Daddy longlegs, not real spiders but close enough, tap-dance on his cheeks. Either the spiders' man doesn't notice or he doesn't care.

Past parted lips, his wide, pearly-white smile greets me.

At least no spiders emerge from his mouth.

The spiders' man's eyes, cleared of tiny mite-sized arachnids, draw me in, cocooning me in judgment. "He who brung you here before?"

I nod. The memory comes easy. It always does, at least the outline of it. But this time's different. This time, new details surface and weave their way into the tapestry of my mind.

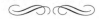

"Yo, 'Toine! Listen, dawg!" Martin calls to the front of the Grand Cherokee, putting on his "Black" voice, sounding nothing like the aw-shucks country boy he is back on campus. "This fool says he ain't never seen Voodoo Village."

It's me. I'm the fool.

Before Antoine responds, Martin's browbeating me for my apparent offenses to the appreciation of local spooky landmarks. "Man, how you live in Memphis and ain't never gone out to Voodoo Village?"

I don't get to retort. Antoine cranks the Pink Floyd to ear-splitting levels on his stereo and Martin keeps right on talking, not even pretending to care about my answer. "Yo, we gotta go check it out!"

Without missing a beat, Antoine takes both hands off the steering wheel and lights the glass pipe filled with some of the weed he'd sold Martin and me. I watch the green and brown nugs turn a radioactive orange, glowing in the dark confines of the car. Martin and I smoked before we went to Music Fest, the annual outdoor concert festival by the Mississippi River, and we'd passed around a one-hitter amid the unwashed moshing masses. Combined with all the beers I drank between sets, I'd made a vow I wouldn't partake when the pipe came around.

Except it's in my hand. And I've got Antoine's transparent blue Bic lighter turned upside down, its flame leaning sideways and scorching my thumb until it blisters.

But I don't mind.

There's no time to consider how the pipe got from the front passenger seat where Eduardo (who, despite his name, looks whiter than me, but whatever), this guy Antoine brought along, sits, to Martin, and then to me. I exhale, trying not to cough too much—Martin always gives me shit for not handling my weed—but someone's soft fingers on my left arm prove too shocking a distraction and I belch out thunderclouds of dope smoke that roll through the Jeep's interior. Damn this is strong. Martin laughs, saying my name. But the sound comes slow and muddied. Like when your parents talk outside your childhood bedroom before you fall asleep at night, their words transformed into the murmured lapping of the evening tides.

The soft fingers belong to Suzie.

Did I know she was here? Was she at the concert?

Suzie is Martin's on-again-off-again . . . something. We're not at the friendship level where I'd ask him to define his relationships.

But she's got a hell of a smile.

I'm not jealous or anything.

Except . . .

Smoke curls around her head after she exhales. "It's okay if you're afraid," *she says.*

"Of you?"

No more smoke. No one's even passing the pipe.

Did I take another hit? Where are we? What time is it?

Suzie's laughter doesn't hurt like Martin's. She leans close in the dark back-seat. Her cheeks red, her nose short and curved. Her green, gold-flecked eyes spar-kle, like we're sharing a secret, a stolen moment none of the others will take away.

"No, silly. We're here. At Voodoo Village."

"A'ight, y'all," Antoine says from the front. He makes his announcements loud and clear but long and drawn out, like some stoned tour guide. "We gotta watch out. My friend told me his brother heard they got human sacrifices and devil wor-ship shit up here. So y'all shut up."

The spiders' man keeps silent while I tell my story. He nods along, moving his head up and down a few more times than necessary. Like the bones in his neck have atrophied. My words slow at the sight, and he catches me watching him. He leers from his spot on the dusty ground.

Then, he gives me the universal signal to *get the hell on with it*, spinning his fingers around and around, wrist rotating in the same loose-jointed manner as his neck. Spiders—four, maybe five of them—spin webs down from the hood of the school bus to the dirt and rocks below. They dash and dart, in and out, missing the spiders' man's twirling fingers by fractions of inches.

At this point, I figure out what the rope he's holding is made from.

I wonder how many spiders it took, working together, to weave that length of cord—thick, yet malleable.

"I . . . I . . . I . . ."

"Aye, aye!"

The spiders' man stands close, clapping his hands to get my attention. The earthy decay on his breath overwhelms a slight hint of peppermint also present. The burst veins of his bloodshot eyes look like more spider webs, red and slick with sticky serum. He switches to a salute. He fires it off like an old pro, suggesting he served somewhere long ago before com-ing to wait outside the gates of Voodoo Village with his spiders.

Waiting for me.

He takes another step forward, hand extended. I scramble backward. Finally, the fear gnawing at the back of my mind bursts forth in full bloom. I'm sure the spiders' man's reaching out to strangle me.

But then, he's standing behind me.

His hand brushes across my shoulder. "It's okay," he says, his voice no more than a whisper. "These stories of yours, they always the same. Right?"

I nod.

"You drove on down this road. That one right here. Lights turned off?"

At first, I nod, but soon course-correct and shake my head. "No, uh, not after a while. Antoine turned his high beams on."

Like a Magic Eye illustration stared at for hours and hours, possessing a desperate need to be seen, my memories of that night twenty-odd years ago appear whole from within the haze.

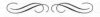

Antoine, Eduardo, and even Suzie shared their campfire-style stories, retelling the urban legends about the commune-like establishment out by Memphis's Orange Mound ghetto. Lots of talk of voodoo, curses, spirits, ax murderers. The usual for one of these infamous local "haunted" places.

Then, there was Martin. He grew more incomprehensible by the second. His head tilted against his shoulder, a sure sign he'd gone black-out drunk or was at least well on his way.

Imagine him up on the yellow pole. Drooling. Eyes glassy.

He reached up to the front. Tried to grab Antoine's steering wheel.

There's the part I forgot.

Antoine batted Martin's hand away. "Yo, man! Can you grab him?" he asked. Me. He asked me.

I reached out, hands shaking the whole time, and hooked a finger through one of Martin's belt loops on his jeans. When the denim brushed against my skin, I pulled back. But he was strong. Stronger than me at least.

Martin made one last desperate lunge for the steering wheel. His palm slapped down on its middle, compressing the horn. It yelped a high-pitched bleating call. Like a lamb lost in a forest filled with wolves.

Martin collapsed against the seat. I pulled my hand back at the last second, otherwise, his full weight would have crushed against my wrist.

"Martin, what the hell?"

Suzie spoke up when none of us guys in the car could work up the courage to say a goddamned thing.

Then, the orange lights flashed behind us. Eduardo pressed his forehead against the passenger window, staring into the dark. "Someone's moving out there," he said.

Everything went quiet.

No more fun. I got the distinct impression we needed to leave. Everyone else seemed to share my unspoken conclusion.

It's strange how, in relating these events to the spiders' man, I send myself back there, taking the same breaths, eyes straining against the same darkness, tasting the same salt-tinged sweat and tears.

Antoine tried to navigate in reverse down the long gravel road we'd taken to Voodoo Village. He was searching for a spot where he had enough room to turn around and keep an eye on the yellow school bus at the same time. Dreamcatcher-like metal and wire-frame constructions covered the bus's front windshield. I couldn't tell if there was anyone in the driver's seat of the bus. But there was someone, a figure keeping to the shadows, moving at the edges of the jeep's taillights. This someone was out there, rolling the bus across the road, preparing to block our exit.

The spiders' man moves his hand down to my arm. I flinch, shivering with the certainty I've lost time again. *Or had time taken away.* The moon's full and the setting sun's bleeding, like the trees double as razorblades shoved through the lumpy, malleable faces of star and satellite. I'm forgetting parts of the story again. The way you try and tell someone a dream and it falls apart in the telling.

The spiders' man laughs. "Right. So, that's where your story splits, ain't it?"

My eyes give me away and the spiders' man keeps talking. "Let me tell you your story," he says. "What you *think* happened and what *really* happened. Gonna leave it up to you to decide which one's which."

He moves fast. Next thing I know, he's scrambled up the front of the bus, more agile and limber than any man his age should be. Than any *man* should be. He brings his ass down hard onto the curved and dented hood, producing a hollow *thunk* at the point of contact. His pupils become oil spills, fluctuating in size. "Okay," I say. I've come this far, and I want something, anything, for my trouble. "Tell me what happened to us that night."

When the spiders' man speaks again, I fight back the urge to drop to my knees. As is, I give serious consideration to clapping my hands over my ears and screaming until someone, anyone, rescues me.

The voice coming out of the spiders' man isn't his, and it's not an imitation, but a one-hundred percent genuine match. Speaking in my voice, he finishes my story one way. The way I remember it.

Antoine hadn't looked at me once after we climbed into his car post-Music Fest. I wasn't sure I wanted him to now. "Yo, man. We gonna make it?"

He was talking to me. He was asking if there was enough space on the road behind us for his jeep to get through without running into the school bus. Someone was crying in the backseat. But it wasn't me. I was too scared to cry. On my left: Suzie was fine. She rushed through her Hail Marys in a husky whisper. But her eyes were dry.

Martin was the one sobbing. Tears and snot dampened his chin, hanging down like a gooey, transparent goatee. He wasn't saying anything, so much as he was repeating a choked half-syllable over and over: ". . . guh guh guh . . ."

"Yo! We clear?"

My depth perception's horrid enough under normal conditions. But stoned and scared out of my mind, trying to gauge distances through a tinted back windshield and into the black night beyond? Forget it.

Still, I had to try. I had to say something.

"Yes!"

Up in the front, Antoine pressed his foot down on the gas pedal. The wheels spun, rocks flying. Eduardo leaned out the passenger window with both hands extending twin middle fingers for whoever stood behind the school bus. The force of the jeep screaming over the rocks and asphalt pressed me, Martin, and Suzie back against our seat, holding us there like a giant's sweaty palm, grinding us into the black leather.

I held my breath.

And I didn't exhale until we were free.

The spiders' man stops and addresses me in his true voice. "That how you remember it?"

I want to nod my head the same way he'd done. Up and down. Up and down. But something's stopping me. I stare at my feet. Furry-legged spiders tiptoe and tap-dance on my shoes. The more adventurous ones are already scaling my pants legs. Obsidian and scarlet-dotted eyes appear luminescent under the moonlight. I'm standing still. Not perfectly still, but as close to it as I can. Except something's wrong with my fingers.

I raise my hands to my face. The crisscrossed pattern of lines on my palms looks more and more like webs. It's a tempting thought to push these spider-woven hands over my eyes and surrender.

But my body has different ideas.

I seize forward, grabbing my chest. I'm wracked by coughs from the stomach up. Soon enough, I'm on the ground, dry-heaving. This time, the spiders' man keeps his distance. Waiting until I finish.

Rotten stomach acid, blood on my lips tasting like pennies, I seek the spiders' man's mercy. But I know he'll have none to give.

"You done?" he asks.

I nod.

"Well a'ight then. Now let me tell the *other* way you remember that night. Let me tell you how you remember that night in your dreams."

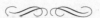

Antoine won't stop looking at me. The car fishtails backward away from the open gates leading into Voodoo Village. I want him to stop. Stopping. Giving up. They're the only things left that make sense to me.

"We're not gonna make it," I say.

His expression crumbles from fear to acceptance in a breath. Something syrupy-thick and warm soaks the shoulders of my t-shirt. I run shaking fingers through my hair. The blood comes back flaky and already dried out in the summer heat. It's not my blood.

Sure, some of it is. But not mine alone.

On my left: Suzie's gone. Her absence hasn't sunk in yet. They made us stay outside while they took her into the temple. We watched as they dressed her in robes, chanted, and then made her eyes bleed. No one present touched her eyes, not with their hands or knives or anything of the sort. But those scarlet tears showed up clear as day all the same.

Martin's dead. One look to my right reveals where the blood's coming from. An open wound throbs on his neck. His chin dips down against his chest, giving him a goatee of gore.

But at least he's stopped screaming.

Antoine stops the car.

"No."

Up in the front seat, he's having a crisis of faith all his own. The car's in neutral, but Antoine presses down on the gas pedal and spins the tires regardless. Rocks fly from beneath the jeep. Something slams against the vehicle from the passenger side.

It's Eduardo. No. It's the other . . . thing. The shadow-creature that pulled itself up from the rust-hued bloodstains on the temple floor now plays the part of Eduardo.

It moves as though it came up from underground, slithering past dirt and debris and now crawling through the open front passenger window. The shadow pretending to be Eduardo is too long. Too long by far. The long nails of its over-segmented fingers scrape against the paint.

I exhale. I exhale. I exhale. Shadow Eduardo sits in the passenger seat looking back at me, watching as I hyperventilate in Antoine's backseat.

We're caught.

The spiders' man stops the second corrupted dream-logic version of my story. He slides down from the bus's hood and onto the ground. The light and shadows give him phantom arms and phantom legs in excess, bringing the count to an even eight. "That the ending you wanted?" he asks.

He's not smiling. For once, he's stone-faced serious.

"No. You . . . you made it up. It's a lie. Some urban legend bullshit."

I've got a wife. Daughters.

I recite facts, things dug up from my internet search. "Founded in the 1960s by spiritual leader Wash Harris, the community at Saint Peter's Spiritual Temple adhere to a form of worship combining Christianity with aspects of Freemason . . ."

The hard lines crack and crumble from the spiders' man's face as he laughs, long and loud, until it's not laughter, but something like a car horn. Many car horns. All pressed at once. Their shrill, gassy chorus echoes through the woods. When the spiders' man stops laughing, the noise continues.

"Where you think you at, boy?"

"V-v-v-v-voodoo Village. I know it's not real. All those urban legends, tall tales. It's private property. A piece of folk art. It's—"

The spiders' man's shadow limbs move against the black of the night sky, nothing pressing against nothing, and I'm shocked by how little resistance reality gives.

"You ever wonder if those directions you got sitting back in your front seat might've been wrong? Ever consider your boy Antoine got hisself too goddamn high to drive the right way that night?"

He holds his hands up, feet on the ground, but his shadow limbs pull me in and hold me close.

"Maybe you've never come to Voodoo Village at all. One time, or maybe two times, you turned down a wrong road you wanted to believe was right. Wanted to believe so got-damn bad.

"Well, here we are now. Here I am.

"You all come, and you bring pieces of a story. Pieces of *your* story. Pieces of this place's story as you want it to be. As you think it *should* be.

Y'all give the pieces to me and want 'em all sewn up into something. Something meaning *something.*"

Uncertainty fills the break points and blank spots of memory, extending from the night in May lifetimes ago to this present moment.

I've got a wife? Daughters?

The unbelievable parts read as no more than mundane facts. The bland details of domestic bliss tinge with nightmarish surrealism.

"I hold a mirror up to the world. What it takes, it takes." The spiders' man puts his hands on my shoulders and turns me around. Whatever fight I might've had left slips out of me. I let him put a hand under my chin to take in the once-empty way down which I traveled.

Cars, minivans, trucks, a highway-sized traffic jam, all waiting on the road to Voodoo Village. The line stretches back for miles and miles.

I call it *Voodoo Village* because that's what it is for me. "How long have they waited?" I ask.

"Long as they needed to," the spiders' man says.

Then, he turns me back to face the waiting open door of the bus, to face the open gates leading into the Village. He leans in close and something tickles the insides of my ears. Whether it's his curly white mustache hairs or the furry legs of another spider, I'm not sure. He whispers, "What you give me, real or a dream, I keep it all. You wanna go in again, you can. But there ain't no leaving once you commit. Understand?"

I nod, imagining a thousand eyes on me like knives held inches from a mortal wounding.

I'm waiting in my seat on the bus. There are so many seats. More than I expected from earlier glimpses through the dust and graffiti-covered widows. Still plenty of room for anyone else who comes to take the spiders' man up on his offer. I hope some familiar faces board soon.

They can tell me if I'm still who I've always been or let me know if my limbs are longer than they're supposed to be. They'll tell me if I'm still me or if I'm a shadow, an imperfect copy made where the light strikes the darkness.

No matter who comes or what they tell me, I'll welcome the company.

It's always better when you can share an experience, find someone who looks you in the eyes and says, "This is all real. This is all happening."

This is all real. This is all happening.

See?

PUTTING DOWN ROOTS

From day one, Tom knew marrying Cat came with a certain amount of *shutting the hell up and going with the flow*, where "flow" represented whatever her latest flight of fancy might be.

So, when he came home on Thursday after teaching his last class of the week and found their bags packed for a road trip, he wasn't surprised. Cat loved planning spontaneous excursions, and he'd found he could tolerate them, assuming there was a hotel bar and decent Wi-Fi on hand.

Cat, a full head and a half shorter, stretched up on stocking-covered tiptoes and gave him three quick kisses, one for each stubble-covered cheek and the last on his lips, before pulling back and holding up a yellowed parchment-like piece of paper. She held it *just* out of Tom's reach. An overwhelming earthy aroma wafted from the page, strong enough to almost trigger Tom's gag reflex.

"You never told me Jefferson had an Arbor Day celebration. Arbor Day! How neat, right?"

Jefferson. Now, that was a surprise. Tom had expected a candlelit dinner in colonial Williamsburg or a drive down to Virginia Beach. But not the hometown he'd left at eighteen and never set foot in again. Not that place.

There's nothing there but bad memories, he wanted to say.

Instead, he said, "I didn't? Does it? Uh, is it?"

Cat stuck out her bottom lip, her expression falling halfway between playful pouting and taking offense. Tom knew how much she hated the so-called "walls" he put up around his past. But in truth, he was reticent to speak of Jefferson because there wasn't much worth remembering.

A month after Tom had left for college out of state, the local paper company had been bought out and his dad had been let go from his sales job as part of a downsizing. He ended up taking a new position with a company in Tennessee. Before she passed, his mom kept in touch with her friends in Jefferson, but when she got too sick to do so, neither Tom nor his dad picked up the slack.

As the years passed, Tom let his old Jefferson friends become acquaintances who then became strangers. He didn't even follow any of them on social media. The distance in years left fewer and fewer reasons to even think about his birthplace and whatever small-town traditions the declining mill town continued to carry on after his departure.

"It says here, on the last Friday in April, Jefferson holds their Arbor Day celebration where they ask everyone, including guests, to plant a tree in observance."

Bet they don't need to look far for most folks, Tom thought. He counted himself as one of the lucky few who'd managed to get away from the dream-crushing gravity of Jefferson.

I wonder how they even found our address?

He recalled something his dad had texted, a brief mention of "a new tree thing in Jefferson," but he'd buried it inside some paragraphs-long screed about Democrats eating babies and turning guns into homes for immigrants, so Tom had breezed past it. He let it serve as another reminder of why he'd stopped talking to the old man after Tom's mom passed from her bone marrow cancer. Thinking about his dad, the fact that their last text was from over a year ago, and the lingering pain of that severed connection, got Tom more agitated.

He wanted to grab the invitation and throw it away, settle down for a quiet evening at home afterward. Watch a movie or a show on Netflix. Start working on the "special project" they'd talked about. The special project they hoped would lead to a future tiny occupant for their spare bedroom soon enough.

But he knew the drive down to Jefferson took no more than a few hours, with all other traffic diverted to more compelling destinations by the end of the trip.

"Looks like someone in Jefferson found out about your books and they want you—well, you and me, I guess—to come for the actual tree-planting event. And, you know my friend Elvin whose boyfriend Raul works at the garden shop? He's getting Raul to set aside two dogwood saplings for us. We'll put 'em in the trunk with our bags. He sent me pictures. They're the cutest things. Oh my gosh. It's gonna go great, honey. I get to see where you grew up."

"Yay."

She wrapped her arms around his midsection, hugging tight. "I'm so proud of you, Tommy."

"Hope they read my first book and stopped. Dunno how my last one reached 'em unless they pulled all the remaindered copies from some landfill."

Cat tilted her chin back and arched her eyebrow, unwilling to put up with her husband's self-deprecation. Tom made himself wink, letting her think he was kidding. Even though he wasn't.

"Well, I'm excited for you. Small-town boy makes good. Who doesn't love that story?" Cat asked, letting go of her hold on him.

Tom kept his eyes steady, making sure he didn't roll them until she'd turned away.

Growing up in Jefferson during the 1990s, Tom always heard the trees described as the heart and soul of the town. He didn't agree with such fanciful descriptors. He only thought of the trees as the town's *currency*. There wouldn't be much of a Jefferson without the trees—oaks, willows, firs, and pines. Every adult he'd known back then worked in either lumber or forestry at the logging site on the outskirts of town or the sawmill. That, or the pulp and paper mills. If you didn't work with the trees, you were at least related to someone who did.

Tom sat in the passenger seat daydreaming about boarded-up buildings and trash-strewn streets as Cat took the exit for downtown Jefferson. He tried his best to tune out Cat's narration of everything seen from behind the wheel.

"Oh my goodness. Look at the trees! It looks like, let's see, one, two . . . three on every block. Wow. So green. Oh, I bet it smells incredible! I'm gonna lower the windows and—"

Her last remark yanked Tom back to the present. "Honey, no, stop!"

If Tom retained one thing from mill-town life, if one element remained etched in his primal sense-memory, it was that you *never* rolled down your window in a mill town unless you'd prepared for what came next. The sour smell of burning pulp hung in the air all the time, and when the wind hit from the right direction, you'd end up with full-blown foulness. He recalled those windy days driving to the mill when his dad put down the windows in his Ram Charger and let in the overpowering aroma, reeking like a thousand hairy shits set ablaze.

Tom knew the smell downtown wouldn't be as bad, but newcomers often had a hard time with even the slightest whiff on their first exposure. They'd complain about it smelling like a manure farm. Tom didn't get to share his explanation before Cat rolled down all the windows in the car.

"It's not—"

Too late.

With the windows down, Cat tilted her head back, nostrils quivering, and drew in a long, deep breath. Her eyes opened wide and a smile turned up the corners of her glossy pink lips.

"Oh my goodness," she said. "It smells so . . . good."

She elbowed her husband across the console, driving the tip of her elbow into his gut. She got the job done. Tom sucked in an expected mouthful of diseased, chemical-rich air.

But like his wife, Tom opened his eyes wide—his in disbelief. "It smells . . ."

"Good, right?"

Cat finished his sentence, and Tom couldn't argue. The scent outside came in as strong as he'd remembered. But it wasn't a paper mill stench. Instead, he detected pine needles and woodchips, campfire remnants. It carried a hint of foil-wrapped meats, leaking juices onto bits of charred wood. It made his mouth water.

From the passenger-side window, Tom took in downtown Jefferson. Sure enough, all the trees were there. And then some. He was no expert, but Tom thought they looked like maples, their branches like giant stags' antlers. They spread across the sidewalk, so the façades of the old downtown buildings peeked out from behind the dense foliage. The slivers of old downtown, exactly how he remembered them, surprised Tom. He found no trace of the rundown, derelict structures he'd expected (and hoped for).

Cat reached across again and whacked her frowning, brow-wrinkling husband across the chest. Looking away from the road, she gave Tom a goofy, impossible-not-to-love smile. It made him putty in her hands, as it had ever since she'd taken a liking to him at the sports bar trivia night they'd been dragged to by mutuals five years previous. "You never told me about the trees, dummy."

But Tom couldn't have told her about the trees. He didn't remember there ever being *any* downtown. Which didn't line up with the gray and brown colossuses dominating the sidewalks. An outside observer might think the trees had grown for decades. Centuries even. But Tom knew better. He knew the trees here didn't make any sense.

"What's up, butter-butt?" Cat asked him.

"It's—Jesus Christ!"

Tom took the wheel and wrenched it hard to the right. At the same time, Cat's foot came down on the brake.

Tom's ears rang. He couldn't tell if it came from the squeal of tires against asphalt or the shrieks both he and Cat emitted while avoiding a head-on collision by inches. He shook his head once, then twice, trying to get the cobwebs loose. The sudden stop jostled the two saplings in the back of the car, leaning them forward with thin branches draped across the top of the back seat.

The obstacle that made Tom's heart drop to his ass and set off their tire-squealing chain reaction was a tree standing right in the middle of the road, unencumbered by any barricade, median, or other indication someone had placed or planted it there. The tree grew fat and tall up through the asphalt. Thick limbs, like the kind you'd hang tire swings from, grasped for the setting sun.

Cat's hands trembled, as she pulled over and parked. Tom unbuckled his seatbelt and pushed open his door. He planted his low-tops on the ground, steadying himself. On the other side of the car, Cat did the same. She mumbled something about how the "tree came out of nowhere, swear to God I looked down the road and I didn't see any tree there a second before." He left her to it.

Tom grew more concerned with the quiet.

Other than Cat's mumbled excuses, his heavy breathing, the scuff of their shoes against the pavement, and the thrum of the car's engine, everything else sounded too damn quiet. *Even for a small town.*

Up and down the street, along the sidewalk on both sides, everything appeared . . . *fine.*

There was Hank's Burger Joint and Soda Shoppe, whose mustachioed owner used to pull quarters from behind the ears of every child who had a birthday dinner there. The lights hummed and buzzed. A neon caricature of old man Hank waved patrons in. But no one sat inside the restaurant or waited outside. The same nonstory unfolded up and down the block, from the bank with the extra-large gumball machine in the foyer to the town hall with its marble-columned entrance.

Everyone was gone.

Tom held his hand out, index finger extended, trying to count all the trees. But he kept failing at the simple-seeming task. He lost count every time.

"Tom, look!"

Cat stood below him, her eyes wide with manic energy. He knew that particular expression all too well. She got it whenever she'd determined everything was fine, everything would be okay, and they had to believe and push ahead for the good time they deserved. She took his chin in her hand and tilted his head back for a better view.

Above their heads, stretched across the street from one lamp post to the other, a paper banner—made from what seemed to be the same paper from the invitation—spanned the distance from one side of the street to the other. Multiple sheets stitched up like a book's binding rather than stapled together.

WELCOME HOME, THOMAS BURNS:
JEFFERSON'S OWN BEST-SELLING AUTHOR

Tom didn't know what bothered him more: the fact they tried to pass off his mid-list sales performances as "best-selling" or the fact they'd dared to claim him as their own.

Cat wrapped her arms around his midsection again, pulling herself in tight. She nuzzled the top of her head along the crease of his armpit, purring like her namesake. "Aww, they remembered you. How sweet."

"But where is everyone?"

Cat shrugged her shoulders. "At some evening mixer before tomorrow's tree planting? Nothing on the invite I recall, but you never know. Or maybe everyone's in bed. I didn't expect Vegas nights when we drove down here, babe."

Cat opened the passenger-side door and slid into Tom's old seat. She raised an eyebrow as if to say, *You coming or what?*

Tom sighed and got behind the wheel. "So now what?" he asked.

A smile broke out across Cat's face. "Let's go see your old house!" she said.

Tom frowned. He'd expected his wife would want to see his childhood home, but he'd hoped to avoid the experience until morning.

"But we don't even know the folks who live there now and, I mean, who's to say they'll be cool with some strangers ogling the front of their house?"

But Cat was having none of his excuses. She shook her head and cracked an imaginary whip in his direction. Tom knew she expected mock terror in response, but the best he managed was a defeated shrug of his shoulders. "Alright," he said. "Let's get this over with."

The canopy of trees magnified the effects of early sunset. Tom turned on the headlights and peered through the darkening bruise of downtown stretching out in front of the car. Had the huge tree they'd almost crashed into moved further away?

No. Impossible.

Cat bounced off her seat, the top of her head brushing the ceiling. "Let's go home," she said, with a wink.

If downtown Jefferson had more trees than Tom remembered, its residential streets were something else entirely when it came to their arboreal populations. Massive willows lined the roadways. The simple streets on which Tom had ridden his Schwinn were transformed into leafy tunnels. Of the already diminishing light above them, little made it past the cover of the trees.

Of course, Tom didn't *need* any signposts or landmarks for navigating to their destination. He didn't need Greg Schmitt's canary-yellow house his mom called an eyesore or Lisa Collins's modern colonial with the blue-black wooden shudders making the windows look like they'd wound up on the losing end of a fight. He could've driven past them blindfolded.

The streets sat as empty as downtown. Tom tried bringing it up to Cat, but she rebuffed him again. "I'm sure it's fine," she said. "They're all in their houses sitting down for dinner and some family time."

She trailed off as she gazed out the window, coming face to trunk with yet another tree. "They're all right behind those trees. Gosh, they couldn't have picked a better spot for an Arbor Day celebration, huh? I can't wait to see what this place looks like in the morning."

"This doesn't seem at all strange to you?" Tom asked, letting his exasperation get the best of him. "I told you, I don't remember any Arbor Day Fest. Christmas? Sure. Easter? Yeah. Thanksgiving, Halloween. Hell, I know we even had a Veteran's Day Parade where they'd drive around all the old-timers from the VFW Hall. But Arbor Day?"

Cat pouted. Tom knew the sour attitude curdling her typical warm and welcoming features was genuine. It was rare for Cat to give such a response.

They'd made it to the traffic light marking the turn to his old house, the one Tom's dad built almost all by himself. He'd even hauled the lumber, made from trees chopped down at the mill's logging camp on the outskirts of town. Tom recalled going through pictures packed away in an old mildew-smelling photo album at his parents' house after his mom's funeral: baby Tom bundled tight to her chest while Dad sanded planks laid across twin sawhorses.

If Tom kept anything from the Jefferson days, it was his memories of love experienced inside the old house.

The old house was safe. The old house was *his*. The old house was . . .

"Gone?"

"Tom?"

Cat's quiet inquiry kept him from forgetting to park the car. Without it, he would've stepped out from the driver's side and let the car roll to a stop against the curb right in front of Ms. Deirdre's place, the one with the rose bushes. Except there wasn't any building there.

There wasn't a single house on the street.

Searching high and low for a glimpse of a porch, some windows, a dented garage door, anything, Tom couldn't locate traces of the neighborhood homes imprinted in his head like childhood lullabies.

Cat jogged to keep up with him. "What's wrong, Tom? That's where you lived, right? I remember the photo your mom put in the rehearsal dinner slideshow. Those are the street signs at the corner you lived on, right?" It sounded like she'd come around to sharing in Tom's uneasy feeling.

More trees covered the spot where Tom's family home should've been. They pin-cushioned up through the soil like the tree they'd almost hit downtown, the location and size of these overgrown behemoths matching no timeline Tom comprehended. Too tall, too wide. He'd been gone for a while, but not long enough for a mob of ancient-looking sentinels to grow in the place where his house should still stand.

Tom remembered sitting on his father's knee. His dad had pointed out the men operating machines to chop down trees—one, two, three, four at a time. "Before they cleared most of the land, Jefferson was all woodlands," his dad had told him. "Nothing but trees far as you could see. Old lumber-jacks sat around like us, telling stories from their father's father's father or however far back it goes. Said those trees screamed with every swing of the ax. Back then, you see, they cut 'em up close and personal."

Tom stood crying like he'd done with his dad all those years before. Cat's nails dug into his wrist, pulling his tether back to the present. "I don't understand. I wanted to surprise you," she said. Distress colored every syllable.

"What? Surprise me how?" Tom stepped off the pavement and onto the soft, wet ground. His knuckles brushed against the bark of a tree, and he drew his hand back fast like he'd touched an electric fence.

"Someone sent a clipping from the Jefferson paper, a For Sale listing. I remembered the address. I thought we'd buy it for cheap. Fix it up. We both work remotely anyway, and I—and I—I wanted to surprise you. I wanted you to remember what you'd loved about this place."

Tom wasn't mad. He loved his wife's impulsive, take-charge approach to life. Moving to a tiny middle-of-nowhere burg like Jefferson made sense for Cat. She was his big-city girl daydreaming a fairy-tale version of small-town life. He'd never had the heart to tell her it wasn't all it was cracked up to be, or that whatever so-called upstanding character he had to his name came long after he'd left Jefferson.

But it didn't matter. There was no house to buy. No house to live inside. They walked between trees marking where the front porch had stood. They ducked under branches where the stairs to the second floor had risen. One mighty pine, its green needles gleaming like knife blades, marked the site of the fireplace. The tree's trunk stretched up higher than the house's chimney ever had.

"This doesn't make sense. This doesn't make sense."

In the middle of his latest panic attack, Tom caught Cat folding back the pages of the *Mid-Atlantic Journal*, Jefferson's oldest (and only) news periodical. Printed on the same yellowed paper. Same as the invitation, same as the banner.

He stopped walking and stood between two poplars indicating the spot where the back deck wasn't. "Let me see that paper," Tom said, taking a sheet from her before Cat responded.

It felt unlike any paper Tom had ever held. It had a leathery texture, like a tanned hide. Like cave people painting scenes from the hunt on the dried skins of their kills.

Then, he found a patch of faded ink on the Sports page sitting beside an article about the high school football team's winning season. The article included a photograph of the football field covered in trees, their branches bare for the coming winter, but not a single player or coach on the field. No one in the stands either. At first, he dismissed the splotch as nothing more than a printer error. But on closer inspection, Tom recognized the distinct shape of a heart, twin curved lines descending to a point. Letters written across the heart spelled out, "HOME."

Tom knew a girl from his sophomore year of high school before leaving Jefferson. Erica. They'd dated for a few months, enough time to make out and feel each other up playing "seven minutes in Heaven" at friends' parties. She'd showed him the tattoo her mom had let her get. Over her left breast. She'd seemed so cool. He always figured she'd get out of town and become a rock star or experience some other cool-sounding fate.

Guess not.

Tom dropped the page and slapped the other sheets from Cat's hands. "Hey!" she said, turning. "What the hell?"

The pages fell like dead leaves. But not before the edge of one piece of "paper" sliced across Tom's palm, raising a tiny cut, like a spinster's thin lips in the fleshy part of his hand where thumb met index finger. Without thinking, he brought the wound to his lips and sucked in the bright red blood spilling out.

"We've got to get out of here. Now." Tom grabbed Cat's wrist and took a step past the poplars, back into the inexplicable forest.

Like he'd touched poison ivy and the plant had worked its unbearable magic on his brain, Tom found his mind awash in inescapable glimpses of the terror that had befallen the citizens of Jefferson. He wondered if Cat saw the same things, minus having the context that he brought to the visions. Tom wasn't sure if that made her luckier than him or not. His head swam with images, real memories forcing away wild visions his subconscious fabricated. His third-grade class field trip to the paper mill, where they'd made the kids wear masks to block the chemical fumes. He'd watched the trees get cut up, pulped, strained, drained, pressed flat, and cut again. Except there weren't trees on the conveyor belts or in the vats or under the knife in his nightmare visions. It was Mrs. Willoughby, the mean substitute teacher, and Miss Ling, the nice one. It was Virgil Rowan, the ex-Marine who painted portraits, and Stumpy, the town drunk who'd acquired his nickname long before any cultural sensitivity made its way to town. Everyone appeared older than the last time Tom had seen them. Terror appeared to have that effect on people.

"Zachary, Tammy, Curtis, Vanessa, Jaron, Cole, Jordan, Jameson, Ashton . . ."

Tom rattled off the names of other classmates he hadn't thought of in a long forever. People who'd stayed behind. He wondered if they'd screamed like the old trees when their time came.

Cat held her phone up, letting its flashlight cut a path through the trees. Tom watched her dial 9-1-1. She held the phone to her ear. She walked around in a widening circle, waving the phone from side to side. But Tom knew her chances of getting a signal standing under all the trees were slim to none.

She screamed, but it wasn't her scream that set Tom on edge, it was the silence that followed. *No, not silence.* Old branches creaked overhead. Leaves rustled. The wind whispered through bristling pine needles. Cat swept her phone in front of her. Reaching, reaching. Until she stopped. "Oh my God! I saw someone! I saw a face out there! Hey! Hey! Can you help us?"

Tom couldn't grab her in time. She ran before he even thought to move. Last fall's leaves crunched under her shoes. Twigs snapped. Tom slapped at his jeans pocket for a minute before accepting he'd forgotten his phone back in the car. He ran after his wife. Her phone's light, like a will-o'-the-wisp, led the way through the dark.

The trees surrounded Tom.

"Honey, wait!"

His call echoed off trunks, ping-ponging until it circled back to him: "Ho-wai!—Ho-wai!— Hooray!"

A celebration.

That's what they're having, Tom thought. After all, Arbor Day *was* a day for the trees.

Tom crashed into branches, shoved his way through brambles and vines that caught on his shirt and tore the bared flesh of his forearms. He gave his blood, his skin, his cries of pain, whatever they wanted to take. He didn't care.

When he made it through, Cat hung suspended in the air between two trees. Their branches pierced her skin. Their leaves shook from her open mouth and eye sockets as she shuddered her death rattle. Her cellphone lay on the ground, its flashlight shining up at her. Falling blood droplets, like cherries shaken loose, got caught in the white, artificial glow.

Something groaned. It took Tom a precious, petrified moment before he understood the cry hadn't come from his lips. Or Cat's—she was already dead. The ground trembled under his feet. The two trees holding onto Cat parted but didn't let go of her. They pulled her apart like a paper doll.

Tom's choked whisper of her name was an inadequate eulogy for the woman he loved.

Then, the "Old Man" Tree came for Tom.

Cat must've seen its face in the dark. A gray and wrinkled old man, its peeling bark like infected skin. An awful visage he remembered from too many sleepless nights in his youth.

The "face" was nothing more than a twisted knot jutting from the trunk of the tree outside his bedroom window. But it looked like a rotten old man's sourpuss face.

I don't like the "Old Man" Tree, I don't like the "Old Man" Tree, I don't like the "Old Man" Tree . . . Tom's old nighttime mantra came back easy.

When the bark peeled itself from the aged trunk, the "Old Man" Tree revealed a new terrifying detail. Below the false face that had haunted Tom for so long, a second face—the near-mummified visage of his father—lay flat against the inner layer. "Dad?"

Except Tom didn't get the chance for tearful apologies and reconciliation. The "Old Man" Tree closed its bark over the dead man's face. The spiteful taunting seemed to say, *You should never have come home again.*

The "Old Man" Tree, with its witch's claw branches and its hollow opening wide into a scream, had waited for Tom's return. It slid over the remnants of his wife. Its blue-green leaves drank a bloody baptism. Fat pink and yellow roots, like the tentacles of a giant squid, dragged behind on the ground, stretching back into the dark.

Tom ran away from home again. But the second time differed from the slow-motion escape of some twenty years prior. Chased by the "Old Man" Tree, Tom ran for real. With no light to distinguish the army of trees, every branch, every root, every leaf seemed to move in unified purpose, intent on stalling his progress. At least they stayed in the ground. In his fevered mind, Tom guessed they were leaving him for the monstrosity unspooling more and more of its root system in pursuit of its prey.

Tom had no idea where he was going. But he knew he had to run.

Something caught his foot. He sprawled, chin and palms grinding to raw-hamburger pink as they hit the asphalt. His tears fell heavy, weighed down with relief.

He'd found the car, right where they'd left it.

Tom stood on unsteady feet. His pulse pounded like a heavy metal bass line. He turned back and raised two middle fingers to the trees. "Fuck your Arbor Day!"

His hands, slick with blood, sweat, and fears, fumbled with the latch on the driver's side. But he got it open and slid into the seat, cranking the key in the ignition. He threw on the high beams and hit the gas.

Speeding through the empty streets of Jefferson, Tom laughed and cried in equal measure. Snot caught in his stubble, but he didn't care. Every second brought him closer and closer to escape. Then, he'd be done with Jefferson once and for all. This time, he'd leave it *all* to the trees.

A rustling, shuffling noise came from the back of the car.

"Catherine?" He called her name before remembering she was gone. He checked the rearview.

The saplings had waited until he was almost free before making their move. Their branches touched his hair, then his ears. Tom slammed on the brake and threw himself against the door, thinking he could run the final distance to freedom. But it was too late.

The trees had him.

The next morning, all the trees of Jefferson attended the Arbor Day planting ceremony. Freed from the suffocating confines of the car and the burlap sacks pressing stale soil against their roots, the two dogwoods wriggled across the open field until they found their perfect spot. Roots dug down through rich soil. They drank from the blood and bone matter of the humans who'd called this land their home, foolishly believing there was no one or nothing to oppose their claim.

Despite the calm, windless morning, the other trees shook their branches with exuberance. Leaves clapped against each other and branches beat together in a primal rhythm. The new dogwoods stretched branches across the space between each other. Twigs, like fingers, linked together. The knots on their trunks were round and deep, black against the gray of their bark, mistaken at a distance for pleasant, smiling faces.

MELVIN AND THE MURDER CRAYON

The black crayon—the one School Resources Officer Gary swore looked like a gun ("or maybe a knife; definitely *something!*")—rolls out of Melvin Jenkins's limp hand. It comes to a stop under the water fountain outside Miss Beverly's classroom.

Blood, splashed across the white porcelain fountain, drips down. Droplets splatter against a black vinyl tile in the elementary school's checkerboard hallway. The black crayon—its gray paper wrapper peeled away—blends in with the floor.

Later, as more police officers, EMTs, school staff, and administrators filter through, someone will step on the camouflaged crayon, grinding it against their heel, as they try to lean in and take a quick sip from the fountain.

"What the hell are you doing?" someone will ask, trying to sound like they're in control.

School Resources Officer Gary can't put down the gun in his hand. After all, there's protocol to follow. With his free hand, he wipes unanticipated tears from his cheeks.

He looks down at Melvin. He's so small. School Resources Officer Gary blames the shadows, the way they fall, long and black, across the hallway at this time of day. They made the boy look so much bigger.

And then, there was that thing in his hand. Why didn't the boy just drop that thing in his hand?

School Resources Officer Gary will take early retirement and start a new after-hours security job at the local for-rent storage facility lot. He'll never know the "thing" was a crayon.

School Resources Officer Gary can't even remember the last time he fired a gun. It's been years since he had time for recertification. But he knew someone who kept pushing his paperwork through.

Melvin's construction paper—with the drawing he'd hoped to finish at home while his mama watched the local news for her Lotto numbers—rests beside the boy's body on the floor. The paper showcases black crayon marks and faint gray boot-print scuffs.

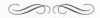

In the days ahead, that drawing—boot prints and all—will sit center stage for countless hours of news coverage. Talking heads will split time between extolling the artistic significance of Melvin's monochromatic palette and holding it up as indication of a third-grade time bomb ready to explode (if not for School Resources Officer Gary's quick thinking and even quicker trigger finger).

"I'll be right back. Please stay in your seats," Miss Beverly says. She's surprised by the calm behind her words, even as fear pounds needles into her brain. It makes her want to scream.

She steps into the hallway, keeping her eyes on the ceiling and the flickering fluorescent light fixture overhead. The clanging fire alarm that someone's pulled does the screaming for her.

She can't look at Melvin. She's afraid she won't recognize him if she does. Not because of any damage from School Resources Officer Gary's bullet, but because she's unsure if she ever really recognized Melvin before everything became *everything*.

She only knows his name because Sadie—the best artist in class and a young lady with an incredible amount of promise—asked, "Miss Beverly, did someone mass shoot Melvin?"

The principal, assistants, and some of the teachers who want to be seen as doing *something*, circle around School Resources Officer Gary. They speak in hushed and urgent tones about hushed and urgent next steps to take.

Miss Beverly picks up Melvin's drawing from the floor. She holds it close, inches from her nose. She still can't look at the dead little boy—the dead little boy who traded a chocolate milk for a Capri Sun at lunch earlier in the day. "Put that down, that's evidence," one of the older teachers says.

She drops the paper. Her eyes follow its descent, and she spots the gray paper sleeve that once encircled Melvin's black crayon.

She returns to her classroom to cry with the other children.

The DA will hold a press conference to announce he's considering possible policy changes. He'll hold another press conference to address the protests that spread downtown once news of the shooting hits social media. He'll plead for peace and understanding, while also insisting that SWAT's presence and the newly mandated curfew are necessary for community safety.

He'll hold a final press conference weeks later to announce that his office has found insufficient evidence to press charges.

On that night, someone will throw a brick through the DA's windshield with a Xeroxed copy of Melvin's black crayon drawing taped to it.

The clean-up crew will pick coin-sized shards of glass off the silhouetted form rendered in a child's sloppy, yet careful hand. A gap of paper-white separates the black crayon scrawl in a surrounding frame.

Melvin won't be around to explain what he's made. But most "experts" will agree that it looks like a chalk outline of a body on asphalt.

Mrs. Jenkins will ask to bury her son with the drawing. But the DA will insist it has to be held for evidence and that she shouldn't make such unreasonable requests.

Melvin Jenkins dies in the school hallway. His drawing's never finished.

He hates using the black crayon. Thinks it's too boring. But the teacher—Miss Beverly (always calling him Marvin, but at least she smiles at him sometimes) only passed out black crayons to Melvin and his classmates.

"What's that in your hand? Drop it! Drop it!"

Melvin recalls a flash of yellow, orange, and red coming for him. He dies wishing he'd had those kinds of colors for his drawing.

The next year, the school board will vote to cut the elementary school's arts budget, a necessary sacrifice following their decision to add two additional school resources officers.

They'll unveil the memorial at the start of the year: a locked glass case filled with drawings of Melvin made by his classmates.

People will comment on how beautiful it is. "What a touching tribute."

Even still, someone will ask, "But why did the children have to use so much black?"

THERE IS NO BUNK #7

Dee-Dee doesn't know she's the only one left alive. Long past "lights out" in all six log-cabin-style bunks (three for the girls and three for the boys), moonlight illuminates encroaching trees. Heavy with forgotten divinity, the moon casts a glamour on dirt paths that meander through the campgrounds, making the well-trod earth under Dee-Dee's flip flops appear bone-white.

She traverses these skeleton paths and her fear builds on itself with each step.

Mr. Carlson, the camp supervisor (the camp's "real" grown-up, as opposed to counselors like Dee-Dee, who play-act the role from mid-June to early August every summer), still had creamy white zinc oxide slathered on the tip of his nose when he had sent Dee-Dee to wait for help by the camp's front gate. "I called the sheriff," he'd said, hands hovering just above her shoulders in an approximation of inoffensive paternalism. "They'll send some deputies. We'll get everything sorted. We'll find where those kids and counselors got off to."

"I know where they are!" Dee-Dee protested.

But her words were met by the back of Mr. Carlson's head bobbing down the path, headed in the opposite direction from her destination.

"I'm telling you," she said, "I saw Jenni and Jesse go into Bunk Number Seven! There was an extra bunkhouse behind the fire circle. I think that's where all the others are too. Mr. Carlson!"

"There is no Bunk Number Seven!"

That's when Dee-Dee heard a sudden, swift sound, something that could have matched the tone and tempo of a long-bladed weapon swung from the shadows and embedded in the neck or chest or stomach of the unfortunate and unbelieving Mr. Carlson. After that seemingly definitive thud broke up the nighttime cricket chorus and snuffed out the fireflies' lights, Dee-Dee ran.

If she hadn't run, then maybe, she could have considered other potential sources for the noise that'd made goose pimples rise in defiant rebellion against her skin. Could the blame lie with a raised cabin window, shaken loose by time and subpar construction, that dropped shut on a windowsill, spilling dust and dead flies instead of blood?

Perhaps.

Dee-Dee sees the light ahead. It's not the floodlights illuminating the gated entrance by the service road or the promised rotating blue and red squad car lights as expected. Instead, a large Coleman lantern hangs from a railroad spike that's hammered into the front of a bunkhouse that has no business standing where it does. Orange flame flings itself against the glass and metal enclosure, testing the limits of its prison again and again.

On quick inspection, this new building matches all six of the other bunks back down the trail. Dee-Dee sees the same cedarwood façade and the placard displaying the bunk's number beside its screen door. If she turned around and went back to camp, she'd see the same features in the six familiar bunks. But this is Bunk #7, not 1, 2, 3, 4, 5, or 6.

And that can't be right. Because there is no Bunk #7.

Dee-Dee *knows* that. Everyone at camp knows it too.

Everyone at camp knew it. But everyone is gone.

Dee-Dee's all alone. She's got no one to tell her if she's crazy or not. And she still sees the building dead ahead, somehow moved from where she'd seen it last. It stands in the middle of the path. Which makes no sense because how did the old bus get them to the campgrounds if not down this old road?

But the building *is* Bunk #7. That's exactly what she sees on the placard. She hears the harsh winds teasing a summer thunderstorm, blowing through the open windows. She smells stale sweat, wet beach towels from lakeside swimming, and campfire smoke, the same as she might smell from any other bunk.

Inside, shadows stretch from the cabin's ceiling down to the floor. The dark outlines remind Dee-Dee of bodies from some slasher film, trussed up nubile teens hung from the ends of meat-hooks red with rust or blood or both.

She's held in thrall by her fear and doesn't consider that shadows don't always resemble their sources. Could those sinister shapes belong to backpacks or bunkbed posts?

Perhaps.

Last time she'd seen Bunk #7, Dee-Dee had watched Jenni and Jesse, a pair of teenage lovers—the kind she had only seen in dreams she didn't tell her Mom about—find the seventh bunk behind some brambles backlit by the dying glow of their last campfire.

From the shadows, Dee-Dee had watched them approach the cabin. *Where are you going? Everyone's gone, and you're off to do God knows what? Don't go in there!*

She'd kept her warnings and admonishments to herself and had looked away when they'd opened the door. Staring down at a sprouting poison ivy plant, Dee-Dee shivered to hear a killer's footsteps stalking behind her friends. Boots rattled floorboards in a relentless pursuit.

But don't old wooden buildings groan and quake with the settling, adjusting for the added weight of new inhabitants?

Perhaps.

Dee-Dee picks up the lantern from its hook outside Bunk #7. She raises it with one hand, feeling its weight try to drag her arm down. Before she can talk herself out of it, she grabs the screen door's rusted, crescent-shaped handle and looks inside.

If the deputies' cruisers pulled up at the spot, short of the camp's padlocked gate, they might mistake the squeal of a screen door's hinges for a girl's scream, some high-pitched whine of terror in harsh contrast to the night's peace and quiet. They'd get out with their service weapons drawn, imagining themselves the heroes arriving at the last minute to dispatch some masked psychopath offing counselors and campers inside Bunk #7 in brutal and creative fashion.

But what if there's no Bunk #7 to find? Would those would-be heroes be content with finding nothing?

Perhaps.

IGGY CRANE AND THE HEADLESS HORSE GIRL

Overdressed for the muggy weather spreading across the Hudson Valley like a damp weighted blanket, a hungover Iggy Crane arrived at the Sleepy Hollow Girls' Preparatory Academy at 5:05 p.m. on a Sunday in early June, the night before summer session started. Leaving behind an overpriced and overcrowded Brooklyn apartment, Iggy brought two pieces of luggage—a lilac-colored suitcase stuffed with clothing, toiletries, and assorted miscellany, and an extra-large raincloud-gray duffel containing horse-riding gear, a saddle, and her riding outfits. She also came blissfully unaware of the specter rumored to haunt the trails around the posh private institution: the so-called Headless Horse Girl.

When agreeing to the summer post, Iggy refused to accept its advertised *temporary* status. The offspring of a Mississippi oilman and a woman whose parental oversight extended to placement on the society page and no further, Iggy Crane came with an expectation of things "working themselves out."

Owing to a miscommunication with the town car driver hired to bring her from the city to the school, Iggy stumbled to the academy's administration building with sore thighs, her hair in a tangle of humidity-ravaged curls, and a sinus headache pounding behind her eyes like an explosion of horse hooves on tight-packed soil. Cigar smoke and the sound of balled-up racing slips slammed against metal bleachers would've completed the illusion of a life she'd believed was left to her past.

Emerging from the tree-lined walking path and approaching the old brick steps of the admin building, Iggy's complaints sat forgotten on her tongue at the sight of Headmistress Catherine van Tassel's smile.

If cruel eyes gleamed in hyena-pack formation from the surrounding grassy commons, Iggy didn't see. If bare hands or feet slapped against the paved ground, if blood splattered on the grass, Iggy didn't hear. The smile drew her forth from the dark. She was planetary debris pulled into the matter-destroying interior of a deep-space black hole.

Reality and conversation slipped back into focus. ". . . delighted you're here to help our girls with their horses, Ms. Crane."

Another flashback took hold, a scene replayed from Iggy's own student life. On acid at a frat house Halloween party, she'd watched a friend take too many shots of Everclear before falling headfirst into a jack-o'-lantern. She remembered how he'd come back wearing an upside-down orange grin and how the plastic-handled carving knife made a twanging sound, like a plucked banjo string, when it jammed through one of her wasted friend's eyes. He'd flopped his arms and skittered around like a demented marionette, screams muffled by unscooped pumpkin guts.

Like the sight of her friend's shuddering dance of pain, the Headmistress's smile had a similar stupefying effect on Iggy. "Thank you, Headmistress," Iggy said.

"Please, call me *Cat*. All my friends do."

Call it lust, call it infatuation, Iggy Crane's quest for sustained employment at the Sleepy Hollow Girls' Preparatory Academy took an immediate backseat to her pursuit of the affections of Headmistress Catherine "Cat" van Tassel. Backlit by the twin sconces on either side of the admin building's main entrance, the Headmistress's short blonde hair glimmered under the soft lights. The swoop of ghost white set against the top of the woman's head reminded Iggy of the new wave pop stars whose photos she'd cut from her big sister's old punk-rock magazines. She used to hide them in shoeboxes under the bed.

"The Bones Girls" got their clique name when, during their first week at school, the four young ladies each broke a bone in separate incidents and met in the Academy's infirmary. The breaking of their bones kick-started an inseparable friendship and alliance. United by pain, they rocketed to the top of the school's social food chain. Not the prettiest, not the most studious, and not the nicest, the Bones Girls were rowdy, boisterous, and unapologetically united.

Daring the faculty to oppose them, the foursome never submitted projects, book reports, or even pop quizzes as individuals. Instead, everything became a group project. Britney, Rosa, Olivia, and Meredith even signed their joint tests with a tiny skull and crossbones symbol, the quality of which varied depending on what Girl happened to hold the pen or pencil at signing.

Headmistress Cat gave Iggy a nighttime walking tour of the campus, pointing out various buildings older than both tour guide and guided, and sharing a somewhat restrained version of the Bones Girls' story along the way. "They mean well," she said as if the potential explanation excused their strange behaviors.

Iggy nodded along with every word, but not too hard. Not so much she'd draw attention to herself. Even still, her focus on achieving the correct level of nodding caused her to bump against her new employer when the latter stopped at the end of the path they'd taken through campus. "Well, I suppose there's one more place you'd like to see," the Headmistress said, brushing off the contact with restrained ease.

Iggy took a slow breath in, the scent of peppermint from her brief contact with the Headmistress tickling her nostrils. "Bed?"

The Headmistress's laughter wasn't dismissive. She stepped aside and revealed a dirt path extending to the grassy meadowlands behind the school. Instead of peppermint, a foul combination of dried manure and damp hay stampeded over the young teacher's senses. Iggy wrinkled her nose.

"Okay, well, two things you want to see. I assume you want to inspect our stables. Right, Ms. Crane?"

Iggy unwrinkled her nose and returned to nodding.

"Of course," she said. "I love horses."

The next day, the first of summer session, Iggy Crane woke alone in her bed in the teachers' dormitories. Having showered and dressed in her riding gear before bed (a habit picked up from her father, who'd slept in his best suit on the eve of every major business deal or life-changing decision—except for his last), she applied makeup and pulled her mass of tangled brown hair into a tight ponytail before starting her day. She left her room a good hour early, giving herself time to partake of the buffet-style breakfast offerings in the cafeteria. Croissants, muffins, links of vegan sausage, fruit wedges pooling sticky pink and green juices around the rim of her plate. Sitting at a small bistro-style table facing the entrance of the cafeteria, Iggy watched summer-session teachers and students steal glances at her, the new face in their tiny enclave.

Iggy wondered if any of the faces cutting eyes in her direction belonged to the Bones Girls.

After polishing off breakfast, Iggy arrived at the stables five minutes early. She found the four horses assigned to her students already fed, brushed, and saddled, ready for a day of galloping through the fresh-cut grass and trotting down dust-cracked trails. The black heels of her riding boots sunk into the straw-scattered dirt with each step. In stall after stall, Iggy found a horse ready to ride, but no riders.

Approaching the next-to-last stall, Iggy heard the murmuring voices of her new charges.

The Bones Girls ignored their new riding instructor standing in front of them and paid no attention to the tired old nag in the stall behind, instead giving their full attention to a video playing on one of their smartphones.

Iggy missed getting a good look at the video, given the tight circle formed by the Bones Girls, but she caught glimpses of an empty horse arena ringed by tall hedges. She didn't see any horses.

Iggy stepped into the fray, still trusting things to work themselves out. "What're we watching, ladies?" she asked.

The phone went black after their thumbs flicked across the screen like the darting tongues of fly-crazed frogs. Eight eyes looked Iggy up and down, four faces imperceptible in their study of their new instructor. The synchronized judgment made Iggy stop short, with one foot still raised to move forward. She planted it back in the dirt at an awkward angle and rocked back a step.

"Okay." Remembering the Headmistress's warning about the girls and deciding not to push too hard on her first official day, Iggy fell back to her favorite safe subject: *herself.*

She went through her introductory spiel, listing riding schools she'd attended, naming winning jockeys who'd taught her how to take turns on the track in the most efficient ways, and recalling dressage experts obsessed with form and style.

When she finished, Iggy paused before pulling out a piece of paper where she'd scribbled the Bones Girls' names for attendance-taking.

"Britney?"

"Here."

All four spoke at once. Polished and practiced in their "I am Spartacus" routine.

"Rosa?"

"Here."

Again, all at once.

The behavior repeated for the last two girls. All four answered for all four names, making it clear: where one went, the others walked alongside.

"So, why'd you want to take this summer's Equestrian Fun course?"

"We like horses." There was a slight delay as they attempted to sync their off-the-cuff answers. Iggy found comfort there. It showed their speech as affectation rather than any supernatural synchronization.

"We *love* horses." Each took a deep breath in before they continued. "Though not as much as the Headless Horse Girl."

Pitch-perfect, even down to their trailing silence at the end.

Iggy peered inside the next-to-last stall, giving some consideration to the worn-out old mare chomping with relaxed but insistent vigor at a pile of straw already splattered by ricocheted chunks of her expelled horse turds. "Hmm," she said. "Let's see if there's something else over here."

Iggy's singular voice rang hollow and tiny in her head. When she stepped toward the last stable, the polished black and brown boots of the Bones Girls kicked up old straw chunks and gravel. They moved in formation, blocking Iggy's path and shaking their heads together.

"Sorry ma'am," they said. "There's no horse in there. You've gotta ride Vanna White over here."

They pointed to the nag. The horse didn't bother to lift her head at the sound of her name. Her tired bloodshot eyes rolled back white.

Iggy's displeasure registered on her face.

"She's a good horse. Faster than you'd think," the Bones Girls said. As a way of further convincing their new instructor, they added, "They keep the last stall empty. There's been no horse in there for a long time."

The Bones Girls walked from Iggy's stall and split apart, the way sparrows dart from their migratory V, a temporary separation before inevitable reunion. They moved into their stalls, each claiming a horse as their own, leaving Iggy alone with Vanna White.

Iggy kicked loose rotting straw over a turd and made a mental note to make the Bones Girls clean the stables later.

Iggy's past-her-prime horse gave a strangled cry as she found someone else inside her stall-sized world. The noise reminded Iggy of a car alarm left screaming and screaming against a busy curbside on a hot summer day. She reached out and touched the surrounding wall, the part shared with the supposedly empty final stall. Her warm palm touched the peeling white-painted wood and became clammy, slicked with sweat. She considered a quick peek over, just to make certain the last stall really was empty.

An insistent nudge at her elbow pulled Iggy away from her investigation before it could even get underway. She turned to face her steed, stifling a bemused chuckle at the sight of sagging horseflesh wrapped around a fat, bloated head.

By the time horse and rider made it out of the stable and onto the field, the Bones Girls appeared bored atop their mounts. Iggy forced a grin, unwilling to let the girls intimidate her. "Okay," she said. "Let's ride."

When Iggy held her hand up and signaled for the foursome to return to the stables, she dropped it quickly to reestablish her double grip on Vanna White's reins. Even the slow and steady gait of the nag proved too much for the worn-out instructor. Iggy winced remembering her first conversation with the Headmistress when she'd commented on the recency of her equestrian experience. *My last time around horses? Oh recently, very recently. Always, really.*

The Bones Girls received no points for style and grace, but they made up for those deficiencies with their raw power and stamina. They ran their horses hard. Iggy looked back across the open field and picked out the furrows made by each horse and rider combo.

Iggy pulled up to the stable and found all four girls off their horses and all four horses back in their stalls. In turn, Iggy led her aged mount by the bridle, grateful for the girls' absorption in their post-ride tasks. They missed seeing the way she winced with each step or how her knees knocked together like dull wooden blocks played by a toddler in nursery school music class.

Absorbed by her pain, Iggy walked too far, stepping past Vanna White's stall and heading for the end of the line. She faced a shadow on the final stall's far wall, something resembling one of the ponies from her childhood. But the proportions, even in shadow? All wrong. Its back legs were longer than the front. A disjointed outline replaced the expected swooping curve from neck to belly to tail. *And the head?*

Horse teeth fell heavy on Iggy's shoulder. Not enough to tear clothes or break skin, but enough to get her attention. Vanna White pulled her rider back from the dark. With a frustrated sigh, Iggy dragged the old horse into her stall, giving her the most perfunctory of brushes and rubdowns. After she'd crammed a sugar lump between yellowed teeth, Iggy exited the stables and didn't check if the shadow remained.

The Bones Girls were already gone.

When Iggy returned to her room to change into her "civilian" clothes, she found two text threads waiting on her cellphone. First, a group text, four other numbers besides her own making it easy to guess the senders' identities. Three messages and one link, each item from a different number.

Here's what.

We were.

Watching.

The last message's URL opened a video file when Iggy clicked on it. She recognized the same horse riding arena she'd glimpsed in the video the Bones Girls had been watching back in the stables, but it looked different somehow. Undersaturated, drained of life and color, emerald-green shrubbery became inky black blobs, and the girl—of course, there was a girl—appeared pale white like a funeral shroud on-screen.

And yet . . .

When the girl at the empty horse arena dropped onto the ground on all fours, Iggy covered her mouth with her free hand to stifle the giggles. The girl wore a "My Little Pony" t-shirt, a genuine vintage number from the 1980s, and jean shorts.

Her uncovered limbs, arching back, taut neck, and shoulder muscles all stood out. The girl's arms and legs were muscular and sinewy, but also gangly. She got into position, like a foal taking her first afterbirth-covered steps fresh from her mother's womb.

Everything changed when the girl moved. She took off at a trot, navigating around the nearest obstacles in the arena. She pranced around the first gate, shaking her long black hair from side to side like a show pony displaying her coiffed mane for the judges. Her backside twitched like a phantom tail. And then the girl picked up speed, moving from a trot to a full-on gallop, heading for the first jump, a fence set two-and-a-half feet tall.

Iggy found herself invested in the strange athletic feat being performed onscreen. She gripped her phone with both hands.

The first fence sat low to the ground, easy enough for a person on two legs to cross it. But someone galloping, their limbs moving in the same synchronous motions as a horse's legs?

The girl's shins pressed against the undersides of her upper legs like a spring-loaded chamber being prepped. And then? The explosion, the girl leaping up and over the obstacle. Her body stretched across the screen. The Horse Girl filled in the sky, like the sun's last light show before settling in at dusk. There was no sun, only the Horse Girl.

She cleared the fence.

"Yes!"

Iggy caught herself cheering for the strange young woman's feat. She bobbled the phone from her hand. As it fell onto her tossed aside comforter, the sound of something like thunderous applause rose from the video.

When she picked her phone up from her unmade bed, Iggy found the video app closed. A second set of texts caught her eye, pushing the Horse Girl from her mind.

From the Headmistress: *Hi it's Cat.*

Sorry. Van Tassel. Sorry.

How's your first day? Want to come around for cocktails after dinner?

And then: *This is my private personal number.*

Iggy Crane's summer plans proceeded as she'd envisioned.

And yet . . .

In the meadow, the crowd of students, teachers, and staff who'd gathered to watch the Fourth of July light show dispersed. Across a full-moon sky, the last of the fireworks burned out like dying stars.

Iggy Crane watched the colorful explosions while leaning against the railing of the Headmistress's balcony. All alone. "The best view on campus to watch the girls riding their horses. Second best place for me to see you," Cat—*no, not Cat, not anymore for me*—the Headmistress had told her weeks before. Her long arms had wrapped a flannel blanket over Iggy's bare shoulders and had pulled her in close to whisper breakable promises in the younger woman's ear.

The soft, sweet tones she'd used were now a distant memory for Iggy. More often, their conversations escalated to screaming without argument in between. They threw dishes across kitchens like goddamned clichés. Hours before the fireworks, the Headmistress had moved from tipsy to exasperated and mean. "Fine, Iggy, I admit it: I *only* hired you because I hoped your family would underwrite some of the developments intended for . . ."

Nearing black-out drunk beneath a smoke-streaked sky peppered by fizzling sparklers, Iggy found the details of the few hours previous came with a certain fuzziness. She held onto moments, feelings—the way her heart sank into her stomach. She remembered the Headmistress's eyes, her dawning realization of what Iggy's trembling lip meant.

Iggy had forced out every word. About her father's gambling debts. About how he'd gone to "settle up" with the bookie to whom he owed their family fortune, Iggy's inheritance included. About what her dear old Daddy had meant when he'd said he was going to "settle up," how he'd actually meant he was going to "take a swan dive off an oil derrick." About the pictures of the final bloody tableau sent to her family, the earth stained black enough to mistake her father for oil leaking up from underground.

The Headmistress had tried talking while Iggy ran through her confession, but there had been too much to confess. Iggy figured she had slipped away at some point, leaving to host the fireworks for *her* students and *her* teachers. Once Iggy got around to confirming her family fortune's depletion, nothing had mattered. That's when she'd walked to the balcony and watched the first whistle-and-bang explosion.

She suddenly remembered the horses, probably scared out of their minds in the stables. *How're they holding up, I wonder?* The Bones Girls were staying with them while the fireworks went off. Not as a punishment, but as part of their "Equestrian Fun."

The Bones Girls.

They pushed me to watch the rest of the Horse Girl video. That ruined everything. Why'd they make me watch it? What was even in it for them?

Recklessness and indiscretion swam in Iggy's gene pool. Following an afternoon tryst, she'd faced the Headmistress's open doorway, giddy with satisfaction. Greedy for more, she'd leaned in and grabbed the other woman by the shoulders, pulling her halfway out the door for a kiss.

"Ms. Crane!" The Headmistress pulled back, retreating into the supposed safety and secrecy of home. Iggy licked her lips and waved goodbye. But as she'd walked away, she heard voices, some persons whispering out of sight, footsteps following. Not one pair of feet or two, more like three or four.

The texts from the Bones Girls picked up again, confirming Iggy's earlier suspicions. Except no blackmailing over her affair with the Headmistress followed, not directly at least.

Did you
Watch the
Whole video
We sent?

After each text, they'd re-sent the video link. Like a finger poking Iggy in the chest over and over: *poke, poke, poke, poke.* Raising their eyebrow like, *you see? Do you see?*

Iggy wandered to the stables. Absent class time and free-riding hours, she had the building and horses to herself. She made a beeline for Vanna White. Iggy found something comforting in the old gal's orneriness and flatulence. "Hey, can I buy a vowel?" Iggy asked. Vanna White paid no attention whatsoever.

Iggy shrugged. *Nuts to you, then.*

She figured she'd put it off long enough and pulled up the Horse Girl's video on her cell. Her index finger pulled at the on-screen progress bar, moving past the parts she'd watched. *There's the arena, there's the girl. She's on all fours. My Little Pony. Trotting. Trotting. Gallop. Gallop. Jump and . . .*

Iggy picked her finger up from the screen and the video resumed. The Horse Girl touched back down from her first jump, her breath whooshing out like a prizefighter taking a body shot to prove their toughness. Not breaking her stride, she kept up a galloping pace. And good thing too, considering the next fence stood a full foot taller than the previous. Iggy checked the time left on the video. A few minutes remained.

As she checked, she missed the Horse Girl vaulting over the second fence. Her eyes flicked back to the action in time for the landing. From behind Iggy, Vanna White snickered and whined in her stall, stomping with her forelegs, mashing her old straw into the muddy soup of the ground. Iggy tried to ignore her.

She focused on the thunderous applause she'd heard before. Except this sound came with a tougher, heavier quality to it.

The Horse Girl's bare palms and soles slapped on the manicured grass, but their movement doesn't quite match the sound either. Then it all clicked into place. Not applause, but the sound of horse hooves stampeding, barreling through the arena. Splintered remnants of a jumping fence flew forward into the path of the camera. An equine shadow hung above the Horse Girl.

Iggy watched it get closer, closer, and saw fear in the Horse Girl's eyes. Slick from nervous sweat, Iggy's finger slipped against the video's progress bar again. She went too far ahead.

The video played from a point where Iggy caught the thick burnt-tree-trunk back legs of a massive stallion thundering out of frame. The Horse Girl slumped on the ground, frozen in time. Her back arched at an unnatural angle. Her head was gone, replaced by a blossoming red and pink bouquet, like someone had sprinkled middle school Valentine's carnations in the arena.

Rewinding, Iggy watched what happened to the Horse Girl in reverse. The shattered pieces of her face stitched back together. The black stallion's massive hoof pulled up from the ground, traveling up through her chin, back out the top of the Horse Girl's skull. Every drop of blood, every bit of brain, every hair put back into place until the horse was gone and the shade remained.

She played it through again, confident she'd already experienced the worst. Egged on by those texts from the Bones Girls, she put herself through the sight of the Headless Horse Girl's creation once more. A white banner fluttered across the frame like some massive mythological bird, either side of the cloth flapping like wings ready to take off and fly away, up to the full moon.

But that didn't happen. Instead, Iggy watched the winds bring the banner down slow, giving her a chance to read the words printed in shiny golden script across the blood-splattered fabric: VAN TASSEL RIDING ARENA.

The campfire smoke blurred Iggy's eyes, tracers of light appearing behind every popping spark from the crackling wood. The mushrooms Iggy had taken in the middle of the fireworks show kicked in. She stood in the dark, watching her riding students passing around a bottle of Malibu rum taken from the Headmistress's liquor cabinet.

When she studied the fire-lit faces of the Bones Girls, Iggy found their mouths closed tight, like someone had used needle and thread to sew them shut. But she heard them, talking together, inside her head.

"The Headmistress's family owned the arena. It closed after the accident."

"It's nearby?" Iggy touched her lips, making sure they still moved.

"It's right behind the school."

Iggy looked up from the eye-watering firelight. She put a hand above her eyes and peered past whirling, pinwheeling shapes. Dull stadium lights glowed around the trees.

It didn't make sense. Iggy had never noticed those lights before.

"We're surprised you haven't been. Considering how much you love horses."

Iggy nodded.

"I *do* love horses. Don't I?"

The Bones Girls shrugged their shoulders, a rippling wave of indifference. Iggy blushed, realizing she'd spoken her question out loud.

Iggy changed into her riding clothes. Her hands rubbed grass stains and dirt on the black cloth of her riding jacket. Her legs tingled, warm from the fire baking its way through the khaki jodhpurs. "Okay, let's all go," she said, looking around the campfire circle, seeking the buy-in of the Bones Girls.

They gave her a slow clap. Let it grow and grow, rolling like thunder-claps on a late summer evening. Iggy stared into the flames and noticed the upside-down pumpkin grinning on her old friend's head. Blood spilled from both his triangle eyes and from his jagged, smiling teeth.

When Iggy stepped inside the empty arena, the Bones Girls were gone, slipped away in the night. *Were they ever here at all?* Iggy let go of the notion, knowing her nightmare was of a more recent vintage.

"Hello?"

Her question echoed off the bleachers. Her hands touched the hedges while her eyes fell upon something else.

She was not alone.

The Headless Horse Girl ran in circles, kicking up dirt and grass on the other side of the arena. Iggy took slow, measured steps, weaving her way around the obstacles, inching closer to the phantom. Iggy watched blood droplets flung from the long-dead girl's ruined neck wound, the space marking the absence of her head. Iggy stepped closer and closer.

The Headless Horse Girl's My Little Pony shirt darkened from white to a blood-soaked pink, then red. It stuck to her pale skin. The sight of her affected Iggy beyond mere disgust. Something hideous yet beautiful remained in the sleek, powerful limbs of the dead girl bucking in headless arcs like a wild rodeo bronco.

She can't see me, Iggy thought. But when the Headless Horse Girl's shoulders lifted upward, her stubby neck tilting like an animal regarding some unnatural intrusion, Iggy doubted that conclusion.

She stopped in her tracks, regretful of all her decisions made along the way. Moving closer and closer, for the first time, Iggy Crane worried she was mistaken about everything working out. Not just this once either, but all the times before.

The Headless Horse Girl reared up on her front legs, phantom tail twitching, blood spray angled to form a temporary mane. She took off at a full-speed gallop, heading right for Iggy. The riding instructor looked left to right, back behind her too.

My last time around horses? Oh recently, very recently. Always really.

Iggy recognized the sound of horse hooves thundering like applause. From the thinnest of the surrounding shadows, a pitch-black stallion burst from a pocket of nowhere and into the arena. Iggy fell to the ground, staring up at the muscular, savage beast. Its eyes glowed red and threw sparks like fireworks, like out-of-control campfires catching the dry wood of old horse stables ablaze.

For the first time, Iggy glimpsed a rider atop the phantom horse. It was cloaked in dark garments, wearing the same grinning pumpkin face as her bloody friend from school. The rider pulled back on the reins and spurred his steed forward, heading right for Iggy, who scrambled in the dust with nowhere to run.

Corpse-cold hands found Iggy's skin. They pulled at her pressed white shirt, at her coat. She gazed back into the bloody stump of the Headless Horse Girl. Dirt clods exploded from the black stallion's hooves, spraying Iggy and her ghostly savior. Blood baptized Iggy and she nodded her head in quick acceptance.

Iggy swung herself up and over, rider mounting steed. She clung to the My Little Pony t-shirt fabric as the Headless Horse Girl leaped clear of the stampeding charger. Then, they rode on—away from the arena built in the path of old ghosts, heading back to the school.

Later, everyone at the Sleepy Hollow Girls' Preparatory Academy noted how lucky they'd been to escape the roaring flames tearing through the tinderbox buildings. Someone let the horses out from the stables, thank god, leaving them to gallop in panicked circles, digging furrows in the burning grass.

One person remained unaccounted for, though—the riding instructor the school had hired for the summer term. Spurred on by the Bones Girls dropping conspiracy theory morsels to anyone who'd listen, students and teachers would soon whisper about sightings of Iggy Crane fire-touched and moonlit, pulling back on the shoulders of the Headless Horse Girl.

The pair rode out into the night-world, loping into the moon-soaked dark.

THE DECIMATIONS OF CORN-SILK SALLY

1. Corn-Silk Sally and the Pumpkin Patch Massacre

Anguished cries of the dying echo across the picked-over fields of smashed pumpkins. Under a late October moon, blood stains the corpse-pale innards of neglected gourds judged unworthy of Halloween porch displays.

Beams of light, like agitated fireflies, move with the flicked wrists of every police officer who's come too late to save Corn-Silk Sally's victims.

From the corner of his tired eyes, Sheriff Jones spots her in a tattered, dusty dress, watching between the rows of corn.

"Stop!"

But she's gone. The sound of her skirt sewn from corn silk brushing against the yellowed husks serves as her retort.

2. Corn-Silk Sally Teaches the Worst Girls in School about Revenge

Breanna and Cayden watch from under the loose hay. The damp strands now reek with the tangy odor of bloodletting.

Believing the violence over, they recall Corn-Silk Sally placing a finger against chapped lips, her damaged nail like a lit black-flamed candle. The darkness danced in the girl's eyes, ready to spread.

They climb off the creaking trailer, avoiding the hollowed-out chest cavity of Annie Previtt, the pumpkin patch's owner. Her eyes are forever opened wide, asking, *What did I do?*

The girls know. The girls always know.

3. Corn-Silk Sally and the All Hallow's Grieving

Gam-Gam's tears dry on fallen leaves. Her body trembles, sobs like small earthquakes tearing her apart. When she stands, bare feet crunch eggshells into the grass. Toilet paper soaked red with blood dangles from the front porch eaves.

She stops short, peering up at sweet Sally's room. No lights appear there, no candle burns on the windowsill. Her not-so-friendly neighbors watch, judging her from a safe distance.

Many don't understand what the women in her family are capable of, and those who know aren't in a position to share.

4. Corn-Silk Sally: Trick or Die!

The costume-wearing children stand beneath the willows, spilling candy on the lawn. From surrounding houses, screen doors slam and heavy feet stomp onto porches.

Names drift down shaded streets.

"Benji!"

"Sarah!"

"Antoine!"

"Leah!"

"Carl!"

On and on.

No children turn from their vigil.

Perhaps if those parents, drenched in panicked sweat, wondering why their children's beds sit empty, called for:

"Ghost!"

"Witch!"

"Cowboy!"

"Cat!"

"Devil!"

Maybe then they would be answered.

Finally, someone's father, wearing flannel pajamas and fuzzy slippers, grabs a child and asks, "What're you doing here?"

"Corn-Silk Sally's gonna die," they answer.

5. Corn-Silk Sally and the Harvest Dance with the Devil

"Come dance under the full moon, Sally," the Devil says.

Sally wipes blood off her face, picking dirt from long, black hair. Something rubbery-wet comes loose as she brushes out debris.

Principal Martinez's eyeball.

Sally smirks, recalling the sound her handscythe had made wedging, freeing, twisting the orb from its socket.

The Devil clears His throat, offering a hand. He never introduced Himself as the Devil. But Sally knows without needing a name.

Stray dogs howl behind them.

The music swells, approaching the grand finale. The Devil whispers, "Here's to a new beginning."

6. Corn-Silk Sallies

Deputies keep away from Sheriff Jones, leaving him to moan over the body of his only son. Jordan Jones, varsity football captain, lies across the ground like a tattered costume.

But there's no one to slip on his skin and ring doorbells, singing, "Trick or treat!"

Instead, they search for Corn-Silk Sally aka Sally Perkins aka the Sopho-more Witch. Radios chirp. Dispatch puts through anyone who's seen a pale girl with black hair, a dress made of corn silk, and a handscythe trailing blood.

No way all reports are true. No way she's in so many places at once.

7. Corn-Silk Sally: Trick or Die II: The Trickening

Heavy downpour washes fresh blood down storm drains, into the over-grown grass of ditches bordering small-town front lawns. Winds, thunder, and rapid lightning crashes drown grief-stricken howls and the final moans of dying children.

Tiny broken bodies bleed while dark clouds pass over the harvest moon. The siren on Sheriff Jones's cruiser drones on, waiting for someone to smash the glass, reach over the Sheriff's ruined, shotgun-blasted face, and switch it off.

Until then, the neighborhood listens to electronic screams as red and blue lights pass over the living and dead alike.

8. Corn-Silk Sally's Hayride to Hell

They tear her handmade corn-silk dress. Rough and smooth hands alike, dirt under some nails and others manicured to idealized perfection, her classmates leave her bare beneath the harvest moon. Bleeding within and without, her eyes closed, dreaming. She opens them, hot with fire.

Except this already happened.

Back on the hayride, she steals a glance at Mr. QB himself, Jordan Jones. She picks out the school gossips whispering farther back on the trailer. Sally wonders what they'll say when the night ends.

Everyone's already dead, though. Why do these things keep happening to me?

9. Corn-Silk Sally: Another Origin Story about Revenge

Gam-Gam never talked to Sally about the girl's daddy. Never told her what Sheriff Jones, then nothing more than quick-to-anger, ambitious Deputy Jones, did to the misunderstood man, Gam-Gam's baby boy.

She didn't talk about rinsing the girl's corn silks in enchanted oils before feeding them into the sewing machine, stitched with needles hexed to prick the skin, the corn-silk drinking her blood.

She loves the girl, her sweet grandbaby. But she loves her boy more. She'll have her vengeance, even if it means destroying her line, the Sheriff's, and everyone else's besides.

10. Corn-Silk Sally in Space

Sally, not the same Sally as before but close enough, wishes on a dead Earth. The field-trip rocket's left. Classmates locked her in the corn silo during boarding.

But she's high enough to touch the dome around her lunar colony home. Ears of space-grown corn shuck themselves, revealing golden silk amid kernels off-white like rotten teeth.

A shooting star, she falls. Her dark hair covers the explosions of pain behind her eyes. A blade waits by her injured hand. Sickle-shaped, a crescent moon.

Shadows fall, forming a mask. An appropriate costume for the next Halloween party.

SHATTERED

From his hiding place in the walk-in pantry, Norman watched Cheryl. She maintained a firm grip on the broken shard of glass (a long, thick piece from one of the toasting flutes at their wedding, a gift from one of Norman's aunts).

"Are you watching, honey bear?" Cheryl asked.

He shivered at the sound of her pet name for him. As he clasped a bloody hand over his mouth and tried his damnedest not to make a sound, he tasted dirty pennies.

"I know you men like to watch." Not waiting for or even expecting a reply, Cheryl continued. Still holding the glass, she dropped her hand to her exposed midriff.

As she pressed the jagged edge of the glass to her stomach, the skin gave way. It split open, a willing and able participant in what followed. Cheryl twisted and turned the glass against her skin, following the curves, one and two, of a "B." Then she pulled out the glass and jammed it back in to form a short line across, then made a longer one down, and followed with another short one across for the "I." More lines cut deep for the "T." A curve for the "C." And she finished it off with the deep gashes of the "H," making sure to dig the glass deeper at the bottom, as though adding punctuation.

The girl who'd once flinched at a papercut now stood in their demolished kitchen and branded herself a *BITCH*.

None of it made any sense to Norman.

Because the whole time, as she stabbed, cut, sliced, and tore at her flesh,

Cheryl never reacted to the work done by her hand. Not a single cry of pain escaped her lips.

No pain, no crying, and *no blood*.

Regardless of whether she knew Norman's hiding place or not (and he suspected she did), Cheryl kept her attention on her handiwork. Manicured hands, pin-pricked all over with bloodless holes, stroked the open wounds across her stomach the same way she'd rubbed her swollen belly months before.

Back then, her smile had been a beautiful thing, something holy. Her smile in the kitchen held a sickness, the final, corrupted image from a bad dream tattooed inside the eyelids.

"Doesn't it look nice?" she asked, as though she'd complimented a perfectly raised cake before taking it out of the oven.

A rattling sound distracted Norman. His teeth chattered behind his hand. Cheryl turned away, her back to the pantry, and stomped out of the kitchen. A bare foot—a dancer's foot (*and, man, could she dance*)—came down on another broken sliver of glass, this piece kicked out from the oven door earlier in the evening.

The glass went in and she kept right on walking. Like a magician's trick, an illusion. But the glass was *real*. Norman's blood leaked from cuts, scratches, jabs, and stabs. The sticky, wet foam from a busted Budweiser bottle turned from white to red as it drip-dropped down his face, proving the reality of the glass.

"Here you go, dollface. This Bud's for you," Cheryl'd said before chucking the bottle at Norman's nose earlier in the evening. She'd never met her husband's father (he'd passed years before they'd met, romanced, and married way too fast). But her impression of his old man, how he'd talk to Norman's mom after coming home from those late-night "business" meetings?

Uncanny in its similarity.

"Thanks again to the doctor for telling me all about his new book *The Glass Ceiling's All in Your Head: A Man's Guide to Women's Progress*. I know *I* never put my copy down."

By this point, Norman could lip-sync along to the cheery voice from the TV. It'd echoed off the walls of their home enough times. Nothing else played on the TV—nothing else on broadcast, cable, or even streaming.

He turned the pantry door's handle and poked his head out into the kitchen.

Bland go-to-commercial music plays as the camera pans across the studio audience, mostly women, which matches the show's demographics. A hot mic picks up the sound of breaking glass. The camera swings back to the main stage. The operator zooms in on a smashed flower vase scattered across the coffee table.

The co-host—the blonde one you'd call "sassy," "spunky," or even "sexy"—stares into the camera. She speaks, but not with the bantering, fake laughter, and forced concern for trivial daytime bullshit repeated five days a week.

Not this time.

"Did you all know my co-host, Mr. Former Failed Sitcom Star Turned Latest Flavor of the Month Male TV Personality, makes more money than me? It's true. That's your glass ceiling at work. And if it can happen to me, well, imagine what it's doing to all of you. All the years I've put into this show, and what do I get in return? The chance to keep on being another pretty face? And how long's that gonna last?"

The studio audience "oohs," because it's all they know how to do.

Norman tiptoed like a trespasser down the hallway of his own house, keeping close to the wall. The debris of smashed glass along the way—mirrors, picture frames, and light fixtures—let him know he was following Cheryl's path. A million tiny, shiny pieces of glass glittered like diamonds at his feet.

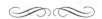

"What's she doing?"

The original broadcast stopped there. But once the change spread, it wasn't long before someone uploaded the uncensored version. Norman first experienced the uncut version in their house. He glimpsed a second of it as he crossed the kitchen to pull a beer from the top shelf of the fridge. Cheryl huddled by the island with her friend Debbie. (Debbie with the bloodless scratch across her forehead, the one Norman noticed too late after he opened the door because he'd started off staring at her rack instead, Debbie who waved off an offer of a bandage, saying, "No, that won't be necessary . . . for me."). Debbie and Norman's Cheryl watched the clip from the smashed-in screen of the other woman's smartphone.

The TV Lady continues talking. Her voice remains flat, steady, like the tick-tick-ticking of an old watch swinging back and forth. Back and forth. Back and forth. Tick-tick. Tick-tick.

And the whole time she talks, she uses a piece of the broken vase to cut.

She starts cutting below the bangs. Then, down goes the glass, shy of her ears on both sides of her face. Her fingers—fingers that should drip with syrup-thick blood—appear dry. She finishes the circuit at her chin. "They used the glass to stop us, to keep us in our places, in cages. But the glass can't hurt us now."

A noise follows, the way pancake batter sizzles when it hits a hot, greased griddle. The camera goes dark for a moment. A man screams, his voice sounding high-pitched like a girl's. "Oh my God! It's her face!"

A different camera takes over. It swings around to the audience again. The women rise to their feet. They applaud. And then, the audience descends on the stage, pawing for pieces of glass so they too can transform.

Who knew how far or fast the footage spread? It spread far enough to reach Norman and Cheryl's house. Norman knew that fact all too well.

At some point to come, CDC scientists will stand in front of an official-looking backdrop propped up deep in some "secure" bunker somewhere people would go seeking safety. A bleary-eyed, five-o'clock-shadowed scientist will explain. "The phenomenon appears to affect primarily women aged around ten to forty. We believe the trigger commands activate something . . ."

Before he's able to finish, a female-presenting scientist will run in front of the camera. She'll scream, displaying her shredded shirt and lab coat. Her breasts will bear their own open, bloodless wounds, like the spokes of a bicycle's wheel. She'll turn around with her back to the camera. The off-center image of broken laboratory test tubes jammed into her spine (self-inflicted, of course) will be the last thing most people get to watch on TV. The people still left, that is.

But that will come later.

Norman leaned against the wall and performed the mental calculations, walking through all the possible escape routes: front door, back door, even the windows. "Gotta do *something.*"

When he reached the back door, Norman spied scratches on the glass window inset. He pictured a kitten scratching on a bedpost, urging its owner to get up and come play. Except Norman knew the playtime Cheryl had in mind for him was the kind that'd see him *gobbled up* in the end. Backpedaling from the danger he believed waited for him outside, Norman sought sanctuary, a moment to regroup and plan his next move.

The open door to the bedroom beckoned.

Norman stumbled inside and pulled the door closed behind him. The resulting click sounded like an explosion in his ears. He felt grateful for the thick walls of the house. Even with all the changes Cheryl and the others had undergone, super-hearing didn't seem to be one of the new abilities they'd achieved.

Inside the room, a window was open. At her rampage's onset, Cheryl smashed the window glass with one of Norman's golf clubs—his nine iron. Muggy night air slapped him across the face. A thin sliver of moonlight shining across the carpet provided the sole source of illumination.

Norman huffed and puffed, catching his breath inside the bedroom—*their* bedroom. They slept in that room, they laughed, they cried, and, one night before (or was it already two?), they'd made love in the room. He eased his sore, bleeding body down flat onto the end of the bed. All he wanted was a moment to catch his breath, to think up the best way to escape the house without detection, or to check his phone again, to see if the network was back up and running. He wanted something, *anything*, other than running, hiding, and feeling helpless.

He flexed his hand and winced at the glass splinters lodging themselves deeper into his palms. His bloody handprints decorated the down comforter. He breathed through gritted teeth. Glass pieces poked into his sides from under his sweat-drenched t-shirt.

Someone giggled—*tee-hee-hee*—from too close by.

Norman sat up, his legs dangling off the bed, calves brushing the dust ruffle. Cheryl laughed again. "Oh God," he said, realizing both her location and intention too late and trying in vain to pull his legs out of her reach.

Norman screamed as Cheryl dragged the glass across the tendons of his ankles. He flopped forward onto the floor, twisting as he fell, crumpling like pie-in-the-sky plans on cocktail napkins. When he landed, he came face-to-face with the woman he once loved.

He watched her reflection in the shards on the floor.

She crawled from under the bed, bringing more glass with her. Cheryl's wide-eyed junkie grin reflected in a long, sharp piece—taken from the mirror they'd once hung above a changing table in a now-abandoned nursery.

When they'd first dated and couldn't keep their hands off each other, they'd fall to the floor over and over, collapsing into a sweaty heap of tangled limbs, lying face-to-face (right beside Cheryl's roommate's indifferent cat).

Cheryl straddled his chest, parted her lips, and spat more glass into his face. The teeniest, tiniest piece got caught under Norman's eyelid. He howled, thrashed, and flopped. He smeared blood—his blood—across their carpet. He wrenched his head from side to side.

With blood running from one eye and the other squinted and weeping more tears than he thought possible, Norman caught a shadow falling over him. He assumed it was Cheryl, looming over him on her knees, a kitty-cat ready to pounce on an injured bug. *This is it*, he thought. *She's going to kill me now. She has to kill me now.*

"Come here!" It came from outside, through the open window. His savior's voice sounded familiar, but Norman couldn't place it.

Glimpsed from the corner of his injured eye, Cheryl slithered back under their bed, moving like a scolded cat, returning to clean herself and plot revenge. More glass shards covered the carpet like fresh-fallen snow. They marked the space between the bed and the open window, between continued torture and potential salvation.

Norman stretched out flat across the carpet, extending his arms. And then, he pulled himself forward on fists balled up like cinnamon rolls glazed and frosted with blood. Norman stretched out again. His teeth were gritted, but he still found a way to scream.

Stretch and pull. Stretch and pull. The glass cut him again and again.

Nearing the window, Norman turned back—Orpheus taking one last fate-filled glance at Eurydice. The moonlight fell onto Cheryl's glowing eyes as she stared back from her under-the-bed Underworld.

Norman couldn't wait any longer. He slapped bloody palms against the bottom of the window frame. Then he stretched and pulled again, this time hoisting himself up.

With his tendons severed, he became a dangling marionette abandoned by his puppeteer. But it didn't matter. Hands, soft and smooth, wrapped around his wrists. At their touch, Norman shuddered. His savior's skin was soft and smooth, but cold.

He pushed up as hard as he could, ignoring the searing pains all over his body. Whoever waited on the other side of the open window pulled back in response. Norman went up, up, over—and through the open window. As he passed through, glass grazed his stomach where his shirt bunched up to his chest. It cut him in a lazy, unremarkable way. Nothing to even scream about by then. He'd grown used to the feeling. It wasn't gone as it seemed to be for all the women, but its constant presence turned to so much static in his mind. What was one more cut among hundreds? Thousands?

Then, he fell. The momentum sent him flying forward, performing an unintentional somersault before landing on his back.

Sounds—the songs of a world ending—washed over him. First came screams and sobs like the ones Norman had made inside his house. Next, car alarms went off, one after the other in a cacophonic, staccato symphony. Between each moment of potential peace, glass broke all around him.

Norman found his voice and said, "Thank you."

It didn't take long to locate his rescuer. She stood a few feet from the house with her back turned to him.

She wore a ball-gown-length wedding dress with a neck halter extending so far it left everything to the imagination. Even her hands and arms were covered by long, silken white opera gloves. The one part of *her* made visible was her hair. It fell the length of her dress in bouncy, golden curls.

"Aww, aren't you the sweetest?" the woman replied. In the time before, Norman might've found her words to be nothing but more clichéd, sugary-sweet sentiment from another blonde bimbo. Tonight, they sounded *wrong*. They came through muffled, muted. She turned to face him, and Norman understood why.

With no eyelids, her eyes popped, even under minimal lighting. They were black and fat, alien things. Bared red flesh surrounded them. From forehead to chin to the top of her dress's halter, not a trace of skin covered an inch.

Her skinless face appeared to be made from raw hamburger patties. The Meat-Faced woman in the white wedding dress kept her eyes on Norman. It took another moment before he figured out why her ground-chuck face glimmered under the moonlight.

The glass. He watched as she brought a hand to the crystalline mask. She stroked a silken finger down a shining cheek. "Do you like my new face?" she asked.

Lipless and raw, her teeth clinked against the glass as she spoke, each word punctuated by a *clink!* like she was giving a toast at the wedding for which she appeared dressed. Norman knew her voice. He'd heard it before—on the morning TV as he'd rushed out the door for work. Back in those days, he'd kissed his wife on the forehead and told her not to cry so much about silly little things that didn't matter, that they didn't have control over. He'd tell her to think of something new to do with the nursery, since they weren't going to need it after all. Then he'd remind her to be good while he went out for another late-night "business" meeting.

The flesh-bearing bride with the new glass visage knelt beside him. Norman watched as her hands worked their way up her face. He watched her bloody red cheek sink in as she swallowed. Her gloved fingers wormed their way into the open eye sockets of her mask. Her eyes—those disgusting, ebony orbs—popped right into her fingers.

She held them out for him, each one pinched between thumb and forefinger of a hand. "Eat," she said.

Norman squeezed his eyes shut tight. She pressed the slick spheres against his dry, chapped lips. "Eat."

When Debbie came over, Cheryl was in the kitchen making dinner, like always. Debbie pushed right past him with her "something to show your wife." He didn't even get to eat his dinner. But he didn't want this offered meal.

He twisted his head this way and that, trying to resist but feeling the weakened state of his body working against him. The woman's cold silken hand covered his nose, smashing down his nostrils, an indelicate blockage of air.

Norman opened up. Gasping for breath, it sounded like he'd said, "Ahh."

She fed him, gentle as a mother coaxing her baby to please try some new solid food, please, you'll like it! Pushing a little, but not too hard. Then, her hand free of the eyes, she pressed it under his chin, working his jaw.

And they weren't even eyes. Not human eyes, at least. They were doll's eyes. Doll's eyes, made of glass.

Once Norman's chewing became reflexive, she stood back and watched.

The woman pressed a gloved finger to the place where her lips should go, shushing Norman. He understood. It didn't matter that he didn't want to. It didn't matter if he said no. His pain was irrelevant.

So, he bit. He chewed. He swallowed.

He did as he was told.

THE GIALLO KID IN THE CATACLYSM'S CAMPGROUNDS

On the last night of summer camp, my little brother Randy put on a cheap plastic Homer Simpson mask and killed all the camp counselors, except for me. When he finished, he cornered me by the lake in the middle of the property and tried to kill me too. Surprisingly, though, something even more sinister manifested in the background that evening. While I lived through one waking nightmare, something far worse called "the Cataclysm" occurred, bringing the civilized world to a sudden and definitive end. What I'd undergone with my murderous masked brother paled in comparison to the world's demise. I suspect he agreed and stopped trying to kill me as a result.

Or hasn't killed me yet, at least . . .

The summer camp murders and the end of the world: both events went down about a year ago. I lived every day afterward under a blood-red stormy sky. One gaping wound slashed across the horizon. Pockets of lightning throbbed like veins, in and out of rust-colored clouds.

After the first wave of *what-the-fuck?* panic shook me like a ragdoll and left me convinced I'd never see anyone outside of the boundaries of Camp

Diamondhead Lake, I'd get excited whenever strangers would cross into the campgrounds. But I'd hardly get out a "Hello" before Randy appeared behind any luckless interlopers.

When Randy stopped trying to kill me, I chalked it up to my saving his life. If I hadn't found the bunker under Diamondhead Lake and pulled him through the submerged gate, who knows if he'd have made it. Saving his life bought me at least a year's reprieve from whatever slaughter he'd planned. Anyone else who stumbled onto the campgrounds didn't fare so well.

The last batch arrived in Hazmat suits. Tinted facemasks and bulky uniforms gave them the appearance of aliens from some low-budget monster movie. I knew what would happen. So, I gave no signal and shouted no warning.

On the top of our old capture-the-flag hill, I couldn't hear everything the visitors said, but bits and pieces made their way up to me. They spoke another language, Italian, I think.

Some of them carried Geiger counters along with an assortment of other ticking, whirring, beeping instruments. Peering through the cracked lenses of binoculars scavenged from the old Lost and Found box, I made out some type of rifle-like weapons in the arms of the others. Despite all the precautions they'd taken, those strangers remained fools.

Once the screams started, I knew it was a matter of time. Shouts echoed across the campgrounds in a never-cresting tsunami of terror and helplessness.

"Giallo! Giallo!"

Without warning, the screams of my brother's latest victims came in much clearer. Sharp cries stabbed at my eardrums. That one word, *giallo*, came in crystal clear, drilled into my brain.

I groaned as the sounds of dying filled the space behind my eyes, a physical presence inside my skull attempting to shove its way back out. In pain, I fell to the ground.

Quick as it started—*click*—the noise stopped. No, not stopped. Whoever or whatever had hijacked my brain and let in those screams had kept their broadcast on but changed the channel.

"Know what they're saying, Chas?"

I didn't.

"*Giallo!*" A whisper this time, sounding worse than any scream.

Laughter followed. I imagined the giggler's full cheeks reddening and her short button nose wrinkling with every exhalation. A chill ran through my body, rattling me from the top of my head down to my toes. My lips trembled, thin, dried-out, and redder from dried blood than any lipstick I'd ever worn pre-Cataclysm.

"*It means 'yellow.' The last thing they're seeing is the yellow mask on your brother's face. That damned mask and your baby brother's black, dull eyes. Remember? Remember, when he dragged me out from those canoes we'd hid under?*"

I knew the voice. It belonged to my best friend and fellow Camp Diamondhead Lake junior counselor, Sheena. On our last night of camp, she'd celebrated her promotion to head counselor for the following summer—a summer none of us would ever see. We all partied, but none harder than Sheena. Sex and booze and pot, the combo seemed so risqué to us, living in an isolated world called "camp."

Thanks to her promotion, Sheena had been the last of the head counselors Randy killed that bloody night. Bad luck that the Giallo Kid picked her overturned canoe instead of mine. She'd sobbed and screamed, begged me to tell her mom she loved her. Then, Randy's machete blade had taken her head off.

My Sheena died. Gone before the Cataclysm, she didn't belong to the campgrounds of this new world.

I refused to let a ghost—or some persistent bit of survivor's guilt—stop me. I rose to my feet. "Leave me alone."

When I opened my eyes, my brother stood in front of me like a child contemplating a butterfly whose wings he'd torn off.

Whoever or whatever the Sheena voice was, they were right about one thing: I noticed my brother's eyes first, last, and always. They were the only part left I believed was *him*. As a result, they terrified me the most.

Don't misunderstand, the rest of my brother's body, after its post-Cataclysm changes, was nothing short of horrifying. Start with an old Homer mask seared into flesh already scarred, burned, and shiny-slick from popped, oozing blisters. I couldn't tell where the cracked and jagged mask started and my brother's ruined skin began. Before the end of the world, I'd grown accustomed to seeing Randy looking up at me. At the start of summer, he smiled. He followed me and the other counselors around like a puppy dog starved for attention. I never asked why he didn't try and make friends with the other campers his age. With the Cataclysm, I now suspected it wouldn't have made a difference.

After a while, the looks he gave me changed. Those black eyes glistened with tears, like the surface of a wishing well dug too deep to see where the coins land. He begged and pleaded, "Please Chas, don't let them hurt me!"

One year later, I'd grown used to being the one who looked up at him whenever we crossed paths. His camp shirt, the one meant for the freshman in high school he'd never become, hung in rags across his freakishly enlarged body. A solid mass of death-dealing flesh. Strong, but not muscular. More like villain-from-a-fairy-tale big. The giant on top of the beanstalk or the troll under the bridge with flesh between its teeth and piles of bones stacked high, where no one sees them until it's too late.

Another of the head counselors, Jared, had been the first to die at Randy's hands. He'd stumbled into the light of our last campfire holding his heart, freshly carved from his chest, inside impossibly red hands. "Boogeyman." His last word. No goodbye to Mom or Dad, no profound statements on what waited on the other side of the veil. With a blood-speckled cough and an urban legend's name on a tongue already heavy and loose between cold lips, he'd fallen into the fire, sending sparks into the sky.

I don't know whether the Cataclysm brought about the physical changes in my brother or if they'd come from some other evil already growing inside him, desperate to complete the transformation from sweet but too trusting kid to killing machine personified. I thought I'd pulled him into the bunker before the Cataclysm hit, but I wasn't sure about my timing. After we followed the tunnels up to the camp's entrance, Randy grew an inch or more every week. Both height and width. From a safe distance, I'd watched his inhuman growth spurt and transformation.

"In a few years, I'll make counselor like you, Chassidy." He'd said that over and over during the first half of last summer.

He'd stopped after Jared and his meathead goons Levon and Marty lured him into the woods the last night of Spirit Week. Who knows if they'd been high or drunk or fucking sadistic assholes with no care for any physical, emotional, or mental trauma they'd inflict? They'd shaved Randy bald, then took out spray paint cans and a Halloween mask leftover from the 1990s. When they'd finished, Randy stayed quiet.

Since then, he hasn't said a word to anyone, not even me.

His skin stayed the same jaundiced hue they'd sprayed onto him. Again, I suspect the Cataclysm played no small role in maintaining this change.

After the initial "prank," the Homer mask disappeared. I think everyone figured Randy'd thrown it away. Thinking back over those last few days of seeming normalcy, why hadn't I been more worried about the damn mask? After all, when the last night came, Randy made sure we'd never forget it.

He hasn't taken it off since then. In many ways, I think of it *as* his face now.

"So?"

Randy didn't answer. No shrug or head-tilt. One year into the post-apocalypse and my brother's refusal to give me anything—not a signal, grunt, or sigh—drove me a tad crazy. Not like I had anyone else to speak with. The silent monster became my sounding board for every half-thought-out notion in my head. I gave him everything and he offered nothing in return.

Sometimes, the constant silence and menacing indifference made me want to reach up and slap him, to see if I couldn't finally knock the damn mask off his face. I imagined my palm connecting with the painted-on grayish five o'clock shadow at the mask's chin.

But before I'd ever take the chance, I'd remember the woman—the one who came to the campgrounds a month or so after the Cataclysm, covered in burns and tire tread marks, as though she'd stepped out of some Looney Tunes cartoon. She'd told me she was our mother, but she was nothing like the jolly PTA president who'd waved at us from the rec center parking lot as our camp bus puttered away from town. She'd come at Randy fast, prying up a corner of the mask near his forehead.

I'll never forget the cracking sound or the smell wafting through the remaining trees dotting the campgrounds. Like rotten eggs smashed against a kitchen floor.

Randy ended up stringing Mom, or whoever she was, above the entrance to the old mess hall. Blood soaked the concrete path outside the building, turning it from ashen gray to brick red. Flakes of dried skin fluttered down whenever the winds blew through the campgrounds.

"I mean, were there any supplies? On the . . . the outsiders?"

What should I have called them? His *victims*? *Sacrifices*? Not even *prey* sounded right. Prey implied a chase, some possibility of escape for the hunted. But with the Giallo Kid, anyone he happened upon became little more than an ant in the path of a stampeding elephant. He crushed them underfoot, not from malice but because they were in his way.

Faced with my follow-up query, Randy stayed quiet. "Well, hell."

I said it how our dad used to, like that time we got a flat on the way to Gramma's or when the kids down the street egged our house one year, yellow yolks splattering onto Randy's bedroom window. Saying it like Dad did the trick. Randy turned his head the slightest bit toward me.

Let me tell you, it was a huge goddamn deal.

I cinched my backpack tight, straps pulled tighter and tighter to accommodate a body that'd burned away any excess . . . anything. I sighed and waved for Randy to follow. We headed down to the flatter part of the campgrounds. Randy's long strides matched his tree-trunk-thick legs. Since the Cataclysm, he'd picked up an uncanny ability to cover ground quicker than you'd expect for someone his size. I tried to incorporate his technique into my movements. The results weren't exact, but I improved every day.

The Cataclysm's effects took a bit longer to work their magic on me. After all, I'd made it to the bunker. But eventually I left behind the cold and sterile emptiness of the tunnels, those labyrinthine passageways offering comfort and safety, but also promising misery. With enough exposure to the Cataclysm's lingering effects, I no longer resembled the curvy junior counselor with the pigtails in her hair. Instead, I cut a more angular figure. In another lifetime, I'd marvel at the starvation- and stress-induced supermodel-thin form I'd achieved with minimal effort. But I didn't get to think about anything outside of surviving. I couldn't even mourn my hair, which had almost all fallen out by then.

The wind slapped its humidity-rich hands against the side of my head. Momentum built, bringing me closer and closer to the bottom of the hill. Randy kept pace.

After seeing Randy's "work," I nearly lost the minuscule lunch of snacks I'd scrounged up from under the abandoned beds of the departed campers. I kept trying to convince myself I'd get used to the sight of the bloodied and mangled bodies.

But I didn't.

"Does it get to you, Chas? Does it get to you, the same way your brother got to us?"

I shook my head, pinched hard at the bridge of my nose until my eyes watered. Tried to will the voice in my head away. I opened my eyes and swallowed back vomit. Randy had taken the bodies, or what parts remained, and arranged them across the blood-soaked ground. A twisted torso here, a hacked-off arm or leg there. Viewed together, a message emerged, spelled out in pieces of flesh: "Do u hear?"

He'd used one of the heads, a woman's, with long black hair matted down by her own or someone else's viscera, as the question mark's dot.

I stepped closer to my brother. When he turned his head, his mask's plastic shell crinkled. Black eyes met mine. "You're hearing them? Who do you hear?" I asked.

"Who do you think?"

The voice again. A voice belonging to the dead.

Before I could respond, in my head or out loud, Randy brought his gore-stained machete down with a commanding swing. The blade appeared headed right for me. Randy made his weapons move the way a magician performs sleight of hand with a favorite deck of cards. One second his hands were empty, and the next? The Kid wielded an instrument of death and dismemberment like a natural extension of his body: *Ta da!*

I didn't scream, but I threw my hands up in a half-assed attempt to shield the top of my head from the gleaming edge. Experience enough death and there's no life flashing in front of your eyes at such moments. It's more a simple white-and-black title card, floating in space. "Finally," the card reads.

Except it wasn't "finally" for me. I heard the stab and smack of the blade sinking into flesh, hacking through skin. Droplets of blood turned into a geyser, the stream slicking my face. I opened my eyes and my jaw dropped.

The outsiders' dismembered corpses were moved again. Something had drawn the various severed pieces together, rearranging them like child's blocks until they achieved an approximation of some gargantuan humanoid. Smashed-in torsos sat stacked on top of each other, the remains of cracked and shattered people pressed together until eyeballs dangled like pocket watches from gold chains. "Limbs" emerged from the mass. The dark-haired woman's head sat on top of it all, the angel atop a Christmas tree of flesh, blood, and bone. An "arm" made from two broken-backed bodies took a lazy, uncoordinated swing at me. I ducked, hit the ground, and looked up in time to see Randy's blade sink into the wall of disjointed parts.

"What the hell?" I asked.

Under the shadow of what I guess you'd call the groin, I dodged mix-and-match sets of gore-slick fingers reaching for me. The fingernails of some unknown dead man or woman pinched my skin, grabbing me with a violating insistence. I slapped the hand away and it fell from the patchwork body, freed from whatever force held everything together. It hit the ground, limp and defeated. But then, the unseen force drew the prodigal piece back up, returning it to the unnatural collection of writhing parts never meant to exist as one.

Playing his role in the nightmarish dance, Randy worked to return the composite horror to its separated status. I was considering whether my brother enjoyed having the chance to kill what he'd already dispatched when the creature came close to stomping through my pelvis with one of its feet—its unwieldy, unlikely toes comprised of forearms and jet-black guns. I twisted onto my stomach, hands struggling to find leverage in the remains staining the ground. Once I got a grip, I popped up like a cork from a shaken champagne bottle.

The decapitated head crowning the wriggling mass of parts didn't open its eyes or move its dead, pale lips to speak, but the force controlling the mosaic monster's movements made its presence clear. Eyes were on me. The same voice from before returned inside my head. *"Why do you protect him?"*

Before I could answer, I heard another voice—a young man's strangled drawl preserved in death. Its texture scraped against my nerves. *"You know what he did, Chassidy. You know how to end it. To end all of this."*

"Watch out!"

The assembled creature swung a makeshift arm's worth of Hazmat-suited corpses at my brother's head. My warning reached him in time and he leaped out of the way of the intended blow. The soles of the thick boots we'd found for him in the groundskeeper's shed after his old blood-crusted flip-flops no longer fit, crunched into the menagerie of chests and stomachs. A demented parkour horror show, he bounded up the wall of flesh and scrambled for purchase, the toes of his boots jammed into the gaps between segments and his free hand alone pulling him to the top. He drew back his machete-wielding hand, ready to swing for the fences.

Another hand grabbed my throat. This time, it didn't miss. Whatever force manned the creature's controls showed no hesitation. Fingers pushed in, tighter and tighter, crushing my windpipe. New voices added themselves to the chorus in my head. *The Cataclysm came and brought us back. It's not a one-time event. No one and done. It's happening over and over again. It brought us back because you won't end it. You won't be the Final Girl.*

I used to think I'd cry if I ever got to hear the voices of everyone my brother killed last year. But I did *not* think it'd be while I was still alive.

Randy's machete connected with its target: a direct hit to the top of the dead woman's skull. He struck with such force he split her head in two. Blood, brains, and bits of skull tumbled down the mound of mixed-up flesh, pebbles into a rockslide. The cascade grew to an avalanche and the bodies fell apart again. I ran for cover. Randy fell from his perch but managed to land on his feet. Parts splattered around him while he remained standing. He stretched his arms out wide, palms to the sky.

He used to strike the same pose whenever the first summer shower hit back home. He'd run into our backyard with nothing on but his Superman Underoos. He'd let raindrops fall between his fingers. And he'd laugh.

If he smiled while corpse pieces fell around him, I couldn't see. The mask, sun-bleached pale yellow, never changed its expression.

"Do you see what we're capable of?" Levon or Marty asked. Even when they'd lived, I couldn't tell the two apart.

"What do you want?"

Randy recovered his blade. Gore dripped like tree sap from the end of his machete. He stood stone still. Waiting.

The voices hadn't stopped, but they'd reduced themselves to a buzzing rattle and hum inside my mind. Perhaps they were talking among themselves. My gallows humor at an all-time high, I wanted to interrupt, tell them they should've planned better, should've known what they'd say to me after a whole year of buildup. I held my tongue, though.

One of them spoke, sounding like Jared. *"Hey, babe. Missed me?"*

Jared: King of the Head Counselors. Jared: The Flirt. Jared: The Sweet-Talker, who told me he'd wait until I was ready. Jared: The Guy who fucked my best friend because she was there and willing. Jared: The Massive Fucking Asshole. Jared: the first of our gang to die.

I didn't realize how hard I'd bit down on my lip until blood dribbled down my chin, rolling faster along the sweat-slicked curve of my neck before disappearing down the front of a crimson tank-top that'd started white. I licked my lips, tasting the coppery sweetness. "You're all dead. All of you. Dead."

"Dead in the world before. But the Cataclysm makes a different world."

"Well, good for you. Where are you anyway?"

"Kill your brother."

Randy remained among the corpses. If he'd also heard what the Jared voice had said, he gave no indication.

"What?"

"C'mon, Chas," Sheena picked up the baton. *"It takes so much out of us to communicate this way, from this distance. We know you heard us. You know what we're asking for is right."*

"Where are you?" I wouldn't be deterred.

"You know where. We're where you let him leave us."

They spoke as one in a sing-song chorus, the way we'd lead the campers in cheers at morning roll call. Jared and the boys always raised the flag, and occasionally some unlucky guy's or gal's underwear. We'd stand in uneven rows and laugh. Because that's what happened at summer camp, right? You made people miserable to make yourself feel better. And you laughed about it.

A muffled, gagging rattle came from close by and lasted for a good moment before I identified its source. Randy's mask quivered. The sound he made struggled to escape through the tiny plastic slit the mask-makers provided as an airhole.

The first sound he'd made in over a year: laughter!

My foot slid back, calves tensing. The flight part of my fight-or-flight response took hold, ready for what came naturally. But I stopped myself. I blew a slow breath out, ignoring the stench of gore all around me. I dug one foot deep into blood-soaked mud. I spoke to the others. "He's my baby brother. And the world's ended. It's . . . it's complicated."

I'd spent enough sleepless nights walking the perimeter of the campgrounds, running through every possible scenario—escape, revenge, forgiveness, giving in and letting it end—but finding nothing satisfactory, nothing matching the tenure of the post- (or better to say mid-) Cataclysm world. The "others" didn't share those assumptions.

They let me know it too.

I fell forward, down to my knees. I refused to scream. Even when it felt like absolute hell, like someone's thumbs were inside my head pushing my eyeballs out from their sockets, I wouldn't give them the satisfaction. Randy's "laughter" stopped, like someone ripped the needle from a record player. I dragged my palms over my eyes, tugging at the lower lids. My hands came back wet with fresh blood. "Stop!"

I didn't scream, but I sure as hell didn't whisper.

After another agonizing moment, the force inside my head withdrew, leaving me with bloody tears trickling down my sunken cheekbones.

"Come to us, then. Both of you. Or you'll find there are fates worse than death."

"No shit," I said, no longer the shy, virginal teen they might have remembered, the one who couldn't stand the sight of blood. (Well, okay, one of those things hadn't changed, given the end of the world and its resulting lack of significant contact with other survivors.)

I hocked a loogie at the ground to underscore my point. I stuck my fingers between my lips and gave a quick, sharp whistle. I waved for Randy to follow. I led the way back up the hill. Randy trailed at a distance. Before leaving the massacre scene, he'd set his machete back in the bisected head of the dark-haired woman. A reminder for whoever came next that the Giallo Kid had been there and they should all beware.

"Where are you going? We told you to come here. To us." A new voice interrupted my reverie.

"Listen, Carolyn, I know we weren't close or anything, but I'm sorry for what happened to every one of y—"

"He stabbed me with one hundred arrows like I was some martyred saint!"

She'd looked more like a pincushion.

Christ! I wondered if I'd sounded so pretentious before my brother's rampage and the end of the world. Funny how those events can change your perspective, huh?

We'd almost made it up the hill. I sheltered in a makeshift shed up near my lookout spot. After we'd returned to the surface from our trek through the tunnels, I'd built it with the guidance of shredded remnants of old camping manuals I found blowing across the campgrounds. Not to mention a healthy dose of making-it-up-as-I-went-along. Something inside—not a voice, but a feeling of certainty otherwise alien to me—told me we couldn't leave. It told me there was nowhere else for me or my brother to go. Once I'd finished the shed, I'd dragged a mattress uphill and put it inside. I'd snatch a few minutes of something close to sleep in there whenever I could.

Of course, sleep was the farthest thing from my mind at that moment. I stopped short, right before the ground crested under my feet to form the hill's summit. Randy kept his distance. He always knew where I'd be, when I'd run, and when I'd hide.

He hadn't known when I'd fight back, though.

"If you're so mad at my brother, why the hell don't *you* kill him? You treated those corpses like stacking blocks and made them dance around. How hard is it to kill one kid, huh?"

Like killing a kid was so easy. Like my brother the Giallo Kid remained anything close to what someone would consider a child.

"He wears the mask."

"What?"

Instead of an answer, a loud shushing followed, nearly blowing out my eardrums. Like someone turned the radio dial to static and cranked the volume. I bit down hard for the second time.

I used to get these terrible migraines, which lasted up through middle school. But they'd gone away by freshman year. I don't know what changed. Maybe the baby fat in my cheeks went away, I got tits, and suddenly people who dictated the high school hierarchy took notice. Maybe I became one of the cool kids because I happened to be just smart and just dumb enough to not rock the boat. No matter the reason, I hadn't felt that pain in a long time, like forest fires raging across clusters of synapses. Before the Cataclysm, whenever it happened, I could always count on one person to be there. Through squinted eyes, I reached for his comfort.

I swore he moved toward me. Not a lot, but I swear something stirred. Even with blank, black eyes beneath a fake plastic face, I could still imagine my baby brother reaching a hand forward to take mine. I pictured him giving my fingers a thoughtful squeeze, letting me know everything would be okay.

Instead, he turned around. With plodding, methodical steps, each one like the rumble of thunder, he stomped down the hill. I knew where he was going. How could I not? I only had to think back one year.

I remembered my heart beating so fast back then. I'd convinced myself it would leap through my chest and sail into the darkness, waiting for me to fall on my own exploded organ. I'd die and it'd be all my fault because I couldn't run and I couldn't keep my own heart inside my chest. But that didn't happen. My brother had kept us in front of him, corralling me and Sheena, down, down to where we'd all probably believed it would end.

This time Randy led and I followed. There was one place for us to go. We went back to Diamondhead Lake.

The static of psychic feedback settled to a dull hum between my ears. *"Kill your brother. Kill your brother." "Kill your brother." "Kill your brother." "Kill your brother . . ."*

I let them keep talking, chanting, whatever the hell they were doing. Not watching where I was going, I nearly stepped into the open wound of someone's slit throat.

We'd returned to my brother's freshest kills. The head counselors, the owners of the resurrected voices in my head, left the mangled pieces of the dead Italians alone. Randy strode past them without a second look. After all, they were dead and of no consequence to him.

I *did* stop. Something caught my eye. I approached the dark-haired woman's bisected head. Randy's machete rose from her skull, blood-matted hair pinwheeled around it. The static cries increased in volume, but

I refused to rush. Studying the dead woman's lopsided eyes, I wondered about the girl she'd been before. Who had she been before the Cataclysm and who had she been after, when she came to the campgrounds and lost her life?

Regardless of the answers, here she was, a severed head with a giant knife sticking out the top. My hand hovered near the hilt. Fingers tingled and the voices in my head sang out, *"Randy, Randy, Halloween candy, wear the mask, it's fine and dandy."*

They'd sung it on our last night at camp. As they sang it again, I remembered how I'd failed to stop them.

Up ahead, my brother screamed. A vibrating bellow, like cows dragged to the front of slaughterhouse lines.

I took off running. Each breath strained to make its way up from my chest and out of my dry lips. I could feel them cracking and peeling against the wind as I ran to catch up.

I reached the boat launch. Those same winds buffeting me back drove once-placid waters into a frothing, white-capped mess. Foul, blackened liquid cascaded down onto the algae-encrusted dock.

If you swim across until you're closer to the opposite shore and dive down below those wild waves, you'll find the bunker's entrance and the network of tunnels beyond.

But for the moment, what was *under* the lake didn't concern me. Randy floated *above* the raging waters. He thrashed and kicked, fighting against unseen forces with the intensity of a cornered wild beast.

I heard a shattering crack, like lightning on the water. Then another and another, all coming in rapid fire. I shielded my eyes from the spray for a better view above the water. Something thick and overwhelming lodged in my throat as the realization settled in that I wasn't hearing lightning. It was the sound of my brother's bones snapped back and forth. Broken and reset again and again.

The winds died down. The waters calmed. But my brother remained suspended above the black lake. His wrists snapped up and down, like a marionette with strings pulled by a sloppy puppeteer. Or, better to say, a gang of sloppy puppeteers, all working together in service of long-awaited revenge.

When I reached the water's edge, they all waited for me. Sheena, Jared, Levon, Marty, Carolyn, and every other head counselor from the Camp Diamondhead Lake staff. Everyone awaited my arrival, everyone with the bad luck to not be me, to not be the Final Girl who made it to the end.

More memories, shoved down as hard and as far as I'd been able to push them over the last year, came flooding back. After Randy had separated Sheena's head from her body, he'd held it up for me to see. He'd waited, patient as always for a kid with a big sister who sometimes liked to pretend he didn't exist or acted like she couldn't see him wanting to be noticed by her.

In this memory, I pushed the canoe off me. As I stood and took in what Randy was showing me, water lapped at my bare, cut-to-shit feet. My brother splashed through the mud and added Sheena's head to his collection. No bodies, only heads. A row of heads—every counselor who'd ever teased or laughed or sought to cause him harm. I saw them, dead and lifeless, some with eyes closed and others staring out with bluish-gray glassiness clouding their outlook forever. They reminded me of masks from a Halloween costume shop.

In the year since, I'd refused to set foot anywhere near the lake. I'm not sure what I expected to find when I returned to the water's edge. A row of skulls with the last remnants of skin, muscle, and hair? Bones bleached white?

That's not what waited for me as I stepped forward and left the memory behind.

The "dead" faces of the head counselors remained preserved, not diminished or rotted at all. Somehow, there was even *more* of them. Each head appeared swelled by several degrees. Wrinkled pink and gray throbbing brain matter squeezed up through their scalps like excess toothpaste around the end of the tube. All their eyes opened and stared at me. And their teeth . . . all those teeth. Stretched-out grins on each of their faces showed every canine, molar, and incisor. Blackened tongues rubbed across gleaming white surfaces.

On the first day of camp, Randy had insisted I help him get settled in his bunk. As a result, I missed taking our summer kick-off counselor picture, the seemingly casual but actually quite posed one, where everybody squeezed in tight under the flash of someone's crooked Polaroid camera. The mad-eyed grinning faces in front of my feet resembled a nightmare version of the earlier picture.

Once again, I was the one missing.

"There is a way. The Killer wears the mask. The Final Girl destroys the Killer. The Dead are avenged. The Killer re—"

"Stop it! Cut the shit. Let me talk to Jared."

When would they accept I wasn't the girl they'd left behind? That I wasn't the crying, screaming, most unlikely one of the group any longer? I didn't have time for games, even if the players were the mutated, severed heads of dear dead friends.

After a short silence, Jared's voice resumed broadcasting inside my head. *"Chas, we need your help. This—all of this—it's because of . . ."*

I expected him to say "Randy." I *knew* he'd say "Randy." Randy and his mask. Whenever I thought about my brother, even memories from before he killed or before he changed, all I saw was the damn "animated yellow sitcom dad" mask. All I saw was the yellow. The *Giallo.*

". . . you. It's your fault, Chas."

Even as a telepathic severed head, Jared retained the ability to stab the emotional knife in deep, right through my heart.

"What are you talking about? What the hell is going on?"

Sheena answered for the collective. *"It's a ritual. You had a role to play. Like we did. We were sacrifices. Your brother wore the mask. You were . . . you are the Final Girl. Except you stopped, fell short of your duties. And your little brother followed suit. And so, the Cataclysm . . ."*

I missed the Sheena who'd shared her copies of Cosmo and giggled with me while we filled out sex tests. I kicked up mud, watched it splatter against the tumorous bulging cheeks on either side of her head. I didn't feel any better.

Behind the head counselors' literal heads, I watched them lowering my brother. The soles of his boots crossed the plane of the water's surface. I wondered how much strength it took them all to hold him in place.

"No need to hide the blade, Chas." Jared.

"We know you took it from the black-haired woman's head." Sheena.

I brought my hand forward from behind my back. My wrist ached from my half-hearted hiding attempt. Randy's machete felt heavier, not only from the blood and guts already soaked into the metal, but from the aches and pains of a year of running but not moving, of hiding but always existing exposed under the watchful eyes of these others. Still, I picked up the blade and pointed it toward the yellow cartoon mask and my brother's black eyes. "Is this what you want?" I asked.

"Kill your brother. Kill your brother . . ."

The voices picked the chant back up. My eyes locked with Randy's down the edge of the blade. I swear the grayish five-o'clock-shadow part of his mask moved, as though controlled by the vibrations of my brother's "real" mouth under molded plastic. I wondered if he felt the same as me.

It fell to me to finish it, just like the year before. Could I walk into the water and thrust the blade up, pushing hard until I drove it through him?

I heard the exasperated gasps of the others before realizing I'd started shaking my head no.

I kept holding onto the machete. "Look, I'm not saying I *won't* kill him, okay?"

"Goddammit, Chas, fucking do it!"

I shuffled down the line of heads until I came back to Sheena's. Another migraine hit me, the worst one yet. I spat out what I wanted to say. "Sheena."

"Chassidy."

The way she said my name in full, with the slightest hint of disdain for my trailer park-ass name, helped to fortify me for what came next.

I took a deep breath in, swallowing the fetid rankness of the lake mingling with the fluids expelled from my friend's severed head. The throbbing of her exposed, engorged brain was almost hypnotic.

I averted my eyes from the pulsations of her open cranium. Then, I let it all out. "You fucking bitch! You stole Jared from me! You stole him and fucked him. How could you? How?"

A murmuring search for consensus followed between the head counselors. The winds picked back up. The stiff breeze pushed across my stubbled head like an aggressive aunt tousling my hair after Thanksgiving dinner. The rising lake water lapped against the cuffs of Randy's pants.

Sheena spoke. *"I'm so sorry, Chas. I didn't know you liked him like that. But, I mean, he's so dreamy. How could I not fall for—?"*

I cut her monologuing off with a downward slash of the machete. Hard as I could, right into the brain matter of whatever wore the face of my dead best friend. A loud squelching sound followed, like bare feet pulled from soupy mud. I'm afraid the sound overshadowed the zinger. I delivered breathlessly, "Before she died, I told Sheena Jared was a prick. Then, she told me he had a small one. Neither of us gave a damn about him. C'mon. Use your brain!"

The other voices shrieked as one inside my head. Pain beyond anything I'd felt before followed. I struggled to regain my footing in the mud while pulling the machete from the disintegrating Sheena Head it'd split apart.

I stumbled to the next head, fighting through the agony of their screaming. I let the blade fall. Again. And again. I couldn't tell if the water running down my cheeks came from tears or splash-back from the blood-red water's edge.

"Who are you? Huh? Using my friends? Hiding behind their faces?"

The blade slipped from my hand, resulting in a horizontal slash across the faces of "Levon" and "Marty," before it fell into the mud.

"Enough!"

Something pulled my arms down like lead weights tied to my wrists and elbows. The force pushed me down to my knees. The Jared Head rocked back and forth, shaking like a mad dog, but frothing from his eyeballs instead of his mouth.

The other heads frothed right along with him.

"Final Girl, you know who we are . . ."

My chin snapped down hard against my chest, another part of me controlled by the Jared Head and its fellow head counselors. I struggled to lift my chin back up and glare at them all. "The bunker below the lake," I said. "You'd already gotten out. You were already all around us." I paused, long enough to catch my breath. "You're the Cataclysm."

"We are the Cataclysm. We are the cycle of inevitable destruction."

I laughed. It came out slow and soft at first, but grew louder, more insistent. The head counselors didn't like that. Not one bit. Multiple pinpricks ruptured my skin, up and down my arms, all over my face. But they came from inside me, not out. Blood burst from a million tiny holes all over. Still, I kept laughing.

"Silence, Final Girl. We do not wish to cause you harm. But we will do what it takes t—"

I pulled a hand up from the mud and smeared blood from the puncture wounds across my face. "It looks like this is taking a lot out of you. All these theatrics. Making me bleed? Seems like you might be distracted enough to forget someone . . ."

Randy's foot came down in the middle of the Jared Head. He lifted his boot back up, leaving tread marks across Jared's brain and pancaked skin. My brother picked up the machete from the spot where I'd dropped it.

He went to work.

I kept my distance and watched. I couldn't shake the strange feeling I was seeing something beautiful. My heart pounded inside my chest. Not from fear, but pride. Randy seemed to be everywhere. Killing everything. Eyeballs, lips, noses, all kinds of facial features flew up into the air like fleshy confetti. Pieces landed in the mud with the wet slap of a one-sided kiss.

Then he finished.

I still heard them—it, whatever—inside my head. *"Those are only some of our faces."*

Nothing more than a loser's lament. I knew they were done for a long damn time.

Before I could savor the victory, my brother trained his black eyes on me.

We'd made it back. Back where we'd thought it would end one year before. Randy raised the machete again.

I wanted to keep my eyes open.

My brother stepped into the water. He took another step. And another. And another. Mud or blood or something worse splattered up into my eyes. I couldn't help it. I blinked. Shut both eyes tight. I couldn't lift a hand and wipe it away. So I left them closed, offering up no prayers for my salvation. After all, I'd grown accustomed to waiting for the end.

The longest moment passed. Then, a splash.

I wiped my eyes clean. The yellow plastic mask waited at my feet. He'd left it there. One last sacrifice for me, the Final Girl.

The lake waters were calmed by the time I peered out and tried to find my brother. I didn't even see a ripple across the surface or air bubbles floating to the top.

I picked up the old mask and felt our last summer officially end.

Hours later, I'd packed up all the supplies from my shed and was now left standing at the gates of Camp Diamondhead Lake. I'd tied my brother's mask on a string and hung it around my neck, twisted around so the expressionless, eyeless face of Homer J. Simpson stared out at anyone walking behind me.

Past the camp's entrance, I should've seen a highway. If I caught the right angle, I should've seen the reflected windows of the closest town. But nothing waited ahead, except leaves on the ground and more dirt paths. Cabins and bunks. And the shimmering surfaces of lake after lake after lake.

I tightened the straps of my pack and headed out for the next camp.

I wonder if my brother will come for his mask. I hope he does.

I'll be waiting for him.

ACKNOWLEDGMENTS

For me, writing is at once a solitary pursuit—spent with long moments staring at walls, computer screens, and the nebulous ether, seeking *just the right* word or idea or bit of dialogue—and, at the same time, a cooperative endeavor. Without help, love, support, encouragement, and, hell, without community, I don't think I'd have the opportunity to peer into the void and come back with the words you've just read in this collection.

Unless you skipped to the end because you're a big Acknowledgments-head, and if you are, strap in. And then go back and give the stories a read as well.

First and foremost, I must thank my family. Jenna, your support and patience for the ups and downs of this writer's journey has meant and continues to mean the world to me. Thanks for giving me the time and space to grow and to indulge in stories of the dark, the weird, and the strange, even though they're not "your thing." I love you more than I love you. Grant and Avery, keep tapping those creative veins, boys. Dreams and stories are everywhere you look and everywhere you don't. I can't wait to read your books someday. And, to Juniper: you are not a lapdog, despite what you might think. Walking you gets me out of the house and away from the writing chair for those moments when I need a brainstorming recharge. For that reason, you can get a thanks . . . as a treat.

In making the move from someone who wants to write to someone who writes—who's writing right now, probably—there have been several writers who've played a part in helping me cross that threshold. To Brian Bendis: we connected in a different career lifetime when I was an editor, and I learned so much from helping bring your writing book into the world. Your continued support, encouragement, and kind words about my creative pursuits warm my heart whenever they come across my inbox. To JG

Faherty: Greg, I can trace a straight line from your insightful commentary and straightforward no-BS approach to editing as my HWA mentor to the continued success I've enjoyed when it comes to short-story publications. Thanks for helping me learn to write things shorter, smarter, and better.

And, to Richard Thomas: your mentorship and friendship continue to feel like a VIP pass to the exclusive part of the party, where I've found everyone's still very chill and welcoming and not at all as intimidating as I might have feared. I've learned so much from your classes, emails, and conversations. Having your words at the front of this volume of stories is apropos. Just as you open the door to the readers of this collection, so too did you help open so many doors for me. I'm thrilled to hold these doors open for whomever may be coming behind me.

As alluded to earlier, I spent 12+ years in book publishing before making the move to freelance writing and editing. I'm quite aware of all the hands and eyes and email accounts that go into taking a bunch of words on a computer screen to the book that you're holding in your hand or that's on your tablet . . . which is also in your . . . you know what I mean! The point is, I'd feel like I'd betrayed my publishing roots if I didn't offer up plentiful thanks and gratitude to the team at Keylight/Turner. Ryan Smernoff, thanks for supporting this collection of stories and bringing me into the Keylight stable. Thanks to Gabriel Thibodeau whose line edits have brought this manuscript up to fighting shape. Thanks also to Todd Bottorff, Claire Ong, Makala Marsee, William Ruoto, and Cindy Cavoto. My thanks also to those providing design, production, copy editing, and proofreading services to help bring the book to its current state.

While many of these stories were written, submitted, and published in a time of isolation and pandemic, technology has allowed connections and community to be forged with many of my fellow writers of the dark, weird, strange, and horrific. My thanks to all my fellow scribes on social media and in the writing communities on Discord, like HOWL, Netherworld, Em-Dash, and others. These stories would not have been whipped into shape without the insights of my beta readers Chris O'Halloran, CB Jones, "Frylock," and TJ Price. And my thanks to JV Gachs for being a dear friend from across the Atlantic. Having someone to talk scary stories with, who comes from a similar mindset in terms of what we fear and how we process it—it is an invaluable treasure for me. Muchas gracias, Jules.

Finally, thanks to the readers. You're the final part of the equation. From my head to the page to your head, I hope the transfer wasn't painful. Or at least, it wasn't *too* painful.

CREDITS

"Lost Boy Found in His Bear Suit" originally appeared in *Pyre Magazine*, December 2020.

"A Portrait of the Artist as an Angry God (in Landscape)" originally appeared in *Boneyard Soup Magazine*, April 2021.

"Casual" originally appeared in *Not One of Us* #67, July 2021.

"Rose from the Ashes" is original to this collection.

"Have You Seen My Missing Pet?" originally appeared in audio format on *Nobody Reads Short Stories*, October 2022.

"And Our Next Guest . . ." originally appeared in *Deep Fried Horror Ezine*, August 2019.

"I Will Not Read Your Haunted Script" originally appeared in Divination Hollow Reviews, January 2021.

"The Other Half of the Battle" originally appeared in audio format on the *Tales to Terrify* podcast, September 2021.

"Pre-Approved for Haunting" originally appeared in *Boneyard Soup Magazine*, July 2021.

"The Crack in the Ceiling" originally appeared in *Dose of Dread*, Dread Stone Press, June 2021.

"Return to Voodoo Village" originally appeared in *Diabolica Americana*, October 2021.

"Putting Down Roots" is original to this collection.

"Melvin and the Murder Crayon" originally appeared in Pulp Modern Flash, April 2021.

"There Is No Bunk #7" originally appeared in *Shallow Waters Vol. 7*, Crystal Lake Publishing, April 2021.

"Iggy Crane and the Headless Horse Girl" is original to this collection.

"The Decimations of Corn-Silk Sally" originally appeared in *Dose of Dread*, Dread Stone Press, October 2021.

"Shattered" is original to this collection.

"The Giallo Kid in the Cataclysm's Campgrounds" is original to this collection.

ABOUT THE AUTHOR

PATRICK BARB is an author of weird, dark, and horrifying tales. His short fiction has appeared in a number of recognized horror and speculative fiction magazines and anthologies. His debut dark urban fantasy novella, *Gargantuana's Ghost,* was a part of Grey Matter Press's Emergent Expressions line. He is also the author of the vampire pro-wrestling novella *Turn* (Alien Buddha Press) and the sci-fi / horror novelette *Helicopter Parenting in the Age of Drone Warfare* (Spooky House Press). Patrick is an Active Member of the Horror Writers Association and a Full Member of the Science Fiction and Fantasy Writers Association. Originally from the Southern United States, he's currently living in Saint Paul, Minnesota, with his wife, two sons, and a large dog who thinks she's actually a lapdog.